Vietnam in the Absence of War

One Immoral War, Two Revealing Bicycle Trips

Thomas G. Rampton
Blacktail Enterprises
Nathrop, Colorado

Cover photograph: Woman with a conical hat, near the city of Vinh, 1998. All photographs are by the author unless otherwise noted. Several photographs are by Alan and Karen Robinson, and Gail Lowenstine.

Several people helped with this book. Gail Lowenstine read and offered invaluable suggestions. Wilson Hubbell shared many facts and insights about Vietnam, past and present. My sister Emily Rampton of Portland, Oregon, very skilled in communications and language, read an early version and commented, then edited the final version. Barbara McNichol, a book editor in Tucson, Arizona, edited. Rick Bauman of Portland, Oregon, outfitted the two bicycle trips. Our guides with V.Y.C in Vietnam—Thai, Nhut, Xuan Hung, and Hanh—shared much about their country; the V.Y.C drivers navigated it.

Publisher's Cataloging-in-Publication
(Provided by Quality Books, Inc.)

Rampton, Thomas G.
    Vietnam in the absence of war : one immoral war, two revealing bicycle trips / Thomas G. Rampton.
    p. cm.
    Includes bibliographical references.
    LCCN 2001119479
    ISBN 0-9634799-2-X

    1. Rampton, Thomas G.--Journeys--Vietnam. 2. Vietnam --Description and travel. 3. Vietnamese Conflict, 1961-1975. I. Title.

DS556.39.R36 2002   915.9704'44
                  QBI01-201415

To my father, Donald Rampton,
who started me down a pathway of appreciation for places
that are natural,
and for experiences that are powerful.

Table of Contents

Introduction

This is a book for those who have felt an interest in what the Vietnamese have made of their independent country in the years since our unfortunate military venture there. It also touches upon the early human past, the prehistoric past, the geologic past, and the wild parts of Vietnam.

I had no desire to relive the Vietnam War. I am a veteran only because I was drafted, but while there in 1969 and 1970, I noticed what was around me—Vietnam was a beautiful land. I wanted to know it better.

This isn't one of those books in which the author describes his heroic deeds in battle. Those looking for combat detail or strategy won't find it here, nor are there the standard pictures of muddy, disheveled soldiers. I certainly don't fit the common stereotype of the gung-ho Vietnam veteran—a lot of us just aren't like that.

Even then, I wasn't particularly in favor of the war and I later came to regret what my country had done there. How did my country get so inexplicably on the wrong side? The Vietnam War was a shameful chapter in our history; had we "won," it would have been even more shameful.

Many veterans like me suspected that the Vietnam War was wrong, though we might have had trouble in those days explaining why. It was an unhappy discovery that my country's leaders had lied to us, lied even to themselves, and that our military had done great evil in Vietnam after such heroic performances in earlier wars.

Early on, I relate this particular draftee's experience in the Vietnam War. Some still believe the war was a noble effort against a wicked foe. Others went just for the adventure of it. They will not like what I have written, but I don't care. Many from both countries died because of them.

I was an infantryman (who did no person any harm) and then an Army photographer along the coast near Hue and in the nearby mountains. I knew even then that I wanted to go to Vietnam again someday, with no war in the way of observation.

I did nothing about getting back to Vietnam for most of 30 years. Slides I'd show to high school classes constituted a break from the chemistry and other sciences I was supposed to be teaching. My own best teachers had sometimes digressed and I make no apology. I pursued other interests and took up new ones. I followed news about boat people escaping from Vietnam, but I mostly lost track while that nation changed into a much more open society.

Then I learned of Cycle Vietnam's bicycle trips from Hanoi to Ho Chi Minh City. Though I was new to long-distance bicycling and didn't know quite what to expect, I joined the 1998 trip.

Bicycling through Vietnam, I did not feel like a returning war veteran. No enemies of mine or of my country had ever lived there, so I had no foe-to-friend conversions to make. I was free now to see, learn, explore, experience the beauty of Vietnam again, and rediscover an exotic land.

I met many of the people. At a school, I saw teachers teaching and kids learning. I saw a country being built by people who are energetic, friendly and proud. I saw people helping other people. I saw intelligent and resourceful people who appeared alive with enterprise—certainly not a gloomy population without hope, as may be the case elsewhere. Vietnam isn't a wealthy land, but the people are spirited.

Evidence of Vietnam's past Cham civilization was abundant along the central coast. Inland, there is a wild ecosystem and wild country I have yet to explore. The Vietnamese know the value of these, and are protecting their lands in a system of national parks.

What prehistoric cultures flourished in Vietnam? What mysterious creatures? Geologically, how did the land itself come to be?

Feeling welcome to explore such interests in Vietnam was considerably more positive than being sent there to conduct war.

I knew only a little more about cycling in 1998 than I had about soldiering in 1969, but I was never interested in the latter. Having reduced my initial ignorance about bicycling, I came to like it and wanted more. I repeated the Hanoi to Ho Chi Minh City trip in 1999.

This book is about thoughts, observations, experiences, and adventures in that land, and about meeting the brave people who live there.

An Immoral War
Should We Be Winning?

"I want to go to Vi-et-nam... I want to kill old Char-lie Cong...!" We were supposed to sing this ditty as we ran around the parade field in the dark of morning during Army basic training. For me, it wasn't even a little bit true.

I didn't have the slightest wish to go there or to kill anyone, but as a draftee in the autumn of 1968, I was supposed to play this head-game to the tune of some now-unremembered song. For the betterment of my soul, I didn't sing along. But how did I ever come to such a state? How did our country get there?

Months earlier at the University of Wyoming in Laramie, another graduate student and I were talking about the Vietnam War one evening. I must confess that I still believed the stuff coming from the Johnson Administration in Washington. I said to Joe that we seemed to be winning.

Joe simply asked, "Should we be winning?"

Well, I supposed so, but asking if we should be winning was a new concept for me. I hadn't thought much about the morality of the Vietnam War before then, but wasn't our country doing noble battle with communists who were trying to take over a sovereign nation? That was the U.S. administration's line at the time. I'd learn much more over the next couple years, and over the next three decades, too.

The Vietnam War's moral, procedural, and logical bankruptcy would certainly come home later—some of it much later. My youthful conservative views had been slipping steadily away under the assault of more knowledge and fuller understanding, but the process was slow and still very incomplete. And I've wondered, had our country really been winning, would the public have turned against the Vietnam War as it did? Did the masses at the time care about the morality of it, or was it simply results that mattered? The results so far had been rather poor.

Should we be winning? And had we won, what would have been the effect on Vietnam? I still wonder. Joe was more concerned with social issues than I was. He may not remember asking me his question, but I sure do. Thank you, Joe, for jogging my thinking. Should we be winning, if indeed we were?

Learning of Various Kinds

Back to 1963. After a first semester at two-year Santa Ana College a couple miles from my California home, I still wasn't sure what I wanted to do with myself. Feeling an educational lack that spring, I took the college equivalent of high school chemistry. My grade was an *A*, and I liked that.

Quickly developing further passion for chemistry, I started the locally fabled "rough, tough" college freshman course the next fall, which was team-taught in a direct, clear manner. Professors Brooks and Hayes were responsible for starting me on a path I'd pick up again later and follow for over twenty years of my life.

The next stop was Long Beach State College, where Dr. George Appleton jumped up and down while lecturing to a large group about physics. Calling attention to the force "by George" on the floor, a force by the floor back on George illustrated an important point in Newtonian physics. Unfortunately, the chemistry course I took there was a bit perfunctory. Learning still proceeded, but I only stayed a semester.

Excellence was rediscovered at Chapman College in Orange, California. The school has since changed its name to Chapman University, though it did very well for me as a college. This liberal arts college required some history, music appreciation, and literature. Chapman, with a very nominal church connection, also required study of the Old and New Testaments for purposes of cultural literacy, not evangelism. What I learned would have displeased biblical fundamentalists at the time, and it does now whenever they knock on my door. Chapman had the effect of rescuing me from unthinking conservatism—religious, social, and otherwise—and left me in favor of whatever works, works fairly, and operates with sensitivity. I finished my Bachelor of Science degree in chemistry in 1967.

Thinking to obtain an advanced degree in chemistry, I was off to the University of Wyoming for the 1967–68 academic year. But my former passion had vanished. It wasn't the university's doing; I was burned out on chemistry. I considered changing schools and switching to fine art photography.

In that vein, I participated in a photography workshop in Yosemite Valley, California, during the summer of 1968. I was then, and still am, taken with the fine possibilities of the photographic image, and with particular modes of thought and attitude in obtaining those images.

Ansel Adams conducted that workshop. Looking back; I was 23 years old, unqualified to sit in the presence of Adams or even turn up within his sight. But he made a lasting impression on me as he taught the use of intense excellence, not gimmicks, to bring about a simple, spectacular result. Adams had written about color photography, advising sarcastically that "if you can't make it good, then make it red!" I understood his thought, but have modified my concept of color since then. I usually work in color now, because I think a photograph can be both good *and* red.

I made a point of backpacking into the California Sierra Nevada mountains each summer during my college years. Schemes to build dams on the Colorado River in the Grand Canyon got my attention, too, and I became more active in the environmental organization that stopped this.

Early explorations with my father started my interest in wild places and natural processes. I haven't changed. Wherever I go, that passion goes with me. It would go with me to Vietnam.

I tell of these experiences because they led to my eventual understanding that most things in the world are somehow connected to most other things. These understandings, insights and passions are very much related to the rest of this book.

Off to the Army

Following my year at the University of Wyoming, the Vietnam War was going strongly. Every young male out of school and in sight of the draft board was being called into service. (This was before the days of lottery numbers for draft purposes.) Well, nothing much was happening in my life. I hadn't gone back to school. What would be the harm in getting drafted? With my degree in chemistry, they'd assign me to something interesting anyway, wouldn't they? I'd work in a lab or a technical field for two years and probably learn a few things. I was called for a pre-induction physical in September, then sent a draft notice for October.

So, I showed up one morning in October of 1968 to ride a bus into the Los Angeles reception center with other local inductees. A few were chosen at random to become U.S. Marines, but even then I suspected, correctly or not, that branch was much like a religious order devoted to war. I managed to stay clear of the Marines. Those of us sworn into the Army boarded another bus. It took us northward for several hours to Fort Ord near Monterey, California, where we arrived in the middle of the night. How could I complain about getting drafted? After all, hadn't I once favored the U.S. part in the Vietnam War? Though my support had begun to decline, I chose to be idealistic about this new experience.

"Get yer hands outta yer pockets! It's not cold!" hollered the young man in uniform who greeted us off the bus very late that evening. In this early contact with the United States Army, its first lowly representative probably seemed like the commanding general to some who had just been made privates that morning in Los Angeles. I tended toward a more cynical view of him. After getting off the bus, we were ordered to stand in a rough company formation. Lined up in the dark, we awaited further induction proceedings. We probably would not be killed in Vietnam that night, though progress toward that end seemed unmistakable. This reception company, and the coarse creatures who ran it, would have us in custody for the next few days.

There wasn't much else to do that night, except this: We were conducted past a hole in the wall similar to a post office mail slot and told to deposit any pornography or other "contraband" we might possess. Photographs of one's naked legal wife were allowed, provided they met certain standards of taste that had come down from above. I didn't see anyone put anything in the slot. If anyone did, I've wondered since what became of it. (Years later, I talked by e-mail with a couple of guys who had worked there. One said they burned the stuff while the other said they heartily enjoyed it. Maybe they enjoyed it and then burned it—I don't know!)

We were shown a barracks and told to find bunks. Sleep came, though not for long. A certain individual in the reception company, probably a low-tier enlisted man serving out his last days in the Army, came and kicked a large metal trash can, clanging and banging it across the room. He loudly proclaimed it to be five o'clock in the morning, and encouraged us to rise. Everyone did.

A New Day

While standing in another formation at first light, I marveled at the cleanliness of the area around the barracks. I learned very soon how it got that way. Lined up elbow-to-elbow, we all walked slowly and carefully through the company area. That same trash can kicker was behind us, offering further encouragement. Preoccupied about us locating and picking up each piece of refuse no matter how tiny, he commented critically about each failure he perceived.

With close haircuts and new uniforms, it became impossible to tell which inductees had formerly been hippies. We were given boxes in which to mail home the clothes we had worn there. The Army's purpose was to have us look and act like robots. The challenge throughout would be to avoid thinking like one.

Meals in the mess hall were not the relaxed affairs of academia. The food wasn't bad, but a mess sergeant would walk around the whole time, scowling proficiently and yelling, "Eat up and get out!" This was probably the most power he'd exercised in nearly twenty years of military service, so why not indulge him a little?

A series of immunizations began, often given with a device that forced a stream of fluid underneath the skin where it made a small blister that was soon absorbed. So the procedure would be entirely painless, quick, and clean, we were instructed not to move. But one guy moved during his injection. The tiny stream of fluid acted like a saw, and turned that part of his arm into a bloody mess. He was admonished in a very face-to-face manner for having been weak. *"Dumbfuck!"*

What Job?

We met with people whose jobs were to offer us regular enlistments with guaranteed jobs, in return for three years in the Army. Or, in my case with a recent degree in chemistry, an officer explained the benefits of becoming one of them at Officer Candidate School. "Then they treat you as though you have a mind," the lieutenant told me. But I remained unconvinced.

I checked out the guaranteed job offerings. But there were no slots in any field I was interested in, like becoming an aircraft mechanic, getting into military intelligence, or going into some other field that required skill and even a hint of intellect. Otherwise, I might have taken the offer to stay longer. But I wasn't ready to spend an additional year in the Army doing what didn't interest me, so I clung to what I'd been told about being assigned to a job somewhat in keeping with my education. I chose to continue as a two-year draftee.

One friend with a bachelor's degree had been drafted earlier, assigned to military intelligence, and eventually sent to Vietnam to analyze aerial photographs. Another friend was drafted a little later, trained as an inhalation therapist and sent to Tripler Army Hospital in Hawaii for the rest of his two years. He'd just earned a master's degree in chemistry and that seemed to make a difference. We draftees would not know our eventual jobs until basic training was nearly over.

Lifers and Non-Lifers

After several days of induction processing, trucks came to bear us to our basic training company area on "The Hill." As we tumbled out of the truck with our new duffel bags, drill sergeants hovered around, bellowing in tones of great authority.

Most of us were draftees, some were National Guard trainees, and a few were "regular Army." The latter had enlisted for more time in the Army but for guaranteed training, which probably was not 11-Bravo (infantry). Most who joined the Army in those days did so to avoid being drafted, then assigned as a *grunt*—an infantryman.

A broad distinction was readily drawn among Army personnel: *lifers* and *non-lifers*. Few, if any, of the trainees would stay in the Army beyond their terms of service. But if any did make a career of it, Sergeant James Spitz provided a daily example of what that meant.

Sometimes he and executive officer Lieutenant Barry Wold would appear to joke about Spitz becoming an officer. Wold would call out, "There's still time, Spitz! It's not too late!" Spitz would reply with gusto, "Naw, I wanna fuck, fight and swim!" I'm sure these exchanges were staged, but they illustrated the enlisted versus officer orientations.

Other drill sergeants tended toward crudeness. Only a small number of swear words exist in English and we've all known them since grade school. But these guys knew them in powerful combinations! One particular trainee among us could hardly wait to go home and pay his little brother certain devastating new insults he'd been learning.

Fight! Fight! Fight!

When fights break out, there is generally a considerable component of arrogant, macho showmanship about it. The shouted reason for such battles is seldom the real one.

We conducted a profound experiment once in grade school when a bunch of us gathered in the far corner of the playground and yelled "fight, fight, fight!" Mr. Lieberman came sprinting all the way across the field, probably farther and faster than he'd run for a long time! There was no fight—just us kids yelling in simulation of one. Lieberman said we'd "played that trick on the wrong guy," and invited our presence in his room after school. There, he sternly said for each of us to compose an essay of a designated length by the next day. I didn't do that and nothing ever happened, but this point emerged: fights are most often conducted just as matters of public demonstration.

Not in basic training, though! Our platoon drill sergeant announced that combatants would be taken to a room by themselves, there to fight without an audience. Nobody ever had to do that, though this matter of foolish machismo would come up again later, in several ways, on another continent.

Further Indignities

Winter was coming. Temperatures would drop, unlike those in our most likely destination. Along the coast of California, winter produces mostly rain and mud, not snow. But the cold and wet felt terrible.

Basic training company barracks were all lined up in the same area of Fort Ord, so the various training facilities could be used in common. Besides the parade field used for running and marching drill, there were class areas of various configurations. Several rifle ranges were down near the beach, and there we were taken by trucks to fire our outdated M-14 rifles. After days at the ranges, we'd have to run in formation several miles back. Elsewhere on Fort Ord was a big gas chamber to illustrate the considerable effect of tear gas upon us and to motivate proper use of the M-17 gas mask.

Facilities included a specialized range for hand grenade training, where there was a concrete wall to throw the grenade over. Along the base of that wall was a deep concrete slot into which a grenade could be kicked if it were dropped. Someone stood right there to do the kicking if necessary. We were told to throw the grenade like a baseball and, with maximum sarcasm, instructed not to use the "John Wayne" style! His movies had not burdened my life, so I just threw my grenade over the wall. It exploded mightily out there somewhere.

About the only enjoyable night during basic training was during our *bivouac,* which was a couple of days spent in a more remote and wild part of Fort Ord. I don't recall everything we did, but I do remember getting into that army sleeping bag, on an army air mattress, in an army tent, for a very comfortable sleep. This bit of pleasantness was directly connected to the many outdoor adventures in my past. Similar recollections would occur throughout this Army experience. Some trainees had probably never slept outside before. For them, perhaps it was a night of fear.

The last week of basic training, my name was on a list for M-16 rifle familiarization so I suspected what my assignment for further training would be. Sure enough, when orders were distributed for training, mine were for infantry right there at Fort Ord after a short leave.

Training as a Grunt

AIT (Advanced Individual Training) proceeded with more shooting, first aid, how to set up perimeters, a little bit of strategy, lots more marching around in the mornings, and assurances that our asses would die if we failed to learn. I remember one training location in particular, about advancing under fire at night on a course set up to teach that. We were warned of grim, deadly consequences if we stood up. Then we crawled in the dirt for a certain distance, underneath and toward massive machine gun fire. I suspect, though, the bullets flew high enough for the Army to avoid inconvenience and paperwork if a trainee panicked and stood up.

Flying?

I'd flown airplanes with my father from an early age. He and I rebuilt his Stinson, then we flew this single engine, high wing, four-place, tail-wheel airplane around the country in the summer of 1960, prior to my junior year in high school. We slept outside most nights, right near the airplane.

My concept of geography had already been strong and this trip increased it by orders of magnitude. It did the same for my historical perspective. Flying low down the Mississippi River from Greenville to New Orleans and then over Civil War battlefields, Jamestown, and Boston will do that. Crossing the prairie in a light airplane, while considering a similar journey by wagon train, encouraged understanding about that region. Flying was a learning tool I felt passionately about.

During my first year in college, I earned a private pilot certificate. Later, involved with the University of Wyoming Flying Club, I used its Cessna 172 to obtain commercial pilot and flight instructor certificates. Perhaps I missed a meeting or something, since I ended up club president rather than just the newsletter editor. My duties included the resolution of disputes between warring factions and resulted in my wanting never to be president of anything again. The grandeur of presidencies is vastly overestimated, and this one interfered with the fun of flying.

My dad owned a Cherokee Arrow by that time and I used it to get an instrument rating during the summer of 1968. I would later do some flight instructing in Southern California where I had students who could almost make instrument approaches before they could land the airplane because of the low cloud layer often present.

Could I turn all this into something with the Army? During infantry AIT, I applied for flight training, signed a one-year extension of my time in the Army, and received orders to Fort Wolters, Texas. There, I was put into a holding company to await preflight training.

But something immediately felt wrong. I quickly discovered these guys didn't love to fly, as I did. They loved combat and shooting people. An aircraft was just their weapon—something on which to mount the guns. I was learning a great deal about the military mentality and saw I'd made a mistake. I got back out of that and, as I suspected would happen, received orders for Vietnam.

After thirty days of leave, I would report to Fort Lewis, Washington, for further assignment to the Military Assistance Command, Vietnam.

New Oceans, New Worlds, and the Moon

Liftoff! Looking back at the television, I hung near the door of my parents' home in Southern California, though I needed to catch flights north to Fort Lewis, Washington, and eventually to Vietnam. Apollo 11 was just lifting off, so I watched it power up through the stratosphere. As the lunar mission continued into Earth orbit, I continued out the door to go across the sea.

My parents and sister took me to the airport where I caught my first flight to San Francisco. Another flight would take me on to Seattle. On it, up a couple thousand feet, I felt the four jet engines suddenly power back. Was I going to Vietnam or into San Francisco Bay? I preferred Vietnam right then! But engine power soon returned. Air Traffic Control had probably issued an altitude hold for some reason, then removed it, and we were on our way again. I could visualize the pilot's hand on the throttles. At about that time, the Apollo 11 astronauts blasted out of Earth orbit and were on their way to the moon.

I don't remember much about Fort Lewis near Tacoma except there was much waiting involved. Apollo was just coasting moonward by then. I was just coasting, too. My name finally appeared on a list to board a DC-8 airliner, chartered by the government from one of the airlines. We'd depart from the adjacent McChord Air Force Base for Vietnam. On board, a flight attendant announced we'd be flying to Honolulu, Wake Island, and Cam Ranh Bay, Vietnam.

On the way, those who wanted to visit the cockpit were invited to do so. I knew what airspeed indicators, altimeters, throttles, and instrument panels looked like. Instead of marveling at that, I looked out the front windshield in hopes of spotting Hawaii.

Nothing doing! We still had a long way to go and the Pacific Ocean was broad beyond my imagining. I couldn't tell by looking, but I knew parts of it were quite deep. Seafloor was being forced down into the earth along marine trenches at plate boundaries, as geologists were just beginning to understand. Looking through the windshield of that DC-8 made me wonder how there could be so much water on the earth?

We reached Honolulu and off we got. I knew that passengers were required by regulation to disembark during refueling of an aircraft. This time, it resulted in my being handed a small cup of pineapple juice by pleasant greeters in the airport terminal. After 45 minutes, we were taxiing to the runway, bound for Wake Island.

Rolling down the runway, it seemed the DC-8 would never fly! It was warm in Honolulu and undoubtedly quite humid. Aircraft perform considerably less well under those circumstances. Air molecules are farther apart on average when the temperature is high. When it's also humid, more air molecules have been replaced by water molecules, which have just over half the average mass of air molecules. So the air in Honolulu was less dense for these two reasons. The result? Our wings had to go faster through the air to create the same lift and our airplane had to roll farther down the runway before it achieved flying speed.

Pilots calculate these things in advance and will only take off if they know it's going to work. It worked. Out near Pearl Harbor we flew, and then over water for a long time.

Wake Island seemed the very image of a coral atoll—a piece of land curved in upon itself with water in the center. The gigantic runway took up much of the island. Outwardly, the place wasn't exciting—quite the opposite, in fact. But I'd read about islands in the Pacific for years and about this island in particular. There can be hard-to-explain satisfaction in finally visiting such a place. Now, while refueling proceeded, there I stood on Wake.

Darkness came upon us somewhere west of Wake. I saw city lights pass underneath, but couldn't make sense of it right then. Later plotting on a globe convinced me it was the Philippines. "We're beginning our approach into Cam Ranh Bay..." It was dark, but I could hear the flaps operate and the landing gear go thumping down. Presently, the wheels squeaked onto a runway and I was in Vietnam for the first time.

Late at night we bused to a reception center on the base at Cam Ranh and were advised to bunk in one of several barracks buildings nearby. I walked through one building, then another. Both smelled musty, but this was the tropics. I went outside and lay down on the sand. Back in America, across the date line, it was 20 July 1969.

The moon! Awareness of the Apollo journey came back to me in a flash. I switched on my small portable radio and tuned around. The military in Vietnam, I learned, had a network of broadcast stations. Lying on the sand at Cam Ranh Bay, I could hear the Apollo 11 crew live, descending to the lunar surface. Astronaut Armstrong's famous giant leap for mankind would come a bit later, but Apollo had landed. I had landed, too. Which of us had the better chance of getting home alive? My bet was on them.

In-country Training and Orders North

Those of us assigned to the 101st Airborne Division were flown off to Bien Hoa near Saigon for a week of *in-country* training about how to operate in Vietnam. We received a briefing from a major. How filled with military rapture he was! Just the sort of man we'd heard about in academia.

This was two months after Hamburger Hill, and I'd been assigned to the division that had conducted this costly, bloody battle to capture a hill in remote country very near Laos. Senator Edward Kennedy led the congressional outcry against such senselessness, charging that no purpose—even in military terms—had been served. Was he ever on the command's bad list when I arrived! See *Hamburger Hill*, by Samuel Zaffiri, 1988.

The division, we were told, had recently abandoned parachutes in favor of helicopters, to the discomfort of certain old-timers. It was now called the 101st Airborne Division (Airmobile) with about 400 helicopters. Their shoulder patch was the only one in Vietnam not redesigned in dimmed colors for better camouflage. Leaders of the 101st were quite proud of this *screaming eagle* business, stemming from the division's World War II activities. "The 101st Airborne Division *owns* the A Shau Valley!" declared the major, strutting with pride. Never mind the human cost.

I had passed the tail end of my days as a pro-war conservative, and was growing more anti-war by the hour. The major's words and demeanor helped me along considerably, but not in the direction he hoped. "I suppose you all think you're gonna get hamburgered on Hamburger Hill?"

Several of us were probably thinking exactly that. This Army thing was about to get more real. But he predicted, with a grin of the most dangerous sort, "In a year, you'll be right back here again. Fit! Suntanned! Ready to go home!" Oh really? Home to explain to all those doubters how right and good this war really was? Tens of thousands of draftees like me had already been killed in Vietnam, but he didn't touch on that. I was ready to go home right then.

We piled into a big C-130 four-turboprop transport airplane for the flight north to Camp Evans where we'd join part of the 101st Airborne Division. I was still uneducated about military transport aircraft. These machines are very loud within and their windows are few and tiny. In the future, I would quickly stake out a place near a window and use earplugs of some sort.

I sat packed among live bodies on the floor and watched various mechanisms overhead. Shafts went laterally into the wing structures, turned by small electric motors. Sure enough, one of them appeared to operate the flaps; another, the landing gear. I didn't see much else during that flight.

Presently the power was reduced and the wheels touched down onto a runway. We taxied just a little, stopped, and the great rear door was lowered. We were at the Da Nang airfield. Fighter-bombers came screaming by lined up to land on the runway, probably returning from missions. It was sunny and hot.

But why were we at Da Nang? Because our C-130 had *blown up*. This common term, often applied to aircraft, simply meant the machine in question had ceased to work. It didn't necessarily mean a blinding explosion in the air followed by a rain of spiraling pieces, though that happened sometimes, too. One of our four engines had failed. The C-130 pilots had executed an emergency landing in Da Nang, which was less than a hundred miles from our destination. We all got out and waited near the aircraft. Another C-130 arrived and we continued our journey to Camp Evans.

Camp Evans

At first, I knew little about my surroundings, except that I was "up north" in South Vietnam. Apparently this was a coastal plain since I knew the sea was near and I saw a range of mountains several miles inland. On that day, I knew next to nothing about the regional geography; I'd learn that later by making a few helicopter flights over the area.

We got another orientation, after dark by then, somewhere on Camp Evans, which turned out to be a base for several infantry outfits. A young enlisted man introduced us to the place and finally said, "Look, if any of you have a question about anything, either I or some other non-lifer will answer it for you!" No lifers were listening.

I appreciated this direct talk. It was markedly different from what we'd just been subjected to at Bien Hoa. Indeed, as I'd already seen during training, a major division existed between lifers and non-lifers. The military career types versus mostly draftees. The gung-ho, war-fight-kill types versus those who were considerably less than enthused.

With several others, I was assigned to Delta Company, First Battalion, 506th Infantry—Delta 1/506 for short. In a day or two, we'd be helicoptered out to join the rest of Delta Company at Eagles' Nest.

Somebody above had decided these companies would be called names like "Ass-Kicking Alpha" for Alpha Company and "Death Dealers" for Delta Company, just as athletic teams may have names like the Giants or Cardinals. I never heard anyone actually use one of these names.

Eagles' Nest Overlooking the A Shau

For my first-ever helicopter ride, I boarded the CH-47 Chinook and sat on the floor. I was used to aircraft that roared down a runway to fly, but this machine strangely levitated before it moved forward. That was new. Out across the perimeter of Camp Evans and that coastal plain we flew, toward the mountains. First over flat, grassy terrain and then over rugged, forested mountains.

I would always notice the shapes of mountains in that part of Vietnam. Not craggy with bare rock like the Sierra I'd backpacked in, but steep, more symmetrical mountains that often rose to points. And the trees! Huge individual trees visible on mountain flanks against the sky.

The big twin-rotor helicopter made a slow descent past what I'd soon learn was Firebase Bertchesgaden on the northeastern side of the A Shau Valley. We stepped off the helicopter into a strange world: Eagles' Nest, almost 5,000 feet high, was atop one of the taller mountains surrounding the valley.

All trees and vegetation had been removed from the summit. Bunkers formed a perimeter around it and a helicopter pad had been made. I've since learned Eagles' Nest was a radio site, but I didn't have a clue that day what it was.

Infantry companies took turns guarding it and my new company was assigned there then. For maybe a week, my job was to guard a part of the Eagles' Nest perimeter all night, each night, from one of the sandbag bunkers there. In a few days, Delta Company would move off elsewhere.

The company commander, a Captain Owen Ditchfield, took us *cherries* (new guys) to the perimeter and pointed out the major, visible features of the A Shau. Right across the valley, named for its height in meters, was Hill 937, or Hamburger Hill.

Somewhere nearby was Hill 996 where he said the company had "seen a little action." This was an important place, but I didn't know it then. As I recall, Ditchfield pointed southeast of Hamburger. He indicated a couple of other places that were equally meaningless to me then. We were standing on a mountain overlooking the A Shau Valley, being shown things by someone who knew. I'd sure like to hear his orientation again, knowing what I've learned since!

Perhaps twice each night, at times that were variable and known only by us, we'd have a *mad minute.* We'd all fire down the mountainside from our perimeter positions as rapidly as we could for about a minute, thinking to disrupt and discourage any attack that might have been forthcoming. Looking across at nearby Firebase Berchesgaden, I'd been able to see their mad minutes; red appeared to stream down that mountain. These were tracers (bullets that glowed in flight to make their courses visible), which we loaded every third round or so.

I also learned about being out at an *LP* (listening post). Each evening at last light, two or three of us would trek off down the mountain 50 meters or so. We'd stay there all night, listening for movement. Never heard any. We had a radio and, upon attack, we'd be ordered back up inside our line of bunkers. I was no tactician, but from my perspective this whole idea had grave deficiencies. Would we be able to pull back in time if attack came? I held doubts.

This whole area was important to the military because some of the Ho Chi Minh Trail's many branches were there. The A Shau Valley ran southeast to northwest, parallel to the Laotian border in nearly the skinniest section of Vietnam. By the maps I have today, the sea was only 32 to 37 miles from the A Shau's centerline. Given the crooked border with Laos, Vietnam was only 35 to 40 miles wide there. The valley before me was about 20 miles long and between one and seven miles wide. It had a fat middle that extended toward Laos. The flat floor looked green and lush with native grasses. Mountains, steep and wooded, surrounded it. No Vietnamese lived there then, though maps showed a village of A Luoi on the valley floor.

Fascinated by this wild and rugged land, I had a sense of place and beauty that the military was not going to take from me, though they'd sent me here to be cannon fodder. The military controlled me then, but they couldn't control what I'd make of this Vietnam experience later. They didn't know, nor did I know myself, that this experience would determine whole directions in my life. On Eagles' Nest, the thought first came to me that I'd like to see this place on my own terms, some other time, in the absence of war.

Firebase Currahee

Just a few days later, Delta Company was helicoptered down from Eagles' Nest onto the southwestern side of the A Shau Valley floor to provide security around the perimeter of Firebase Currahee.

Eagles' Nest and Berchesgaden were on peaks of a divide. Water on one side ran directly northeast to the South China Sea. Water that flowed down into the A Shau took a much longer route. I'd learn later that the Rao Lao River headed in the southeastern A Shau Valley and flowed into Laos through a gap in the mountains not far south of Hamburger Hill. The river ran right past Currahee on its long route to the ocean via the Mekong River.

In the daytime, some of us waded and bathed in the small stream. By night, that part of the perimeter was dangerous because right across the river was hilly, forested terrain from which an attack could come—a situation I doubt was lost upon the commanding officer. My night position was in that area. A helicopter pad was right behind us, and Cobra gunships came and went with some frequency.

Also, there was a quad-50 nearby—the equivalent of four large machine guns, mounted and aimed in tandem. This instrument of death was mounted in the open back of a small four-wheel drive vehicle. At night, I saw what it could do. The quad-50 would *fire up* the area across the river during mad minutes as rocket-flares illuminated the area. Saplings were uprooted and thrown twirling into the air. It looked like the whole side of that low hillock was in turmoil, the earth moving and vibrating. This made the slope across the river a very poor place to be, which is what we demonstrated several times each night to whomever might have been watching. One does not want to be on the bad end of a quad-50.

A few of us had been assigned an M-79 *thumper* instead of a rifle. This was a grenade launcher that looked like a sawed-off shotgun with a fat barrel. It opened at the breech and fired rounds shaped like those for a .45 pistol, only larger. The thing made a *thuuump* sound and the grenade portion of the round would fly away and explode on impact. During the time I had a thumper, I enjoyed the trajectorial challenge of lobbing grenades onto the backsides of small hills during mad minutes.

A Cobra helicopter might make a mad minute strafing run with the minigun buzzing. The minigun, mounted below the nose of a Cobra, had rotating barrels arranged cylindrically. The cylinder rotated and brought each barrel into firing position in turn. On just one pass, it was said, the minigun could put a bullet deep into every square foot of a football field.

It did not go *bang, bang*, or even sound like a machine gun. It buzzed loudly. Anyone in front of it tended to fall dead.

The real purpose of a firebase was to provide a home for artillery. Whole batteries consisting of big guns, soldiers, and whatever other equipment they had could be airlifted to a firebase by big Chinook helicopters. They could set up quickly, carry out *fire missions*, and be moved again if necessary. The guns on these firebases would boom away at random times for reasons usually unknown to me.

Dissent

I first heard it during our stay on Eagles' Nest: ongoing grumbling about Captain Ditchfield. I remember one guy leading a chant: "I won't go to the field again with Ditchfield." This was evidently fairly serious, though I was new and had no clue about it at first. A change in command was made while we were at Currahee. Captain Walter Mather came walking around the perimeter one night introducing himself as the new company commanding officer—the CO.

I was beginning to piece a story together. Some of the guys evidently blamed Ditchfield for events on Hill 996. This had been a Hamburger Hill-like battle fought more than a month after the original, shortly before I'd gotten there. Indeed, as I was able to put the story together, I was a replacement in a platoon in which all or most had been killed. I would realize later that during this time, the high command had been telling news media how quiet it was in the area as a result of Hamburger Hill—failing to mention Hill 996. A cover–up? That would not have been beyond our military then, would it? At Currahee, I first started getting wind of this.

"I missed my chance!" One guy ruefully related how he could have shot Ditchfield, who apparently had been walking around outside the company *NDP* (Night Defensive Position) in the field just before dark. Not a very wise thing to have done, particularly by a commander some soldiers hated. I guess he was checking things out, but anyone who felt the urge could have shot him dead without repercussion. In fairness to Ditchfield, I was told later that events on Hill 996 hadn't been his fault. Still, given the rebellious situation, he could hardly serve as company commander.

Into the Beaten Zone

The beaten zone, a term from basic training, referred to parts of the berm behind the targets at Army rifle ranges where dirt was pulverized from all the bullets that struck. Among the infantry in Vietnam, going to the beaten zone meant going to the field. This was off base camp and off firebases, patrolling mostly through the forest. We called it jungle then and so did the media, but it was really forest. Our missions were called RIF*s* (Reconnaissance In Force).

We'd carry most of our food, a means to heat it, about four canteens, an air mattress, a poncho liner for warmth, and a poncho to string up as a *hootch* (rain shelter). Our weapons included a Claymore mine, hand grenades, lots of ammunition in clips, and an M-16 rifle or an M-79 grenade launcher if assigned one.

Helicopters came: Hueys without seats or doors in the back, two pilots up front, and a door gunner on either side. The aircraft commander sat on the left, I learned, while the pilot in the right seat normally did the flying. These helicopters could be flown from either seat.

We'd arrange ourselves on either side of the landing zone so we could board quickly as soon as the helicopter touched down. We'd run to it, climb aboard, and sit on the metal floor. Flying without a seatbelt or a door was new for me, but the helicopter flew smoothly without the bumps that are common in light airplanes. The pilots, after all, were really flying a big gyroscope (the rotor) with the helicopter hanging from its hub. Some guys just sat on the edge of the floor with their feet hanging out, but I wasn't ready for that at first. Instead, I got more toward the center and found something to hang onto. After a short time, though, I was willing to sit on the edge, too.

Upon reaching the LZ (Landing Zone), the helicopters would often hover two or three feet above the ground. It seemed farther down than that, but probably wasn't. Having to jump for it resulted in hard landings with our heavy backpacks on.

Later, I would hear a story (perhaps true, perhaps not) about an infantryman flying in a Huey on a more relaxed mission over flat country near the coast. He had a small camera and wanted a picture of something on the ground, so he leaned way out of the helicopter to take it and lost his balance. While in free-fall, he must have had a fearsome opportunity for a close-up.

Maps, Bullets, and Grenades

It was visually exciting to fly low over tall forest in a helicopter. I could see all the way to the ground directly below the aircraft, but nowhere else. Even a little bit ahead, I saw nothing but leaves. The tree cover there could be nearly a hundred feet deep and my straight-down view of the ground flashed by rapidly. I didn't know where we were going this first time, but the direction was generally down-valley (southeast) through the A Shau and into the forested hills to one side.

Much later, I would do guard duty at Camp Evans at the battalion TOC (Tactical Operations Center). A topographic map near the entrance there showed our entire area of operation from around Camp Evans on the coastal plain, up into the mountains, to the A Shau Valley, and into Laos. Actually several maps mounted together, it showed every stream, hill, road, and firebase. I admire maps in general, topographic maps in particular, and I wish I'd stolen that one!

Our LZ was the abandoned Firebase Fury, another bare place on a low hilltop. The helicopters touched down, one by one. We jumped out and made for the edges of the cleared area. On the way we saw crude booby traps—small pits that someone had dug with sharpened bamboo sticks in them, pointed up. It looked like a very young person had made these, but in any case, someone had been there.

Off the old firebase and down a trail we went, single file, several meters distance between each man. Were we going to walk along in a big group and all get shot instead of just the first couple of us? I don't think so! This had been a fundamental part of our training. The *point man* (the one walking first) needed to be fiercely proud of his job. Walking *slack* meant being second. The other platoons went off in other directions.

Our assignment was to probe the terrain for the opposition, looking for trouble. But presently, our platoon leader didn't know where we were on the map. My squad was detailed to take the map, go out just a little way onto a ridge, and locate ourselves. Off we went. Moving as just one squad was not common. I walked slack right then and Jones was point.

Zap! Zap! Zap! Bullets passing close make a memorable sound. Everyone hit the ground prone, per our training. The rest of the squad, then the whole platoon, came up on-line with us and we all blazed away for several minutes at the most probable location of the NVA soldier. The lieutenant in charge thought he saw something: "I'm gonna throw a grenade!"

I don't remember if it was his first throw or not, but a grenade bounced off a tree and landed right beside me. It was the only dud I ever saw. It is reasonable that a defective item will be supplied now and then, so I forgave the munitions manufacturer this lapse in quality.

We continued to blaze away, but the NVA trail watcher was probably far away by then. His job had been to fire a few rounds and run, and he'd done exactly that. One of the trailwatcher's bullets had torn a large gash in the helmet of our point man, spinning it harmlessly off his head onto the ground. Jones was fairly new at this, too, and I clearly remember him a few minutes later examining his ruined helmet, frowning powerfully and disgustedly about the state of things.

We rarely used first names, but Jones became a friend. I'd like to talk with him again, see how his life has been, and learn his first name. (I tried to find him once, while in his city of Memphis, but looking up "Jones" in a big-city phone directory was unfruitful.)

I don't remember where we set up our perimeter that night, or the next night, or the night after that. Details of all those RIFs run together for me now. But the first time I got shot at in Vietnam was also the last, and the gunman had missed.

A few weeks later, our platoon had set an ambush along a trail. Somebody in command must have thought the opposition was located down one side of the ridge we were on, since Cobra helicopters arrived and fired up that area. Suddenly, a guy not too far from me stood up, eyes wide but the corners of his mouth definitely downturned. He'd been shot through the wrist by one of the bullets from a Cobra's minigun.

Food in the Field

With relatively delightful exceptions, we ate mostly C-rations. These came with main courses, cans of fruit, hot chocolate, coffee (which I dislike), and various other goodies.

We used small can openers, called P-38s, which were a bit larger than a quarter. A blade folded out from an otherwise flat piece of metal that had a notch in it. We'd hook the notch onto the rim of the can and twist so the blade would cut all around the can's top. I thank the military for my extraordinary can-opening ability.

Cold C-rations would have been awful, like bringing a can of beef stew home from the store and eating it unwarmed. Big chunks of white fat—yuck! But we were equipped. The Army gave us heat tabs in sealed, olive-drab colored packages that we tore open. The tab itself was about three inches long and we usually broke it in half. The light blue, crystalline substance was easily flammable.

An empty C-ration can would make a stove. We also had P-39s, commonly known then as beer can openers though modern beer cans don't open like that anymore. With these, we'd make triangular holes all around the outside of a can at its base to allow air in, and more holes around the top for exhaust. We'd put half a heat tab in the can and light it. A just-opened C-ration can put on top would soon be piping hot. We also had metal canteen cups that fit around the outside bottom of our olive-drab, plastic canteens. With mine atop my little stove, I'd quickly have hot water for my cocoa.

The best foods in the field were LRRPs—Long Range Reconnaissance Patrol rations. These came sealed in olive-drab bags, too. Inside were goodies like a candy bar, coffee, and hot chocolate. A dehydrated main course was in a plastic bag, and there'd be a plastic spoon. We heated water in the aforementioned manner and poured an appropriate amount into the bag. It was tall enough for the contents to be mixed up by kneading. I'd roll the top of mine and slide it back inside the larger bag for insulation. After the specified time, I'd eat my meal.

Guys had favorites, so when we were issued LRRPs or C-rations, we'd negotiate trades with each other that maximized our satisfaction. Most agreed that the best LRRP was spaghetti; we could almost measure our wealth by how many of those we possessed. About the only other measure of wealth was the shortness of our time remaining in Vietnam.

Once home again, I resumed backpacking trips in the California Sierra Nevada, and later in the Colorado Rockies. I found these same LRRP rations sold in more attractive packaging by backpacking shops. I believe the inner bag was exactly the same. This was very convenient because I already knew which ones I liked. The backpacking foods came from the same company whose name I'd seen on the LRRP packages in Vietnam.

Sometimes, food would be flown to us in the field. If a helicopter couldn't land, the food would be lowered to us from a hover above the trees. I'm sure this showed the NVA exactly where we were, so it had to be a situation in which it didn't matter much. The food would be prepared back at Camp Evans, loaded into several insulated containers, and brought to us.

Sometimes it rained steadily. Then there was nothing to do during the day but stand and be drenched. Cold wasn't usually a problem, but soaking in the rain wasn't quite like being toasty warm. I saw a Disney film once that showed a large, male, otherwise fierce African lion sitting glumly in driving rain because there was no other place to sit. We looked like that.

One such day, it was our turn to receive a big insulated container of ice cream, and a helicopter arrived with it. Though we were drenched in the driving rain, we ate that ice cream gladly! The military had decided to promote morale among the troops with ice cream, and had built several manufacturing plants in Vietnam. Maybe I should have resented that as an attempt to purchase my soul, but right then I didn't mind.

Blue Lines

We got water from *blue lines,* so-called because streams were drawn blue on our topographic maps. There seemed to be a stream between almost any two hills. We used halazone tablets to "purify" the water. Nothing was purified, of course. Whatever bacteria or virus had been wiggling around in the water would just drift dead in that same water. The water had been disinfected, not purified, as is also true of water most of us drink at home.

One day we walked down a slope to the blue line in small groups to fill our canteens. I remember walking back up with Boyd (whose first name I also don't know) and saying, "There's a trail… I wonder where it goes?" Boyd, in his wisdom, said then, "I don't care where it goes. I don't think you do either!"

"There it is!" We often used this expression in response to a statement of particular truth and profundity. It was a compliment to the insight and outspokenness of the speaker. I hadn't meant that we should follow the trail, but Boyd was right. It wasn't healthy to be too concerned where trails went. Better to just get our water.

Night Defensive Positions—Homes for the Night

Each night, we'd set our perimeter in a big circle, preferably on high ground, usually with a couple of us assigned to each position. We tied our ponchos up with cord to make low rain shelters. This was easy because almost anywhere we reached, there'd be something to tie to—a clump of grass, a branch, or a root. In my mind, the "jungle" would be a slimy place: full of fungi, mold, and dead things decaying. But aside from the possibility of combat, the forest was actually very pleasant.

We set out a Claymore mine a certain distance from each position. This was a mine used on the ground and not buried in it. The device was sealed in plastic, perhaps eight inches long, five high, and two thick. It had little fold-out legs to help stand it up and a hole to insert a blasting cap. We unrolled a wire that extended from the blasting cap to a hand-held squeeze device back where we were. The Claymore contained a layer of plastic explosive, in front of which were 750 steel balls that would burst forth upon detonation.

I knew two things about Claymore mines. One was that the NVA had been known to sneak up, turn them around, sneak off again, and make some noise. I never set one off, turned or not. The other was that old Claymore mines could be broken open and the plastic explosive inside could be torn into pieces. These could be used just like heat tabs to warm our dinners! I did this many times. Not subjected to the detonation of a blasting cap, the plastic explosive would just burn. It made an ideal fuel.

Frequent rain was a problem, particularly at night. Only the careful among us were able to keep things dry. We'd been issued poncho liners, sized to fit into an Army poncho. I never used one inside a poncho, but what wonderful, soft insulators they were for sleeping! I kept mine in a plastic bag until I had my poncho-shelter erected, so it stayed dry. A little dampness would evaporate quickly enough, but some guys actually wrung water out of theirs each morning. As insulation against nighttime coolness, poncho liners worked very poorly when sopping wet.

We pulled guard duty all night long in the NDP, usually just half of us at a time but sometimes all of us, according to orders. Nobody ever came in the night to disturb us.

One telling incident: a new draftee had arrived from Memphis and was sharing news from *back in the world*. It was that certain young women of Memphis had lately been found "dead in their bathtubs," which had caused consternation. Here we were, near Vietnam's A Shau Valley and just a few miles from Hamburger Hill, discussing heinous killings that had happened in the United States.

The same fellow soon discovered his first leech. They live in the United States, too, but I'd never seen one until I got to Vietnam. I guess he hadn't either. Leeches are horrible little things that resemble slugs, except they seem very muscular. Trying to squish one is like squishing a rubber band. They got on us if we walked through heavy vegetation or waded through wet places. Each end of a leech can stick to surfaces. One end strikes out for a new place and sticks while the other end draws up close.

Leeches inch along inside clothing, moving over skin until they find a warm place to their liking. There, they suck blood, perhaps swelling to several times their original, hungry volume. We'd detect this little lump inside our clothing and… The new guy found that first leech somewhere on his person and was considerably agitated. "Get it off me! Burn it! And I don't care if you burn me!"

Captain Mather had noticed that if we put sufficient army-issue insect repellent around the top of our boots, the leeches would go up that far, turn around, and go back to the ground. And I noticed that putting repellent directly on a leech would make it sizzle and perish, much like putting salt on a slug.

Mail, Books, and Learnin'

Mail would be flown out to us in the field. Sometimes a box of paperback books would come, too. My technique was to stand quietly by and watch as the box was picked over, snatching the few good ones as they appeared. Among all the westerns and such were real gems that I still own, like Sir James Jeans on history of the physical sciences. The pants we wore had tremendous thigh pockets and mine always contained a book. I've been criticized in more recent years for always taking a book into a restaurant but that's my style. I carried books with me in Vietnam.

Walking around Camp Evans one day while our company was in the rear, I happened to find a small vial of potassium permanganate. I haven't the slightest idea why a container of $KMnO_4$ was lying on the ground there. The dark, crystalline, powdered, oxidizing agent must have served some military purpose. It was labeled, or I wouldn't have known what it was. Readily soluble in water, just a tiny amount imparts an intense red-purple color.

I didn't know what I was going to do with it, but a plan came to mind when I saw a friend using a pan of water to shave. I put as much $KMnO_4$ as I could under my fingernails and said I had come to turn his shaving water into blood. Then I did that by swishing my hands in the water. One fellow draftee had ridiculed me for having "wasted" my years in college. Just think! I could have been out working, earning big bucks like him, and proud of my ignorance! I wasted those years of learning, did I, now that I could convert water to blood?

More seriously, I'd wanted to learn what I could about how the world works, and that (much more than future income) had been the goal of college studies. My outlook has never changed. True, I felt burned out on chemistry after a year of graduate school. After that year, I thought I never wanted to see another chemistry book even if the Army got me. The Army *did* get me, trained me to be an infantryman, and sent me to this place. What happened after that? I ended up scratching molecular structures and chemical reaction mechanisms in the dirt near the A Shau Valley, largely to make sure I still could.

Academic Motivation

It was amazing what the military experience did for my academic motivation. I never got that advanced degree, but right after those Army days, I went back to college in California. I was thinking to earn a second bachelor's degree in journalism for use in the field of aviation. But the next fall, a friend was offered a job teaching chemistry at a Catholic boarding school in Colorado, on the grounds of a Benedictine monastery. He turned it down, but I was on the phone within that hour and got the job, which included being a dorm prefect. I was soon on my way to Colorado to teach high school, though I hadn't been inside a high school since I was graduated from one.

My predecessor had already quit, just one week into the school year. The monks and I would not see eye to eye, theologically or on much of anything else, and faculty members grumbled that discipline was meted out according to how much money the boy's parents had contributed. Other problems were orders of magnitude worse, and the school would have to shut down a few years later. But the job had included teaching a course across town at a Catholic girls' boarding school. That was rewarding because Sister Karen, who ran the school, had her head on straight.

Because of the good experiences and despite the poor ones, I went back to college the following year in Pueblo, Colorado, got a state teaching certificate, and later found a teaching job in the mountains at a public high school. I don't know what path my life would have followed if absence from academia—and this military absence in particular—had not remotivated me in favor of academic endeavors. Even horrible things can push us in directions we might not have imagined.

Observation Teams

Back to Vietnam: Our whole company was being sent out as six-man observation teams for a while. We'd be inserted onto a helicopter landing zone along a forested ridge, go a short distance, and set up for several days at a time. Our job was to watch and listen. We were in dense vegetation, so we mostly listened. We maintained radio contact with other teams and with our leaders.

One experienced guy agreed that "if Charlie finds you, your shit's weak." That wasn't likely because of our concealment in the forest, but it was understood. Nevertheless, this was a fine time to read books or write letters. Relatively speaking, I enjoyed these observation missions. Each day spent silently in forest concealment was a day closer to home. A different guy once declared, "I've been making it for eight months and I'm going to continue to make it." He did, too.

Set an Ambush?

Another time, my squad was detailed to set an ambush by the platoon commander, who must have gotten orders from Captain Mather, who must have gotten the general idea from the battalion commander. He must have gotten the concept from the division commander, who must have gotten orders from on high about holding down traffic on this network of trails off the Ho Chi Minh Trail. Fortunately for us, though not for others further south, much of the network was across the Laotian border.

We were to go off a little way along the trail in question and set the ambush. During this series of RIFs in hilly, heavily wooded country near the A Shau, we'd destroyed a few bunkers but didn't find much else. Evidently, though, others had made use of the good, well-marked trails that seemed to follow each ridge. The assignment meant we were supposed to find a likely place near the trail where vegetation would conceal us. We'd set a few Claymore mines, then wait with our automatic rifles. The idea called for us to blow away whomever came walking through.

Off we went, but we didn't set up right beside the trail. The squad leader took us onto the side of a gentle hill, still in view of the trail but not too near it. His intention was clear. We were not going to be killed for nothing, at least not that day. Sending just a few of us out on ambush, not knowing how many NVA soldiers might be coming, was using us as though our lives were expendable. Besides, I didn't have the slightest desire to blow anyone away. Our squad leader had gotten us into a position of relative safety.

There was a saying among high-ranking military: "no guts, no glory!" That meant *my* guts but *their* glory, promotions, and careers. No enemies of mine would be walking down the trail, though I could think of several enemies up my own chain of command. I've been told since that our platoon leader, to his immense credit, was not part of this willingness to waste me in the high-ranking pursuit of glory.

I have also been told that after Hamburger Hill, one of the commanders had said, "I could have called in B-52s, but I wanted the glory for my infantry!" Correction: he wanted the glory himself, for which many of his infantrymen died there.

Up on our hillside, we settled in. We ate a little, read, and wrote letters while keeping an eye open toward the trail. Vegetation consisted of small trees and lots of low bushes, not tall canopy as was usually the case. It wasn't exactly poolside at a resort, but given the reality of the whole situation, it could have been much worse.

Crash, crash! Something was moving through the brush a little behind us! What the…? Rifles locked and loaded, very alert now, we looked for the source of this disturbance. Was the NVA setting up an anti-aircraft gun or what? Should we call the company commander on the radio, get a Cobra helicopter on the way, call in artillery? *Crash, crash!* Here came a monkey, swinging along! A cute fellow, he was.

In hindsight, I realize there was a regional lull there at the time. The problem was not that horrible things happened while we were in the field. Rather, it was that we never knew what was around the next bush or down each trail. The high command, on down to battalion and company commanders, clearly hoped we'd come upon another Hamburger Hill. Just as fervently, I hoped we would not.

Base Camp

Every several weeks (or so we hoped!) our unit would be picked up and helicoptered back to Camp Evans for a few days. While there, we were relatively free to lounge around as we wished and many did exactly that. I used the time to walk over to the small base library. Nearby was a photo lab set up for the use of troops.

I went to the library and the photo lab not only out of interest but also to make myself scarce around the company area. Being put on *detail* meant being assigned to whatever little jobs needed to be done. This would happen randomly to whomever the first sergeant saw when he needed somebody. I was assigned my share of them, and that was fine.

I consistently volunteered for what others thought was the worst detail of them all! Each outhouse on the base consisted of a little wooden structure, the configuration of which is familiar to most of us. Below the seat was about one third, including an end, of a 55-gallon drum in which fuel, oil, or some other commodity had been brought to Vietnam. The job was to go around, pull each of these from under the outhouse seat, and burn the contents with liberal application of diesel fuel, stirring as needed with a big stick.

I volunteered to burn shit because it would occupy a fair amount of time nearly alone (we usually worked in pairs) while our unit was in base camp. The few of us doing this would have to return to each one periodically, stir it, and renew the flames with more accelerant. I'd be free to think, and I probably wouldn't be bothered by other requests upon my time. Not just that, but as the holder of a degree in chemistry who understood drying and oxidation under the influence of great heat, I'm sure I could perform this important duty considerably better than many others. It would have been unwise of Uncle Sam to squander this knowledge, would it not?

I also volunteered for base perimeter guard duty on nights like New Year's Eve when there'd be a party in the company area. I wasn't a party person but I knew others were. Plus, I could build up a little credit with the first sergeant in this way.

Marijuana, Alcohol, Armed Face-offs, and Justice

Getting drunk was a favorite pastime of many in the company, while others would get stoned on marijuana. I never knew the source of either, but apparently both were plentiful. I observed that the drunks would become belligerent while the stoned would become rather mellow. I'd stay on a bunk and read, not paying too much attention to anyone.

I don't think we ever came into base camp except that liquor would encourage one drunk to grievously insult another one. Then there'd be a loud, damning, verbal response from the insulted one, followed by body language and words that were even more damning from the instigator. Just a few more seconds and both would snatch up their M-16 rifles for an armed face-off.

What a show of intelligence and camaraderie this was! Two trained (and currently employed) killers who were wildly drunk, each armed with modern assault rifles and several nearby hand grenades. Shouting criticisms freely now, one of them might lock and load his M-16. That is, he'd operate the mechanism that put a round into the chamber while glaring in drunken rage at the other party.

"Lock and load on me, you son of a bitch? I'll...!" Then the other guy would lock and load, too. With rifles pointed at each other, their trigger fingers would quiver. My technique was to move slowly and deliberately out of the line of fire if necessary and observe with detached interest over the top of my book. Which of them would fall dead?

Presently, one would relax and slowly lower his weapon. Then the other would, too. In a few minutes they'd be drinking buddies again. I'm sure this happened in most units, all over Vietnam. If triggers were pulled somewhere, as surely happened, how did the military explain those deaths when the bodies arrived back home? I'm sure there must have been a plan of official concealment, as there was about so many things.

Another time, justice had to be served—a wrongdoing had to be avenged. Near our company area at Camp Evans was a shower. It was in a framed and screened building about the size of a small kitchen, with a couple of showerheads. The water came from a large tank above, which got filled now and then.

One of our men had gone there to shower but had come crawling back, beaten and bloody. Two guys from a neighboring infantry company had beaten the man, but he had escaped. The thugs were still there, so several guys from my platoon grabbed their rifles, locked and loaded, and went off down the hill to the shower. Back they came soon, marching the miscreants at gunpoint to the first sergeant in his office. I know this first part of the story is true because I watched. The following part I heard second-hand. If it isn't all true (and there are crucial details about it that I doubt), enough of it probably happened to maintain the general flow of the story.

According to the story, after the assailants were delivered to our first sergeant, their captors withdrew to the outside. Inside, the company's top enlisted man inquired as to the captives' names and their unit. Perhaps he'd been tipped about what was happening outside.

"We ain't *even* gonna tell you our names! We ain't *even* gonna tell you our unit!"

"Oh really? Well then, I guess I'm just gonna have to let you boys go."

The thugs walked. But they immediately made a discovery: Their captors had already prepared nooses for them both! Back inside they went and told the first sergeant all he asked. I hope sufficient punishment was dealt. Here, summary execution would have been more certain, more final, and swifter than a court martial. It might, however, have set a dangerous trend given the general Camp Evans environment. If this story really proceeded in the stated direction, I don't know where the would-be executioners had found enough rope so suddenly. A firing squad would have been better equipped and easier to assemble. Its members would already have known their business, so the executions would not have been botched. Hanging would have been more traditional and romantic, though I must note that no hangings or shootings would have been allowed anyway.

By far, the greatest danger to our persons was from our fellow soldiers. In retrospect, each such incident of threatened or actual violence was but a bizarre detail in a whole series of these.

Training, Rappelling, and Lieutenant-On-a-Rope

Twice during my time there, we returned to Camp Evans for a week of recurrent training in subjects like maps and weaponry. During one review of topographic map reading, I pointed out to a certain squad leader that a stream couldn't cross the same contour line twice (since that would have had it flowing uphill and then down again, or vice versa). He seriously doubted me, but back in the field thereafter, I was consulted more often about map questions.

Our rappel 90 feet down from a hovering helicopter highlighted the training! This was how commanders would insert small teams of soldiers into areas without landing zones. I hoped we'd never have to do it for real, and we didn't.

We'd rappel down double ropes in training. There'd be two men on the ground below, each holding one of the ropes. If someone got into trouble, the two would just run apart and the rappeller would come to a stop. Such a save wouldn't be available in real situations, but none of us had any problems during training.

We were shown how to tie a Swiss seat, which would be the attachment between our bodies at the waist and the ropes. Then we were shown how to loop the ropes through the carabiner (called a D-ring there) and be ready to go. Finally, we were shown how to hold the helicopter-end of the rope overhead and keep the ground-end tucked against our hips so we could control our descents or stop at any time. Then a Huey helicopter came. It would be easy duty for the pilots that day.

When I got into the helicopter, I knew to make sure I'd be the first one out. I wasn't going to watch the others, except afterwards from the ground. We lifted to a hover 90 feet high—at least we were told it was 90 feet. I sat on the floor of the Huey with my feet hanging out. Once up, a trainer helped me secure the ropes to my Swiss seat. As I'd been told to do, I turned around, stepped out onto the skid of the helicopter, and let myself fall off backwards. Invigorating!

There I was beneath the hovering helicopter, which seemed to move back and forth as I swung. It was my first-ever view of an aircraft in flight from that particular vantage. Then I relaxed my grip on the rope a little and slid down to the ground. All this turned out to be easy and fun, though I wouldn't like to do it while being shot at.

We also practiced climbing down a ladder from the rear of a Chinook helicopter, which was another way we might sometime be inserted into deep forest. (Again, we never were.) I liked rappelling better, partly because my hands became sweaty on the ladder. It was difficult to hang onto the aluminum rungs, which were connected by flexible steel cables at each side. But I did hang on.

How would we get back out of the forest, if it ever came to that? There were seats that hung from helicopters by a long rope, perhaps about three aircraft-lengths long. Once we were sitting on the seat with legs around, and hands holding, the rope, the helicopter would rise and fly away. Most of us didn't get to try these seats. Only our fairly new platoon leader did, as a demonstration. The helicopter lifted him aloft and flew around the area with the lieutenant trailing below and slightly behind in the wind. What a great view he must have had!

Eagle Beach

The "Screaming Eagles" of the 101st Airborne Division had a recreational beach on the coast a bit north of Hue. My company went to Eagle Beach maybe three times by helicopter, each time for about four days. This was officially called in-country rest and relaxation.

At the beach, we had to check in our weapons including grenades, which was good. Drunken face-offs occurred there, too, but at least the disputants were unarmed. One drunk knocked another drunk's steak from the grill and it landed in the beach sand. The wronged drunk picked up the steak and staggered bow-leggedly after the guilty party with the meat held aloft, shouting, "Ya son of a bitch, ya fucked up my steak!" I enjoyed my own steak quietly and privately.

From this beach with gentle surf on gleaming sand, the South China Sea stretched out before us and there was water all the way to California. We all hoped to cross that ocean alive at our appointed times.

A Trip North

Sometime in October of 1969, several companies (probably the whole battalion, though I don't know) had a new mission. President Nixon was beginning to withdraw troops from Vietnam. The Marines operating between us and the DMZ (Demilitarized Zone) were leaving; we'd go up there and cover them as they left. In the words of Captain Mather, this was so the NVA couldn't boast of having "kicked the Marines out of I-Corps" (the northernmost military zone in South Vietnam). As if I should care what the NVA boasted about! Soldiers' lives should be spent to protect someone's bragging rights? In hindsight, I guess the whole war was about that.

When it came time to move out, our company gathered near the Camp Evans airstrip where Mather informed us further. "This whole mission has changed," he said. "We know where Charlie is. We're going there and kick his ass!" Oh good—this was sounding much like another Hamburger Hill in the making.

Top, A Huey carries troops on a "combat assault" mission, though this particular flight near the coast would not involve combat. The photograph was made from the front seat of an accompanying Cobra helicopter.

Middle, the first Huey approaches a landing zone we had just cleared. This LZ was typical of those we operated to and from.

This leech, photographed in Vietnam much later by Alan and Karen Robinson, is more than ten times longer than leeches we commonly found on our persons. Ours were of comparable girth. There are about 650 known species of leeches.

A military band even played for our departure. Why did someone consider that appropriate? What did the command know about my future that I didn't? The reader may have heard the saying that "military justice is to justice as military music is to music." If the expressed relationship to martial music held, I was fortunate indeed to have had no experience with military justice. At hand was a cynical attempt by

the commanders to motivate their cannon fodder. The military band did not honor me, nor did it motivate me.

Aircraft came. C-123s, as I recall. They flew us north and landed at an airstrip that must have been a little west of Quang Tri. There we bivouacked for a couple days, during which there was yet another face-off between two heavily armed, belligerent infantrymen.

Top, I sometimes photographed medical teams that went out to villages. Here, a small boy considers the cure worse than his small scrape!

Middle, Jones inside a small clubroom in the company area at Camp Evans

Below, a view across part of Camp Evans toward the mountains

Top, our periodic week of retraining included climbing down a ladder from a Chinook helicopter. Garrison, having descended, walks away.

Middle, engineers' base on the coastal plain

Bottom, Camp Evans

Helicopters then moved us westward, up a valley past what I supposed was The Rockpile—a large, rocky outcropping just north of present-day QL9, the road from the coast into Laos. We were headed for the general region of Khe Sanh, that former base where Marines had been besieged

in 1968. There, we'd patrol steep, forested hills for several weeks, help set up a couple firebases, and get rained on a lot. That October, we received close to fifty inches of rain.

Top, a compound near what I've called "Village by the Dunes," most analogous to a county seat in the United States.

Middle, a Cobra helicopter in flight, photographed from another Cobra.

Bottom, Warrant Officer Gary Kovelev flies a Cobra helicopter. I occupied the front seat, where a gunner would normally sit.

Top, an idyllic scene in "Village by the Dunes."

Middle, a man holds his child.

Bottom, a local militia member carries his daughter on a motorbike.

One afternoon, a couple of us had been assigned to a small island in a blue line, as part of our NDP. I was starting to read when Captain Mather radioed to another part of our perimeter for a guy to get down out of that tree and quit horsing around. The soldier in the tree was slow about doing so, though any noise or visual evidence of our presence was very undesirable. Turned out, the guy had climbed the tree because of an unexpected confrontation with a tiger. Someone else commented how he wouldn't come down out of the tree either "if there were a tiger at the bottom, wanting me!"

Mather later said that our M-16 rifles "wouldn't stop a tiger." I had no desire to shoot a tiger anyway, and that one had probably fled. I wondered for a long time afterward whether there really were tigers in Vietnam, since misidentification may well have been a factor in this incident. The question would be answered for me much later.

Villagers, some young and some probably not as old as they looked, wait for surplus mess hall food to be distributed in Phong Dien, along Highway One (present day QL1) near Camp Evans.

This boy apparently had run across the military before. It was, after all, a way of life in his country then.

This girl near Village by the Dunes had just found a crawdad and was happy about that!

We stayed up north near the DMZ for about six weeks, but one day we flew back to Camp Evans. We hadn't kicked anyone's ass, which was fine with me.

Engineers and a Thanksgiving Feast

Operating near Camp Evans for a time, we guarded the small base of some Army engineers said to be building a road into the mountains. We also did some patrolling in the surrounding flatlands. At one point, we waded across a good-sized river that exited the

Two views of Hue

Top, the northwest corner of the citadel along Highway One, with moats inside other moats and an airstrip within.

Bottom, Hue south of the Perfume River where the large building with a courtyard and an angled corner (near the end of the bridge) was the University of Hue. It is today's Morin Hotel.

mountains for the sea. I would cross that river again 28 years later, several kilometers downstream, on a bridge.

Thanksgiving of 1969 arrived and a certain helicopter crew had shot a deer with one of the door guns. It was brought to the engineers' base and cooked over a fire, on some sort of big spit. Very good! After that, my company enjoyed some relaxed time at Camp Evans. A new plan came about.

Reassignment—Photographs Wanted

I spent time away from the company area whenever I could, mostly at the library and photo lab. There, I had already met Bob Moon, a photographer at Camp Evans, though he was officially assigned to the 501st Signal Battalion near division headquarters at Camp Eagle near Hue. In short, Bob knew an additional photographer was needed. He was able to get me assigned to the 501st, too, but I'd remain at Camp Evans with the 25th PID (Public Information Detachment). It was January of 1970.

I have a stack of letters I wrote from there, mostly to my parents. I'll quote liberally from them here, changing only misspellings, deleting irrelevant sections, and adding explanations in brackets as needed. Passages quoted may differ in tone, wording, or punctuation from the other text of this book. The letters were either handwritten or typed on a typewriter, so I had no way to italicize certain words. I underlined them instead. I wrote letters home all the while I was in Vietnam, though I can't find the earliest ones. On 21 January 1970, I wrote this to my parents:

> "I'm now transferred to the 501st Signal Battalion, and out of D 1/506 Infantry completely (although I still intercept mail up there). My job is that of 3rd Brigade photographer. I have free rein to go almost anywhere in the brigade, or on any operation in the field for photo coverage. The purpose is to supply photos for Department of the Army records, so that sort of a history can be kept up. News services can draw on this, as can the 3rd Bde [Brigade] Public Information Detachment, out of whose office I'll be working here at Evans.
>
> The first order of business is to make contact with the various units in the 3rd Bde… The desired result of this spadework is to have these units welcome me along, or ask me along, so that I can find out what's going on, do my job, and give them publicity while doing it. They all like publicity—helps the commanders get promoted."

I hadn't been there two days when I wrote this, and I'd already figured out important things about military motivation. Any history to which I might contribute, I soon realized, would be a rather edited version. I was a combat photographer in part, though my enthusiasm for combat was not great. There wasn't much combat going on right then anyway.

We were a small group of writers and photographers (three officers and five or six enlisted personnel) whose job was to produce material for Army publications. I learned that divisions, just like schools, had newspapers, publications, and even yearbooks. We didn't put them together, but we often supplied material for them. This included a publication called *Stars and Stripes,* published by the military and distributed worldwide.

I was only supposed to photograph soldiers who appeared to be happy, wholesome types serving their country in Vietnam and whose 101st Airborne Division patches showed. A list of forbidden terms was once distributed, but the only one I remember said to refrain from calling the daily media briefings in Saigon the "five o-clock follies." This whole public information business was propaganda, but delivering propaganda was perhaps less evil than my previous duty.

My exposed film would be taken to Phu Bai, near Camp Eagle, and processed. A black and white contact sheet would come back. Contact sheets went elsewhere too, so other units could pick up photos as needed.

We propagandists occupied a small building near the middle of the base and had two rooms, several desks, and typewriters. Enlisted personnel lived perhaps 200 yards away in another small building. There was a shower, though it had been set up by another unit and they eventually denied us its use because the water didn't last long enough. Occasionally, though, I'd take a shower just by standing outside in the rain.

Helicopters and Other Flying Machines

Sometimes I'd fly out to firebases in the mountains. I flew in Cobra helicopters with Army pilots and with Air Force FAC (Forward Air Controller) pilots. Sometimes I'd take the shuttle helicopter down to Da Nang and back. I also flew out to villages along the coast north of Hue. I caught rides in aircraft whenever I could.

One aircraft was a *loach,* or an OH-58. The Army mostly used this small, egg-shaped helicopter for observation. One afternoon, I was waiting at a Camp Eagle helipad, looking for a ride back to Camp Evans. The pilot of the OH-58 didn't look like he wanted to give anyone a ride, but I spread my arms with palms up and looked at him. He waved me aboard.

As the OH-58 lifted to a hover, the nose came up and up! We were about to tailslide into the ground when the pilot hurriedly kicked his soft drink from under the cyclic control stick, which emerged in a forward direction from under his seat and curved upward. The cyclic stick in a helicopter makes the aircraft move in a given direction by causing the rotor disk to tilt. He didn't say anything about this incident and he probably hoped I wouldn't, either.

On the way to Camp Evans, the pilot let me fly the OH-58. In forward flight, I soon noticed it flew much like an airplane. It was the first time I'd touched the controls of a helicopter. Like most aircraft, it had dual controls, which means the controls were duplicated at each seat.

Cobra helicopters looked fearsome with a fuselage 36 inches wide, fitted with rocket launchers (Aerial Rocket Artillery, or ARA) alongside and a minigun under the nose. I flew with a Cobra pilot two or three times on missions accompanying troop-carrying Hueys making combat assaults. I'd fly in the front seat where a gunner would normally sit. Told I might have to fire the minigun, I had no idea how to do it. I was allowed to fly the Cobra and it, too, flew much like an airplane.

On one of my last days in the Army at Fort Hood, Texas, a pilot invited me for a helicopter ride and allowed me to attempt hovering in a large open area. I couldn't hover within about two football fields and the situation got worse the harder I tried. Now I understand why. There is lag in a helicopter's control system, so a beginner's control input at first appears to have done no good. Then the beginner (who was me that day) makes an even greater input, and the total finally takes effect with a certain suddenness! Repetition in the opposite direction will probably follow, so hold on!

Later, as a civilian I used my veteran's benefits to learn to fly these ungainly contraptions. I came to understand why helicopters fly a lot like airplanes in forward flight, though hovering is a different story. During training, I knew I was getting somewhere when the instructor finally let me hover in between two parked helicopters and land. The instructor must have trusted that I wasn't going to wreck three helicopters while he occupied the middle one himself.

I passed the examiner's flight test for a commercial helicopter rating on my existing pilot certificate by hovering and doing all the maneuvers she asked for. But it's unlikely anyone will ever pay me to fly a helicopter. I'm hardly experienced. I did it mostly to learn how they work and fly, because I was still thinking in terms of aviation journalism as a career. I took my dad for a ride; in the small Hughes helicopter, he reported experiencing his first feeling of height in an aircraft after having flown small airplanes for about 40 years.

Air Force FAC airplanes operated out of Camp Evans. These were twin-engine Cessnas, called Skymasters in their civilian version, with engines at both front and rear of the fuselage—not on the wings. One pushed and the other pulled. I rode with Air Force pilots a couple of times, and was often able to take the controls. Perhaps these pilots had been trained to fly jets, yet here they were stuck with slow piston engines. Maybe by flying the airplanes, I helped relieve their boredom. In airplanes, the pilots didn't need to be right at the controls, poised to take over in case I erred, as the helicopter pilots must have been.

I learned not to fly straight, lest we provide a good target. The first pilot I flew with asked me to continually make small turns, one after the other. We flew out around the A Shau Valley, and occasionally the pilot would call in an air strike on a suspected gun position. The explosions made the airplane shudder. I noticed a dirt road down the middle of the A Shau Valley, winding easily around bomb craters. We also made a grand circle north over Khe Sanh. As a graduate student at the University of Wyoming in 1968, I had followed news about the battle there.

On one of these flights in the FAC Cessna, the pilot got involved calling in air strikes in support of a ground unit not far into the mountains. He remained on station longer than he should have, over what he said was the highest concentration of NVA troops in all of South Vietnam. The fuel gauges got lower and lower. Still, the pilot stayed. Finally, he radioed that he simply had to return to Camp Evans, adding, "I hope we make it."

I hoped so, too. I'd see the Hanoi Hilton, that infamous "hotel" for prisoners of war, 28 years later. I was in no particular hurry that day.

Another time, I rode the twin-engine shuttle helicopter to Da Nang, actually taking a very long way home from Phu Bai to Camp Evans. While there, the helicopter blew up, as we termed it. I'd been near Da Nang twice at that point and an aircraft engine had failed each time.

I helicoptered here and there quite a bit, getting several good looks at the Vietnamese countryside. Everywhere I went, I took two cameras: the Army's and my own, and I used mine a lot. I often ended up using mine on behalf of the Army, but I made plenty of photographs for myself, too.

One flight was more exciting than most. Here's how I told my parents about it on 24 January:

> "My job got me an exciting helicopter ride yesterday. I went on a "psyops" [psychological operations] flight, dropping leaflets on NVA areas. I thought it would be a high, circling ride around the sky. Shows how much I knew! He flew about 25 feet off the deck at 100[+] mph, up and over bushes and trees, down river valleys, then headed for the mountains. He headed for the <u>bottom</u> of the mountain at the same speed and altitude and I thought maybe he didn't see it, because we were plainly going to crash. We didn't crash, though. The nose came up about 15° and the Huey just floated up five hundred feet or so following the contour of the mountain, and went between two big trees on top. The airspeed fell from cruising to around 20 knots, but to a helicopter, it doesn't matter!
>
> On the deck again, way back in the mountains, we flew along a canyon bottom that got more and more narrow until there was hardly any width left to it at all. Felt like the edge of a knife going through the knife sharpener at home. Remember how we flew the Stinson through the canyon on Lake Mead? [My dad and I had flown his Stinson out to Lake Mead, behind Hoover Dam on the Colorado River, and through Iceberg Canyon on the lake, which I had considered narrow.] Well, it was like turning from the main canyon into one of the smaller ones on the side, and flying through that at 110 mph. Also imagine 75 foot trees on all sides, some of which I think the rotor went under instead of over.
>
> This was considerable fun, and I believe I got some pictures, although I'm going to go again when I get a wide angle lens. That way I won't have to get way on one side of the helicopter to take pictures of leaflets going out the other side. One last bit of fun—some of the leaflets get caught on the skids, and make a big mess on the pad if not removed.

So the pilot found a field of elephant grass, went down and skimmed it, brushing the skids clean! Just like crop dusting, but lower. Fun."

Today I realize dropping leaflets to the North Vietnamese Army had little effect except upon a few individuals. Suppose Cornwallis had been able to rain leaflets promoting the Crown to George Washington's troops as the latter prepared to cross the Delaware? Americans, fighting in America for their freedom, were quite determined, as the British learned. The Vietnamese, fighting in Vietnam for their country, were determined, too, as the United States, France, and China have all learned.

One Less Chinook

Sound from a terrific explosion swept across Camp Evans one day as my co-worker Jim and I emerged from the mess hall. Smoke rose. We turned and walked toward the apparent source, thinking to learn more about this giant blast.

There was a helicopter landing pad where CH-47 Chinook helicopters commonly took on large loads of artillery shells, smaller ammunition, food, and other items for firebases in the mountains. We learned that a pilot had loaded, lifted to a hover, decided he could carry even more, and more had been loaded. Was the aircraft overloaded or out-of-balance? Possibly, but that may have not been the case at all. One of the two engines may have stopped producing power at just the wrong time. Or maybe there was other difficulty beyond the pilot's control.

The helicopter couldn't gain altitude as it flew away. The pilot tried to fly over a low area, but the attempt failed and it crashed. The crew jumped out and ran. The machine burned, and then exploded rather vigorously. Uncle Sam had one less Chinook and his structures for half a mile all around had been shaken.

Contact with Civilians

Phong Dien and another place I'm going to call Village by the Dunes were about as close as I got to the civilian population of Vietnam that year, except for occasional drives through Hue. Phong Dien was just north of Camp Evans on Highway One (today's QL1). I went there once to photograph surplus food distribution. Sent from Camp Evans, it was passed out to villagers. I mostly photographed the villagers.

I helicoptered out to Village by the Dunes two or three times. Northwest of Hue, it was on the seaward side of a large bay that was separated from the South China Sea by a long spit connected to the coastal plain on its northern end. On the side near the bay was a strip of rice paddies, then a road and dwellings, sand dunes on which I walked, and then the sea. It was idyllic, not very far up the coast from Eagle Beach.

Geographically, this place reminded me of the barrier islands along the North Carolina coast (which are much more extensive), though the spit in Vietnam wasn't an island. I've recently discovered that we called Village by the Dunes a wrong name (Huong Dien) in those days, and I still don't know its correct name.

I heard there were about three Viet Cong in that particular area and the residents all knew who they were, so I felt fairly secure out there. I stayed in a small U.S. compound, from where I walked around and photographed. I found the Vietnamese, particularly kids, easy to photograph but I wouldn't realize how easy for a long time. I also accompanied medical teams who treated mostly minor scrapes and such.

Preparations in the A Shau

During the winter of 1969–70, the North Vietnamese were trucking supplies in from Laos past Hamburger Hill and were bulldozing a better road. Our commanders had earlier wasted many lives out there, then withdrew from the area largely because of weather that was predictable and seasonal.

Some military intelligence guys we lived near told us the NVA had a whole logistics company in the valley. Any plans for U.S. troops to retake the A Shau (read: Hamburger Hill all over again) didn't happen. For that, I'm convinced we must credit anti-war activists in the United States.

Too Late

During my basic training, I'd been summoned to the offices of the Army Criminal Investigation Division and told I'd be sent to Georgia for training in forensics. But those orders never came. I wrote this to my parents on 31 January 1970:

> "They [the CID] offered me a job a few days ago running a [drug] lab they're going to build over at Eagle. I told them I'd just gotten a job that I'm happy with, and that I'd rather they pulled in another infantryman from the field. I even suggested one in D 1/506 who is qualified, although he doesn't have a degree.
>
> The job is to sit in a lab and analyze, on the average, one sample of marijuana per day, and get people sent to jail. Not too exciting, and no flying involved."

The Criminal Investigation Division was about a year too late with that offer. Having seen what I'd seen in Delta Company, I had no interest in helping with marijuana prosecutions. Real criminals like muggers? Yeah, I say swing 'em up! Someone could have ordered me to run that lab, but nobody did. A major change of direction: I was deciding what I'd do each day now instead of others deciding for me. I wanted to keep it so.

Flying Around Vietnam Toward Bangkok

The time came when I was eligible for a leave. I'd had R&R (Rest and Relaxation) in Hong Kong earlier. Now I wanted to spend a week in Taipei and the transportation would be free. I had the required $250 for food and lodging once there. On 5 June 1970, I wrote to my uncle about my experiences getting out of Vietnam:

"When I left [Camp Evans] I intended to go straight to Saigon and try to catch a flight to Taipei. However, the Saigon flight was booked from Phu Bai, so I caught one to Cam Ranh Bay instead, hoping to go on to Saigon from there. While at Cam Ranh, I checked with their R&R center to see what flights they might have. They had one to Sydney [Australia] that day, and I decided I'd stay there and try to get on it. I was the first person in line that didn't get on! (Guys on leave went standby behind the R&R people). By then it was too late to go to Saigon, and a Bangkok [Thailand] flight the next morning looked like it might have lots of standby room. So I got in line for Bangkok, and got out. The 707 had twenty empty seats."

If getting out of Vietnam to Thailand had required a bit of flexibility, getting back to Camp Evans required even more—and it came with an aspect of adventure.

"I got back to Evans the long way, landing at Cam Ranh Bay, then going to Saigon, Long Binh, Saigon, Da Nang, Phu Bai, Camp Eagle, and finally to Evans. It [could] have been simpler, but I wanted to go to Long Binh to visit a friend of mine...

That part of Saigon near Ton Son Nhut [Airport, which is actually spelled Tan Son Nhat after the place where it was constructed in 1930] appears to be the roughest part of the world that I have yet seen, although some parts of Los Angeles would have to be considered here also. Saigon is crowded, teeming, lined with barricades, coated with barbed wire, and oppressed by heat and dust. Some of the people are honest and some are not. Several of them are robbers or robber's helpers. One burly guy came up to me while I was heading for the Long Binh bus, offered to take me there for free, and tried to usher me into his beat-up old car. Having just read an article on these Ton Son Nhut "taxis," what part of town they go to, and with what results, I forcefully declined to go with the gentleman. He must have thought I was going to get the guard, because he jumped in his jalopy and departed right then.

The bus ride to Long Binh was bad enough! Traffic is bad in Saigon. It's a vicious mixture of trucks, jeeps, cars of all sizes, Lambrettas, ten thousand or so Hondas, and the remaining space [is] filled with bicycles and people. One drives with fortitude and a horn—a horn so loud, so cutting, so caustic, that the guy ahead will <u>want</u> to get out of your way, even though it may not be possible at the moment. [In] Saigon, it is possible for the natives to drive toward each other in the same lane at freeway speeds, or to be converging at an intersection, or be passing on the shoulder where another car is parked... it is impossible for them not to crash, but they seldom do."

While in Bangkok, I read about a twist in this general no-crash tendency. In another letter, I quoted *The Bangkok Post* to the effect that a bus there had run over and smashed a small Lambretta taxi:

"Not only that, but both the bus driver and his conductor jumped out and ran down the street and neither had been found by the time the paper went to press."

I supposed there must be similar occurrences in Saigon, too, from time to time. In the same letter to my uncle, I wrote about military conditions at Long Binh:

> "Life at Long Binh, the USARV headquarters twenty miles or so from Saigon, is lush. One could be there, or at Fort Ord, or at Fort Lewis, and hardly know the difference. If anyone ever tells you war stories about his year at Long Binh, call his bluff. There is no hardship there. They have hot running water, silverware, a huge air-conditioned building to work in, and a bus to take them there every morning.

> When I got [to] the main gate, I used the MP's phone to dial my friend's office for directions. I had my location by street name, but the man on the phone said that he hadn't been out of his office enough all year to know where the main gate was. He told me a street to find, and directions from it to the office. I memorized the MP's map, and found the place with no trouble. I would think people would be more adventuresome than to not come out of their offices for a year…"

Having visited with my friend, I followed the rest of the aforementioned route back to Camp Evans, considerably more educated about other parts of Vietnam. Educated, at least, about U.S. military facilities in Vietnam. I'd seen some of the country too, but had learned only a little about the Vietnamese people.

Hand Grenade Play

Late in my tour of duty, on 22 June 1970, I wrote:

> "In order to speed the calendar, I'm writing a story this week on artillery for the *Rendezvous With Destiny* [101st Airborne Division publication]. I'm trying to think of a way to illustrate it without having to fly out to one firebase or another… My doing this means that I can fill up my time and someone else gets to relax more.

> So here I sit at 9:30 [p.m.] doing it, when a drunk comes out of the EM [Enlisted Mens'] club 500 feet away and throws a grenade in the gully out in back. Boom. Everybody thought it was a rocket, and turned out their lights and crawled around like snakes on the floor, ending up outside in foxholes and [among] sandbags designed for that purpose.

> After about five minutes, the brigade brass got on the bandwagon and blew the warning siren for the required three minute signal which means that all is not well. That means that every last light on Camp Evans is supposed to go out and everybody prepare for the [NVA] hordes. Everyone knew by then about the drunk and his grenade, so we just sat around outside watching and hoping for his arrest. Eventually the alert was called off, and now I'm back typing again. Made an hour go by quickly, which is good."

Drunks armed with hand grenades had become an old story. By then, such incidents just served to punctuate my time remaining in-country. So did the story I heard about how two infantry companies, while guarding the perimeter one night, engaged each other in a grenade launcher fight. Oh well. I wouldn't be in Vietnam for long. I was said to be *short!*

Boots, Lakes, Air Mattresses, and Home

Walking among hamlets near the coast during a visit to Village by the Dunes, I'd seen a guy floating on a small lake with his Army air mattress. His boots were ashore, so I photographed him with his boots in the foreground. He was, I suppose, part of the U.S. team that was quartered nearby.

The commanding general of the 101st Airborne Division, it turned out, had issued a stern order—I envisioned him glaring all around as he declared it—that troops couldn't float on lakes with their air mattresses. That photograph just happened to be picked up and printed worldwide in the *Stars and Stripes,* but I was safely home by that time! I hope the floater on the lake was, also. I wish I'd taken the photo with my own camera, too. If I had, it would have appeared here.

I heard the thought expressed several times that involvement in the Vietnam War seemed attractive for many youths as a way to beat the boredom of some routine job at home. Personally, it helped me indulge my interest in aircraft and flying. So in that sense, the 101st Airborne Division had been a fortunate assignment.

My strong sense of place makes me want to know the geography (and more lately the geology) wherever I am. I like "wild" and I like "remote." That was the kind of country we mostly operated in. The tiny bit of human history I'd picked up was fascinating, too.

This year in Vietnam had served my purposes of discovery—however involuntary it had been and however perverse the purposes of those who sent me.

A Web of Lies

The Vietnam War was based on a woven web of lies; whole tapestries in which one lie sprang from another and resulted in others. The war was immoral as immoral could be, and so was the process by which its proponents justified it.

Looking back, one power or another had occupied Vietnam for centuries. Once it was the Chinese, so there's little love in Vietnam for China. The French occupied Vietnam almost since the time of Abraham Lincoln. Then the Japanese dominated during World War II, taking Vietnam's rice for themselves and leaving mass starvation. The French returned and stayed until they were defeated by the Viet Minh in 1954.

Partitioning Vietnam after the French defeat was to have been a temporary measure, with elections to be held in 1956. But free elections looked like a win for Ho Chi Minh, so the United States' new puppet regime in the south scuttled them. The "temporary" line of demarcation at the 17th parallel was imaginatively declared an international boundary and South Vietnam was declared a sovereign nation. Ngo Dinh Diem was installed as its leader.

The South Vietnamese government was entirely corrupt. It operated not for the benefit of its people, but for the benefit of rulers and powerful groups. Those rulers quickly learned to repeat the anticommunist line Americans loved to hear. In fact, anticommunism was called South Vietnam's largest export, and too many fell for it. South Vietnam could not have stood without U.S support.

We Did What?

The United States supplied the Viet Cong with weapons. What? There were, by 1962, a number of small government outposts in the Mekong Delta, armed with American weapons and ammunition. To supply itself, all the Viet Cong had to do was overrun an outpost, and that wasn't difficult. The growing Viet Cong were, in fact, a reincarnation of the Viet Minh, the guerilla army that had defeated the French. The Vietnamese saw the United States as just another France and the rulers of South Vietnam as lackeys of a foreign power.

Some point out numbers of Viet Cong or North Vietnamese atrocities, which certainly did occur. But those same people seldom mention atrocities by the South Vietnamese government, or that the United States directly supported a great deal of it. It might have been bloody repression, a policy of indiscriminate fire, or bombing calculated to wipe out whole civilian villages. The cumulative effect of many wrongs turned the rather small Viet Cong into a much larger movement among the populace. Diem's policies supplied the Viet Cong with determined personnel, the United States supplied them with weapons, and U.S. troops were sent later to fight them.

Sharing power were Diem's brother Ngo Dinh Nhu and Nhu's wife, Madame Nhu. She pushed her "Family Law" through the weak National Assembly, making divorce almost impossible and the children of (rather common) second relationships illegitimate. Another measure of hers, a "Law for the Protection of Morality," imposed a penalty of five years in prison for repeated use of contraceptives. We didn't fight a bloody war partly to prevent contraception, did we? I hope not.

Madame Nhu also led a family effort to repress Buddhism in Vietnam where most people outside cities were (and still are) Buddhist. I mean organized, brutal raids on pagodas, and the murder of monks. She expressed joy, "We clap our hands," when monks immolated themselves (doused themselves with gasoline and set themselves aflame) in Saigon. To what extent did we fight a war in support of such intolerance?

After Diem and his brother were shot dead by their own military officers, American troops ended up fighting for corruption and a series of tinhorn dictators. Many "early" U.S. soldiers, having been told a tale, believed they were doing the right thing in Vietnam. Most "late" veterans from about 1968 on—including myself—just wanted to survive and go home. We'd been caught up in something very wrong.

Animosity Toward the Media

Animosity between the news media and the U.S. military/Diem regime started early when the United States only had advisors in South Vietnam. The U.S. command purposefully misrepresented the growing Viet Cong insurgency to President Kennedy, to make themselves appear more effective than was true. By the time I was with the public information detachment about seven years later, the South Vietnamese regime almost seemed irrelevant. Dislike had grown huge between the U.S. military and the media—those damned revealers of truth! Like many organizations, the military tried to project an image, no matter how full of deception. I'm sure commanders didn't like those bright spotlights of unpopularity shining from home. What happened to the days when they could conduct war exactly as they pleased?

Who were the people my government wanted me to kill? Were they the soldiers of Adolph Hitler or of some other fiend? No, they were soldiers of what had the whole time been, despite its faults, the legitimate government of Vietnam. They had come south to put their country back together. They were not my enemies, nor the enemies of my country, though they may have been the fathers or grandfathers of the Vietnamese who would treat us so well 28 years later. Why my country ever made war on their country is a mystery to me, perhaps best studied in the twisted minds of those who directed it.

As Long as the Rivers Shall Flow

In Ho Chi Minh's North Vietnam, the leaders' greatest concern was reunification of the nation. This motivated them much more than communism, though they were indeed communists. A passage attributed to Ho is this: "As long as the rivers shall flow, as long as the mountains shall stand, there will be a Viet Nam." He meant it and he acted upon it. If certain U.S. presidents had put forth the effort to understand what Ho meant, a great deal of trouble would have been saved.

The United States missed several early chances to join with Ho, but instead supported French colonialism in Vietnam. The Vietnamese fought for independence, then for the reunification of their nation, for over twenty years. They won. During that time, the U.S. funded much of the "French War" there, then conducted the "American War," as the Vietnamese call the two.

Life for the Viet Cong and the North Vietnamese Army was much harder than for us but it was their resolve to rid Vietnam of foreign domination. Americans (correctly) seemed a good deal like Frenchmen to them. Their country had been split to satisfy foreigners and they would reunite it, no matter the cost. At the time, I looked upon the NVA in their mountain redoubts mostly as fellow draftees, not enemies. Now, I realize they considered themselves freedom fighters.

We the Vietnamese, Voices From Vietnam, edited by Francois Sully, 1971, gives insight into Vietnamese culture. *Inside the VC and the NVA* by Michael Lee Manning and Dan Cragg, 1992, says much about experiences of the Viet Cong guerillas and the North Vietnamese Army regulars, for whom war was for the duration, not just for a year. *Vietnam: A History* by Stanley Karnow, 1983, tells the long-term story of Vietnam, particularly the latter part leading up to French and American military action. *A Bright Shining Lie* by Neil Sheehan, 1988, as the title suggests, deals mostly with the American conflict in Vietnam and how the United States (and I) got sucked in.

Heroes, Machismo, and Draftees

President Johnson stepped right into an Asian situation with all the intellect he could muster. Our commander-in-chief is reported to have said to his top military people, "Let me get re-elected and then you guys can have your war." Many died so the high-ranking could have their war.

Now it appears that Johnson himself held severe doubts about the success of his Vietnam venture, even in 1965. He said, privately but on tape, to Defense Secretary McNamara that he didn't see "any way of winning." The draft notice I received with Johnson's name on it certainly didn't tell me that. He didn't share his doubts with the rest of us, either. See *LBJ's Secret War,* by Michael Beschloss, 2001.

Our government sent my generation to a worse-than-unnecessary war. Those who stormed the beaches at Normandy or who fought for islands in the Pacific were genuine heroes who did what had to be done. They fought bravely for their country and their sacrifice was great. The results of war were no less tragic then but our military kept us free.

Some World War II veterans and others just couldn't figure out how the Vietnam War was entirely different. Those earlier WWII veterans were dishonored by the subsequent behavior of the country they'd defended so well. Indeed, the Vietnam War dishonored us all. World events, prior and since, have proved how much we need our military, but cool heads must decide its use. No war just for the sake of war!

Regarding heroism in Vietnam, I think of those many soldiers who selflessly rescued others. I think of helicopter medivac crews, physicians, nurses, and other medical personnel. In general, our military performed dutifully, and people reacted to situations as they believed necessary.

Three U.S. presidents (but mostly Johnson) allowed our nation to be dragged through the Vietnam War, and a large group of citizen-soldiers who thought they were doing right got dragged along, too. Most were ordinary guys who had received a draft notice. We ought not blame the ones who truly believed they were serving their nation. The history of their country's wars had, for the most part, been noble. Why should this war be different? But this time, our country was very wrong. That guy who shot at me near the A Shau? I'm sorry my government forced us both into such a position. I hope he made it home, too.

Did the Vietnam War have a parallel in the Korean War, and now it was time for the next generation to save the world from communism? No. Korea involved a clear-cut invasion, in which the invaders did not enjoy the support of the local population. There was no guerilla force analogous to the Viet Cong. Moreover, the defense of South Korea was a United Nations operation, unlike the U.S. misadventure in Vietnam.

Not Volunteers

Some have said volunteers largely fought the Vietnam War. That's untrue. Those who did the actual fighting were mostly draftees, and draftees were usually not the sons of wealthy, influential parents. Certainly, the Air Force, Navy, and National Guard were filled to capacity—because they offered alternatives to the draft. Many jobs in those services were virtually combat-free, though fields like aviation and river patrol were definite exceptions. In general, it's hogwash to claim the United States' war effort was borne mostly by volunteers.

That said, it's true that certain soldiers simply loved war. They volunteered because war fed their machismo. One author had dreamed about war since childhood, as stated in his book. War was a passage into adulthood for more than a few. Some have said Vietnam was the first place they felt like men. Even for some survivors, it may have been the last place.

They found it exciting and adventuresome, which it was. But any war would have served. The "jungle fighter" image attracted them, but the immorality of this particular war often made no difference. Some volunteered for multiple tours of duty. Some wrapped legalized killing in terms of manhood, adventure, and patriotic glory. I've looked through (but not bought) a few of their books with titles that promise lots of death and blood. Those books tend to speak about the alleged thrill of combat, not about patriotic service in defense of the United States.

I'm talking about types of men who fought in Vietnam entirely for macho reasons. War-lovers in the military around Vietnam are said to have commented: "It's not much of a war, but it's the only one we've got." I do not credit this group of willing warriors with being brave defenders of freedom, nor do I call their deeds heroic. A desire to serve their country motivated nothing they did. Rather, they showed up for the thrill of it.

Most of the soldiers I knew in the infantry did not share this macho attitude. I can think of just a few officers and enlisted men who were there for the excitement of it all, though most such soldiers would have ended up in elite combat units of some sort. Ours was just an ordinary infantry company. I've since talked to several people about men they knew who wanted to go to Vietnam and fight. One told me his brother had gone twice, but service to his country was not a motive. He went for "drugs, sex, anarchy, and the ability to do as he chose." That brother is now serving life in prison for murdering a policeman, according to my friend. Some former soldiers simply could not handle the real world when they got back, and ended up in various kinds of trouble.

I strongly suggest that the Vietnam War became a haven for a number of the disturbed. Some of these former warriors may now be telling their grandkids stories about how heroically they fought the brave fight. But how many ordinary soldiers died, so a few others could live out their war fantasies?

More good people than bad went to Vietnam, and some are doing good things there now. I know of a medical clinic recently built at Chu Lai, inspired mostly by former U.S. personnel. Other veterans have sponsored Vietnamese students in the United States. Still others are working on the problem of land mines there, or on various other projects.

Macho Attitudes

I'm convinced macho attitudes influenced our national policy. They were not confined to the enlisted ranks. Officers at all levels, including very high-ranking advisors to presidents, had their own more sophisticated versions of machismo. It is arguable that at least two of our presidents did, also.

There is a good discussion of the military attitude at the time, military training, and misplaced masculinity in *The New Winter Soldiers,* by Richard Moser, 1996. I've seen what passes for masculinity in certain of these men, and I've also seen it in roosters.

Some pro-war veterans love to say they'd have conquered the evil foe if not for those filthy war protesters who didn't love their own country. So, the protesters didn't love their country? What is love of country? Might that include keeping it on a sane path, not controlled by false rooster-masculinity? It wasn't loving to help bring about the deaths of over 58,000 countrymen and to help the U.S. kill several million citizens of a small nation, all for no good reason. Each U.S. death affected a circle of others. In Vietnam, every single person felt the effects of this war.

I can picture two men whose names are now on the Vietnam Memorial Wall in Washington. One young sergeant told me how he and his dad used to pull stranded drivers out of snowbanks in Minnesota. Another was from the warm, swampy country of southern Louisiana. Both were good human beings, though very different from each other. I talked a fair amount with them both, but I recall nothing of their attitudes toward what they were doing in Vietnam. They had been transferred to a reconnaissance company in the same battalion at Camp Evans and their helicopter had landed on some sort of explosive. It's wrong to say they gave their lives for their country. Rather, their lives were taken from them because of a lie.

Hostility still exists toward those who went to Canada or elsewhere to avoid participation. To be sure, some of them would have left even if the war had been just. But it was unjust; those who refused to take part are as heroic as any so-called heroes of the battlefield. Some figured this out a lot sooner than most of us did, and certainly sooner than I. Many, myself included, just weren't ready for a high level of protest then.

There are veterans happy to expound on how we could have won the war. Many talk as though they were privy to councils on the highest level, except they seem to know all the answers. But shown a blank globe without place names, I suspect some would not even be able to locate Vietnam. Any statement, particularly a loud one, beginning with "All I know is…" almost certainly announces ignorance.

Even if the United States had invaded and occupied North Vietnam, as certain war-hawks recommended, the Vietnamese people would have undertaken guerilla resistance. Our troops would still be in Vietnam today. Some just can't get over the idea that the U.S. should control every nation on earth. Some nations may choose governments that we don't like or that wouldn't work here. In the absence of extreme provocation, we have no right to make that choice for them.

The far right will always claim we could have won the Vietnam War if only we'd done this or that: destroying Hanoi, for example. To read certain books and other writing, the people who lived there didn't count anyway. Genocide committed against Asians by means of bombing, invasion, or massacre would hardly have bothered some extremists. But it would have bothered a good many others and rightly so.

Protest, Progress, and Error

Some protesters were in love with protest, just as some soldiers loved war. Any pretext would have served; the Vietnam War was foremost. I knew a guy who was arrested for stealing guns from a store in 1968 or so. It seems he needed those guns to help supply a revolution he and his friends were going to start; the war may have been but a handy excuse.

It's true that several issues, including the Vietnam War, required protest before change occurred. Some things still do. The Vietnam experience triggered a rebirth of freethinking and questioning among many. Those very qualities aroused ire among those for whom thought was difficult. Unrest about the Vietnam War did much to stimulate or perpetuate other activism about women's rights, civil rights, civil liberties, and environmental protection. Our nation has come far in those areas.

In fact, we've come so far that we risk backsliding when we should be moving ahead. Young people forget—or never knew—what atrocities were done to our persons, genders, races, and our lands in the past. What? You mean women couldn't even vote, own property in some states, or do much of anything without permission from a husband? Yeah. During Vietnam War days, black people were still fighting for voting rights in some places, though the nation's draft boards found young black men with little difficulty. Some still believe wilderness lands are for them to conquer and despoil if that's what it takes to make a buck.

Similarly, some don't understand how wrong the Vietnam War was. That ignorance has been overplayed by the far right. Consider *Vietnam, the Necessary War,* by Michael Lind, 1999. If you think the Vietnam War was the best thing ever invented and you want to read in detail what we were being told in the late '60s, here's your chance. Lind also suggests, among other things, that we should have separated the Viet Cong in the mountains from the heavy population along the coast of Vietnam. Well, the NVA may have been in the mountains, but much of the heavy coastal population *was* the Viet Cong! Lind eloquently refutes much of what I write here, but he and others seem to assume that if some national purpose can be stated (though possibly derived from faulty assumptions) then it doesn't matter what we do to a small nation.

No Monopoly on Error

There was no monopoly on error. Having just returned from Vietnam and on leave from the Army, a friend and I backpacked into the California Sierra Nevada. At Rae Lake in early August of 1970, I fell into conversation with two girls. It came up that, only a few weeks earlier, I'd been aboard a helicopter with two captured NVA soldiers who were being taken back to Camp Evans. One girl exclaimed in shocked tones that I "must be mistaken! There are no North Vietnamese troops in the south!" She had swallowed an absolute untruth that had come from North Vietnam, the idealization of which I also resented. Obviously, there was plenty of error in the situation to go around.

Twenty-eight years later, I would bicycle among the rice fields near Hanoi where those prisoners had told our interpreter they'd been farmers. I'd think again about those two North Vietnamese draftees. I hoped they were back there again, as elders.

No Preservation of Freedom

Nothing the American military did in Vietnam preserved freedom, our right to vote, or our proverbial apple pie. Indeed, some who claimed to be fighting for freedom turned out to be the very right-wingers who would take it away if they could, through censorship or other kinds of repression. Those who profited economically from this war (or indeed from any war) are a whole story in themselves.

Some at home opposed the Vietnam War merely because it didn't turn out to be cheap or quick. Let us differentiate—they didn't care what was being done to Vietnam or its people, but only that we were paying too high a price. Their opposition to the war carried no moral weight. Many others, to their credit, certainly did care what their country was doing. A nation so saturated with wrong must be set right again—particularly when that nation is our own.

I had no ghosts to vanquish after the war mostly because I hadn't killed or damaged anyone. Even before I went there, I'd made up my mind that if I had to shoot, I would, if possible, miss. I returned from Vietnam and felt no animosity from anyone. I expected no praise, either, but what if I'd expected to be treated as a glorious hero and wasn't?

Two aerial views of country beween Camp Evans and the coast: An idyllic island in a river was inhabited and farmed. One small village was at the confluence of two streams.

A large Catholic cathedral (just left of, and above, center) stood beside Highway One in the south part of Hue. I rode by on Christmas Day 1969 enroute to a Bob Hope show at Camp Eagle. Parishioners were gathering.

Clerk, Stars and Stripes bookstore on the U.S. base at Phu Bai, Vietnam, 1970.

Mostly I was just glad to be home. Those first Apollo astronauts had preceded me back by about a year. But I'd learned much about Vietnam, which is what I'd resolved to do (resolved in the recesses of my mind, to be sure) way back on Eagle's Nest. Like the astronauts' journey, and to the extent possible, this year had been one of exploration and discovery.

Freedom To Be Like Them

I was stationed at an Army base in Texas after I got back. General ridicule had been directed at the military because "lifers and ex-lifers were gonna do a horsy parade" through town on a certain day. This came from those who frequented a certain local anti-war coffee house.

I was no "lifer" and I don't think there were any horses, but when the day came, I was made by those in command to march. Pro-war participants, civilians too old to have been Vietnam veterans, wore whatever military-looking garb they'd been able to assemble from surplus stores. They would march along with us. This silly group had boots, helmets, ammo belts, and canteens, all in a wide variety of finishes. The officer in charge had us march past the offending coffee house, around the block, and past the coffee house again. He was clearly grandstanding to irritate the assembled hippies, who jeered.

At the time of the parade, I didn't identify with any of the groups represented and certainly not with the Army, but I resented being used as a symbol of militarism. I resented even the slightest implication that, as a Vietnam veteran, I must have been some sort of traditional, crew-cut type who supported that war and who hated those in the coffee house. My attitude was much the opposite and has been ever since, though I was still in the Army and probably looked the part.

It was my understanding that base brass—those self-proclaimed defenders of freedom and free speech—had acted in collusion with officials in the nearby army-town to shut down another such coffee house whose owners had vocally opposed the war in Vietnam. There were, and still are, people around for whom freedom only means the freedom to be just like them.

Boarding our "freedom bird" at Cam Ranh Bay

That extension I'd signed once? I filed paperwork at Fort Hood to take it back, not expecting success. But the first sergeant's phone rang. He said, "Rampton, get down to the [appropriate offices]. They're gonna ETS [End Term of Service] your ass!" Well! After two years and nine days in the Army, it wasn't long before I was driving home across West Texas. Unlike many others, I enjoy that part of the country—and it looked even better to me than it ever had before.

I Did No Such Thing

I must now renounce all Veterans Day commentary about having "served my country" in the Vietnam War. I did no such thing. I was awarded a Bronze Star, supposedly for serious valor. I don't know where it is and I don't value it. I did nothing valorous. I certainly didn't devote myself to soldiering and I wasn't particularly good at it. I regard my Bronze Star more as a dishonor, as though someone thought I must be really vain and dumb. Mine was also a dishonor to deserving past recipients in several wars. The 101st Airborne Division, you must understand, automatically gave us all Bronze Stars.

In 1996, I drove around on the abandoned Fort Ord and found my old basic training and infantry AIT barracks (pictured). Both were in disrepair and surrounded by weeds. These old buildings crumbled rather quickly after the Vietnam War ended.

A Voluntary Journey of Discovery

Starting Out

On the morning of 5 January 1998, I drove away from my house to go to Hanoi. This was not something I did every day.

Enroute to the airport, I conversed with a friend on amateur radio. I have a ham radio license and a transceiver in my car. He asked where I was going. "Hanoi, Vietnam," I answered. Silence followed, after which Ray talked about something else. We returned to my itinerary. "Oh, you really did say you were going to Vietnam!" I told him I'd joined a bicycle trip from Hanoi to Saigon, and ought to be back on 28 January. My bicycle had been taken apart and boxed. Biking and other equipment was in that box, too. I had two other bags, one of which I intended to hand-carry.

Early Plans

I didn't know much about bicycling, though I'd grown up with bikes and owned two. I'd wanted to do long-distance cycling, but hadn't. I didn't even know about proper cycling clothing until the autumn before the trip.

For a long time, I'd wanted to visit Vietnam again with no war in the way, write about it, and photograph it. Here was my chance. My sister had sent me a news clipping about Cycle Vietnam a couple of years earlier, and I'd made contact. I bought a hybrid bicycle—a cross between a road and a mountain bike. I added a few accessories like water bottles and some clothing, then learned what I could about cycling. I paid Cycle Vietnam in the early fall of 1997, did the necessary passport and visa work, received my airline tickets, and here I was on the way to Hanoi.

I'd been a little worried. While riding to get in shape, I came up with a sore knee. My physician recommended an elastic knee brace and it really helped. The braces came in pairs and since the other made my unsore knee feel better too, I wore both on all my training rides and I intended to wear them in Vietnam. Still, should I train hard or should I rest the knee? This was actually just one detail among many.

I have an injured ankle. Would that impede me? It didn't seem to affect bicycling, though it can affect walking at times. Still, I went to Vietnam prepared to bicycle only the first few kilometers each day if necessary. Bicycle-wise, I didn't know how anything was going to work. But despite these unknowns, I intended to explore Vietnam.

Back in 1996, when I'd first thought of a bicycle trip in Vietnam, I'd seen a display in Denver of fine photographs made in Vietnam by Peter Steinhauer. I had talked with him on the opening night of his show about travel there. I'd also read *Sparring with Charlie* by Chris Hunt. He wrote about his motorbike trip down the Ho Chi Minh Trail. Steinhauer said he'd traveled without difficulty in the A Shau Valley, while Hunt reported having been put in jail there.

Underway

"That's oversize!" The woman at the first airline check-in counter was looking at my bike box. I produced the letter from Singapore Airlines sent me by my trip outfitter, Cycle Vietnam. It asked my domestic carrier to accept the boxed bike as part of an international flight. The agent did and commented, "They're really together!" That was true.

A discussion followed about how to check my bike and bag. We'd be given our Singapore-Hanoi tickets later by Cycle Vietnam's Hung Luong at the San Francisco airport, but for now we had no airline or flight number all the way. Unable to check my luggage to Hanoi, she asked if I wanted it sent to San Francisco or Singapore. "Let's get it to the proper side of the world, anyway," I said, and she checked it to Singapore.

Cycle Vietnam and Singapore Airlines were to communicate with each other in such a way that our bikes and luggage would end up in Hanoi, rather than Singapore. We'd been advised to mark the address of our Hanoi hotel on our checked items to help bring about a favorable result in case of difficulty. One woman received her bike but not her clothing until a few days into the trip. Worse than that, another participant received his clothes but not his bike. He rode the trip leader's bike until his own arrived—but not happily.

Aboard the Boeing 737 at dusk, with only a bit of light left in the western sky, a female voice announced that a certain baggage door wouldn't close. It would soon be replaced, she continued, and we'd have a safe departure to Phoenix. The voice spoke with a touch of strain imposed upon the usual airline semi-sweet, but the airplane soon left the gate. When those big jet engines powered up, I was off to Vietnam, considerably happier about it than I'd been the first time. I didn't know what to expect this time either, but the whole enterprise had a much better feel about it than going off to participate in a war.

I continue to hold what seems to be a minority opinion about flying in airliners. I want a window seat every time. This had been the first century in which mankind was able to fly at all, let alone cross mountains, oceans, and go halfway around the world. Am I going to watch some movie in flight? No, if I'm flying, I'll enjoy it. Long ago, seeing me following our course on a map, a flight attendant asked me if I was on my first flight. No, I wasn't. As a pilot, one of my reasons for flying had always been to look down at the earth. Relationships and patterns show up very well from on high.

A change of airplanes in Phoenix was straightforward enough. I soon had my seat on the next flight. But an announcement came from the cockpit about a faulty temperature sensor that would be replaced in about 45 minutes. We ended up changing airplanes, and from my seat on the new airliner I could see my bike being loaded: a positive sign.

When we taxied to the gate at San Francisco, I saw a Singapore Airlines

747 parked. It would turn out to be ours. I hurried to the international terminal, where people with bicycle boxes were standing in a group. I'd come to the right place. Soon, I was acquainted with Hung Luong and a few other members of our cycling group. It wasn't long before we presented our tickets at the counter. There, I was asked to show the agent my recently renewed passport. She asked me if I wanted to sign it, to make it valid? Oh yeah...

There'd been a delay getting tickets for our Singapore-to-Hanoi flight, so our luggage and bicycles still couldn't be checked all the way through. It was handled somehow. My checked items would arrive in Hanoi.

The time came. We boarded that big Boeing, which moved out to the end of the runway nearest the bay at San Francisco and thundered away toward the west across the peninsula. San Francisco is beautiful at night! This three-dimensional city with its hills, buildings, and suspension bridge towers spread gloriously before me. Then it faded away behind.

Using tongs, the flight attendants passed out moist, warm washcloths for us to wipe our hands and faces. This is apparently a custom in their part of the world, where the climate can be muggy.

I had expected we'd fly our first leg straight to Hong Kong, which would have meant a route north of Hawaii, south of Japan, and across Taiwan. But very informative moving map displays on the bulkheads at the front of each section on the airplane (and on small screens ahead of each passenger, too) showed us just off the coast of the contiguous United States, Canada, and then Alaska.

The map showed our intended, very northern, circular route to Hong Kong. It went near the Bering Strait between America and Asia, then south across Siberia. The map display showed headwind and ground-speed, too. This route, I supposed, would minimize headwinds at altitude but the winds were still strong and unfavorable.

Oriental Darkness, Morning Light, and Rain

Siberia had long fascinated me for what I vaguely know to be its rugged and primitive splendor. Was I able to see that geography? No, it was totally dark outside—not even a moon. Occasionally, lights appeared on the ground. I remember seeing what looked like a little village with street-lights all in a line, and perhaps light from several dwellings, too. Who lived in that exotic, though probably harsh, place? What were their lives like? What were they going to do in the morning, which by now was just a few hours off?

We'd departed San Francisco prior to midnight. An aircraft flying west tends to keep up with nighttime, as darkness sweeps around the earth in the same direction. Locally, the time gets later and later because night-time is moving faster around the earth than the aircraft is. Crossing the International Date Line, the day of the week clicks over to the next one, as somewhere on the globe it must.

The map showed us crossing into China and flying just a few miles west of Beijing. I remembered my R&R from Vietnam to Hong Kong years earlier. I'd taken a bus tour to an overlook near the border of what was then the British Crown Colony where we could look across a valley into "Red China." The weather was gray and drab, as I imagined that society to be. But I found it exciting just to be there.

First morning light had barely arrived as we descended across the coast of China and turned back for our approach into Hong Kong. The new Hong Kong airport, then under construction on an island, wasn't quite ready. The old airport was located close to the city and the mountains.

It was reported to be a fiendish instrument approach into the old Hong Kong airport—infamous among pilots around the world because the approach course headed straight toward the mountains! On those slopes were lights, and large visible panels. When pilots descended out of meteorological murk and saw those markers, the moment had come for a hard right turn away from the mountain toward the runway! We didn't have a "hard-core" instrument approach that morning, but I saw those markers on the slope. Thinking as a pilot, just the idea of flying such an approach was riveting.

Morning light spread over Hong Kong as I watched from my airplane seat. After passengers and baggage were exchanged we flew off toward Singapore, which is nearly on the equator at the southern tip of the long Malay Peninsula.

Changi Airport in Singapore is a thoroughfare to the world from that small city-state. Flights to exotic-sounding destinations were constantly being announced. Also, the terminal is a retail capital where almost any consumer item of reasonable size can be purchased. I soon found an "Internet Center" there, from which I sent off some e-mail to friends.

We rode a train to a parallel terminal of similar size and activity, checked in at an international flight counter (what flight from Singapore wouldn't be international, anyway?) and located the appropriate Vietnam Airlines gate. I was glad to see a rather new Boeing 737 and not some other contraption with a questionable record of reliability. Vietnam Airlines was set to depart from Singapore in the rain, near mid-day.

Aircraft taxi distances had to be long at this big airport. Several roads passed under our taxiways but that was as close as I got to off-airport Singapore. Everything I saw looked neat and manicured, with each blade of grass just as tall as all the others. Such perfection may at first appeal, but it reminded me of Fort Ord's scrubbed appearance in 1968. Penchants for neatness and sameness have ways of spilling over into other parts of life where we may desire them less.

Water streamed aft across the windows on takeoff, but we soon broke out on top of clouds. Flight attendants came down the aisle passing out moist washcloths, then cool drinks and a warm meal. We filled out two

Vietnamese customs forms, one of which had barely enough space to write our names. The weather cleared as we flew north across the sea.

Vietnamese Landfall

What were those strange white streaks on the water ahead? Must be the wind. But wait—that wasn't water. It was the Mekong Delta. The land there is so low, it looked like part of the sea at first. Seacoasts, in my experience, meant rocky cliffs and headlands, challenged by surf. Descending, we reached the Vietnamese shoreline not far south of the river's mouth.

The Mekong spreads to the sea in several major distributaries, full of large green islands that stretched upstream as far as I could see. Visibility looked to be about ten miles in the hazy air. Land around the river channels was marked almost concentrically in brown or green, no doubt the leavings of gigantic floods that must arrive regularly. Various small waterways went here and there. As elsewhere, man-made features tended to have sharp angles while natural ones went in graceful curves. A few plumes of smoke rose. Was somebody cooking down there?

Down from the Himalayas, the Mekong heads in China. It briefly forms the border between Myanmar (Burma) and Laos, flows within Laos, and forms the Laos–Thailand border before reentering Laos. Then through Cambodia it goes. From there, it crosses the only flat section of Vietnam to the ocean. Muddy river water represents mountains going to the sea.

We passed a port town (My Tho?) on the side of the river most toward Ho Chi Minh City (formerly Saigon). Ocean-going ships go there, as well as to the city itself. We turned upriver, then right again. Flaps and gear went rumbling down, we were low, then rolling on the runway at Tan Son Nhat Airport. There, we would go through Vietnamese customs though our destination remained Hanoi.

Several groups of hangars, shaped like large concrete Quonset huts, were near the taxiways. Built to protect fighter-bombers, they'd been there 28 years earlier when I had flown into this same airport on a military C-130. No aircraft were within and I couldn't tell what the fortifications were being used for now.

All luggage came off at Ho Chi Minh City and so did we. Blasted full in the face with heat and humidity, down the steps with our hand-carried bags we went, then onto a bus and into the terminal for customs. The building looked familiar. It seemed to be the same one that had been there during the Vietnam War. If so, it had been nicely remodeled inside. Presently, our checked luggage arrived on carts.

Documentation and X-Rays

"Passport!" That was the demand spoken by the stiffly uniformed agent of this communist country, seated within a raised booth. Maybe he was that very guy who once shot at me! But no, he was too young.

Surely this agent, whose chain of command must have extended all the way to the Kremlin, possessed the authority to shoot whomever he pleased! Or was I allowing wild old notions about communism—and relationships between communist nations—to creep into my imagination from the past? Those notions had been crumbling for a while, though incidents that promoted strong revival had occurred from time to time around the world. I was in Vietnam the nation now, not South Vietnam the puppet. My outlook should be forward, not backward.

My passport in hand, the agent examined papers and worked there in his little box for a time. Then he gave me back my documents and commanded me to go. We stopped at another counter to present the other of our two forms.

After that we gathered our luggage, including the bike boxes, and sent it all through a big X-ray machine. I could see that my bike box had come open along the bottom and was now upside down. I'd neglected to tape the bottom, and the glue there had probably gotten wet in Singapore. The cardboard was intact; it looked like things would remain inside as long as it was kept on its side or inverted. I didn't have time then to go through it and I had no tape handy. I could only hope everything inside would get back onto the airplane. Someone had put back items such as my monopod (like a one-legged tripod, for photography) that had been in the bottom. All I could do was trust airline personnel to do their jobs. More than their jobs, actually.

Looking back on this incident, I must comment: It was an insight into the character of a remarkable people. Evidently, somebody had seen to it that my possessions remained in place. Are there any airline terminals in the world where the opposite would have happened? Where personnel would have seen an opportunity to rifle through my stuff and steal? I commend those who handled my luggage in Southeast Asia.

I'd declared various items: cameras, lenses, my small tape recorder, and a GPS (Global Positioning System) receiver. The latter aroused the curiosity of a customs officer who wanted to see the device. What was it? He studied it for a moment, but did not arrest me for attempted espionage as had recently happened to a man using his GPS in Russia.

Nothing could have been learned about Vietnam using the GPS that the Pentagon didn't already know more accurately. The receiver hardly would have served as a spy-instrument, particularly since I never got it to lock on to our constellation of satellites. I took it to help confirm locations on the map, but that failed. My GPS couldn't even locate itself.

What's in a Name?

Saigon has been renamed Ho Chi Minh City, though the Vietnamese seem to use both names. "Ho Chi Minh" was printed on the aeronautical maps I had with me. Airlines check baggage to HCM, but many signs, highway kilometer stones, and wording painted on the backs of buses say Saigon. One name fits on signs a lot better than the other, and the

Vietnamese recognize this. The city was called Saigon for a long time and many who live there still call it that, or abbreviate it SGN.

"Saigon" would fit in a book better, too! But Ho Chi Minh is regarded in Vietnam as the nation's George Washington and, as we know, the United States has a city named Washington. I will respect the Vietnamese reverence for Ho by calling the city its recently given name, though I'll usually follow emerging practice by writing "HCMC."

Jules Verne, I'm sure it was, taught me the city's former name in a book I read while in grade school. Verne would have known about it because his country, in his day, was colonizing "French Indochina." I had only the foggiest idea then where the place was, and I had not the slightest expectation of ever going there.

Natives spell the name of their country differently than we do. It's "Vietnam" to most westerners but "Viet Nam" to a native. "Two words!" said Hung Luong with great emphasis. Each word carries its own meaning in Vietnamese, which uses only one syllable per word. A number of marks that control accent and pronunciation may be used, too. Without them, Vietnamese words can be rendered meaningless.

Hanoi is spelled "Ha Noi" in Vietnamese, with a number of those pronunciation and accent marks. The name means "bend in the river." It's pronounced "Ha-NOI," not "HAN-oi." City names are often two words in Vietnamese, though we in the west may put them together into one. Some are Da Lat, Da Nang, Phan Rang, Tuy Hoa and indeed, Sai Gon. We often shorten them to Dalat, Danang, and so forth. I'll spell these place names to most correspond with western usage. This may or may not correspond with the Vietnamese way.

Spelling in accordance with western usage tends to fit the English language better. But direct quotations in this book will be written in the Vietnamese style, out of respect for the speaker.

Off Again to Hanoi

The airliner flew northeast over a large reservoir that we'd see again many days later, then up the coast of Vietnam. But soon, there was cloud cover that lasted up to about the 17th Parallel—the wartime divider between north and south. Then, using maps I'd brought, I could identify coastal features for a ways.

Keeping track of our location wasn't hard from the air using contours of the coastline and of river estuaries, the shapes and locations of mountains, and of valleys in between. These charts were designed to show features visible from above. But darkness came over the land north of Dong Hoi just after I was able to spot a broad river we'd later cross on a ferry.

The maps were aeronautic Operational Navigation Charts, ONC K-10 (south) and ONC J-11 (north), available through aviation supply outlets. I'm a much happier person if I have a map of where I am, so I'd scanned and printed parts of the ONC maps to correspond with each day's bicycling. When I prepared this book, I found I could use those same scans with only minor sharpening. Some scans show creases that were in the originals, but these were the same maps used on the trip. The red route highlighting was added later.

Any reader with an aviation background will understand the additional information about airports (they're shown with runway alignment for longer runways) and airspace. These are also good topographic maps; just ignore the aeronautical symbols, most of which appear in dark blue.

Hanoi's terminal turned out to be small and functional. Noi Bai Airport is about a dozen miles north of the city on flat, agricultural land. We handled our own baggage as it came through an opening in the wall onto a small conveyor device. We lifted the bike boxes and other checked items off onto carts as they came, and wheeled them outside the terminal to waiting V.Y.C buses. The process was refreshingly simple. No Vietnamese customs here, since we had already been found worthy at Ho Chi Minh City. I took a minute and looked into my box. All bike components appeared to be present.

V.Y.C Travel is a HCMC company whose name, for some accidental reason during their official registration, did not include a period after the last letter. V.Y.C stands for Volunteer Youth Committee. They guide tours inside Vietnam for visitors and out to other countries for Vietnamese. They would support us with two buses and a small Toyota van. Though a bicycle trip was new for Thai, he and Nhut were excellent guides. The government of Vietnam, with which V.Y.C is associated, is very interested in building tourism.

Formerly, travelers in Vietnam had to be associated, however loosely, with one of these travel companies. But times have changed in the direction of simplicity. On the earliest Cycle Vietnam trips, regulations required an ambulance to accompany the group. Restrictions of this sort have eased considerably as cycling groups and the government have come to understand each other. As happens in some countries, we did have to turn our passports in at hotel desks most nights. This requirement eased a bit as we bicycled south.

We drove into Hanoi in the dark, settled into the Kim Lien Hotel on the south side of the city, then bused to a restaurant for a dinner including rice and noodle soup. This fare would become very familiar in the days ahead, except for the flaming bananas served late with this particular meal.

Water puppetry after dinner! For this, most of the stage at Hanoi's Thang Long Water Puppet Theatre was a pool of water, probably several feet deep. Water is heavy, so it must not have been deeper than needed for getting the puppets in and out. Puppeteers controlled the various dragons and other characters from behind a curtain through which they could see, using mechanisms that were underwater. A handful of musicians including drummers and singers were on stage right.

This was Asia, where such performances may hold much meaning. But I had no idea what the meaning was. I suspect it was less transparent than some seemed to think, though I could be wrong—maybe it was just fun. Reviewing the English language program I kept, the program was in 17 segments including *On a Buffalo With a Flute, Lion Dance,* and *Children Playing in Water.*

Puppeteers must be extremely talented and undergo a long training period. The vast majority of those in the audience were not Asian, so many foreign visitors must have had a new experience that evening, too. According to the program, I could have used my camera inside the theater for an additional dollar.

Tripmates

We were a varied group of twenty, plus three Cycle Vietnam people. Hung Luong would be bicycling as an employee. Outfitter Rick Bauman would be with us only for part of the trip. Rick, Hung, Jerry, Wilson, and Bob the bike mechanic had done this trip before.

Only five of us were veterans of the Vietnam War. Wilson had been a helicopter crew chief operating mostly near Qui Nhon. Joe had been an Army lieutenant and combat photographer near Saigon. John had been a Marine officer north near the DMZ, but had been seriously wounded when he stepped on a grenade. Bob had been in the Air Force at Tuy Hoa. As Gail noted, their experiences added a depth to the trip that would have been missing otherwise. Three veterans were making their first visit to Vietnam since the war.

Many were strong, experienced cyclists, but a few including myself were new at it. Our group included a policeman, an attorney, a florist, a bicycle mechanic, a city planner, a museum employee, a few retirees, and a teacher of photography. I'm a retired chemistry teacher. Our ages ranged from early twenties to mid-sixties.

Lost in Discontinuity

Bikes available now, Gail ventured forth into the city. She only wanted to go around the block. But to western minds, Hanoi streets are worse than discontinuous! She finally found her way back to the hotel after a long tour of a very foreign city. Few people outside the tourist industry understood English, but she wisely carried a business card from the Kim Lien Hotel. Eager to help, people were making themselves understood through gestures. Though mildly anxious because she was thoroughly lost, she never felt—with a mixture of surprise and gratitude—that her person or her possessions were at risk. She was carrying, for ordinary Vietnamese people, a large amount of money.

You Don't Wanna Drive Here!

While riding into Hanoi, one of us had jokingly said something about wanting to drive. Maybe it was Hung Luong, a native Vietnamese, who responded: "You don't want to drive in Viet Nam! You'll see why."

A person may ask, "Do they drive on the right, as in the United States?" To that, the short answer is yes, they drive on the right, though such a statement leaves much out. It's tempting to say they drive on the right—except when they're driving on the left or in the center. But that's too simple, and it hardly touches the terror or beauty of the experience.

In Hanoi, traffic consisted mostly of bicycles with a few cars and moderate numbers of trucks and buses. At first, it seemed comparable to the constant, random motion of molecules in a gas, but it's unlike that. Motion was constant, but not random. Bicycles flowed along the broad major streets in vast numbers like water in a river, moving smoothly around obstacles including each other. Each cyclist must have had a particular destination and purpose, though it would be easy to imagine their creation out of nothing on one end of the street and their return to nothingness at the other.

International driver licenses are not valid in Vietnam, for very good reason. A westerner driving a car in Vietnam would quickly cause big-time traffic mayhem. Hung was right. You don't want to drive in Vietnam!

A Trip to the Hospital

Wilson, Gail, and I decided to bicycle about half a mile from the hotel to the Bach Mai Hospital that had been bombed by the United States during the Vietnam War. This involved staying to the right side of the flow eastward along a divided street from the hotel, turning right onto QL1 (National Highway One, which goes to Ho Chi Minh City) at a busy intersection, and riding south just a bit farther. The hospital would be on the right. No problem!

The hospital building was set back a little and had an entry circle with a gate from the street. Against a building to one side stood a monument to those killed in the attack. The U.S. military claimed the hospital's bombing to be wholly accidental, though some people in both countries remain unconvinced.

Before the monument was a container with a few incense sticks standing in it. They'd been burned a little, but weren't burning then since the lighted end just smolders and goes back out. Such incense is common at many roadside shrines throughout Vietnam. Lighting it honors the purpose to which the particular shrine is dedicated. So Wilson borrowed a match from a Vietnamese man nearby. He walked over, lit the incense, took the man's matches back to him, and shook his hand. There was poignancy in this. There sure was.

Wilson had done this Vietnam bicycle trip two years before, and had tried to do it a year before that. His story is this: Wilson had gone to Hanoi with Cycle Vietnam, but nightmares from the Vietnam War overcame him and he couldn't continue. As crew chief and door gunner on a Chinook helicopter, he had seen unpleasantness. Wilson had to leave Cycle Vietnam that first year and fly home from Hanoi. Rick had offered him a second try a year later and Wilson made the whole trip. He'd gone to the Bach Mai Hospital then, too, for a similar purpose. Now he was back again for another Cycle Vietnam trip with Gail (her first). There is more detail about Wilson's experience in *Travels Along the Edge,* a collection of 40 adventure stories by David Noland.

Gail would tell me later about a course Wilson is involved with teaching at the University of California at Santa Barbara. It's about Vietnam and the American experience there. Students express great interest in how our nation got sucked into that war, though most of them had not yet been born. Indeed, about 70% of the Vietnamese people living as I write hadn't been born either at the time of the "American War" in their country.

Soon we were bicycling back to the hotel. This time, our route involved crossing onto the northbound side of busy QL1, making a left turn at the intersection to go a block west to the Kim Lien Hotel, then crossing the busy street there, too. A simple thing? Wilson knew best because he'd been here before, but what I learned in the next few minutes amazes me still.

It Shouldn't Work, But it Does

Bicycle traffic in Hanoi can fill the street from one side to the other. Where busy streets cross, a stream of bicycles may be turning left while another stream continues to flow straight ahead. The streams coming from the other three directions divide similarly. Each stream of bicycles must cross other streams, which pass right through each other as though they were ghosts walking through walls. It is a reality beyond the imagination of most westerners.

Traffic lights exist in Hanoi and HCMC; they are scrupulously obeyed, though we were told Vietnam has no traffic laws. But even at large intersections without lights, traffic flows smoothly. Trucks, buses, and the occasional car mix right in, though bigger vehicles definitely get the right of way. Horns blare constantly, but this is mostly to let cyclists and others know what's coming.

A bus, for example, may slowly back out into the street or move across an intersection with raucous honking. Cyclists see it and just flow around. True, 15 to 17 people are killed daily in traffic accidents throughout Vietnam, commented Hung Luong, but out of how many people on the move? In my experience, nobody—drivers, motorbikers, or cyclists—went very fast. There was little turmoil and an absence of road rage. Nobody seemed perturbed. The universal, vertical gesture of insult was unseen.

Sentient riders guide each bicycle in such direction, and at such speed, that they go where they need to go while missing all the others, though several directions of travel can be involved. They may not miss by much, but they miss. The rippling mass moves smoothly. This works? Yes, it works very well.

My western traffic habits were a liability. I stopped before turning left across the flow, as seemed sane and normal to me. But I ought not have done that! I barely got going again and then had to ride another half block or so before I could finally get over to the hotel's side of the street.

Do not stop! Don't even think of stopping! Move slowly, deliberately, and steadily—or risk upsetting the intuitive plans of a hundred other riders. Cyclists must keep moving as others expect they will. Then, while hardly thinking about it, others see what's happening, arrange their paths accordingly, and flow around even if the cyclist turns against traffic. The goal is to be as intuitive as possible, but that won't come easily. Have faith! Such faith, though infinitely difficult, is absolutely required. It works.

Hanoi traffic seen from a bus is nearly as awesome as from a bicycle. As we'd see throughout Vietnam, our bus would advance against oncoming traffic when passing, then somehow manage to get back to the right in time. Bicycle riders always figured out how to clear the way, however narrowly. Pedestrians did, too. Oncoming trucks demanded a more conciliatory response, but drivers found just enough room. Water buffalo were accorded their space.

Later in the trip, I'd hesitate to follow a large vehicle very closely, thinking I'd probably hit whomever it had run over. But this never seemed to happen. Motor vehicles of every type, bicycles, people on foot, and large animals all kept missing each other. Driving in the United States, for the most part, is calm, uneventful, and routine. Driving in Vietnam isn't! It certainly wouldn't be for westerners and isn't even for the Vietnamese. Thai, our V.Y.C guide, said of our driver, "This guy is working hard!"

Driving in Vietnam, if done right, would be a *flow* experience. This is the state of optimal psychological experience as described by Mihaly Csikszentmihalyi, a professor at the University of Chicago, in his book *Flow*. Flow involves absolute concentration, a feeling of being in control, and peak performance. It can also involve deep enjoyment derived from the activity. Ask a quarterback in professional football how he feels at a peak moment. Ask a pitcher who threw a no-hitter, an astronaut who made a lunar landing, or a precision aerobatic pilot. Why is skiing such a popular sport? Most of us have experienced flow to one degree or another. Some athletes call this being *in the zone.* How about driving in Vietnam? Yeah, that qualifies, and drivers had better be good.

Prison Walls

Tours around Hanoi the next day included what remained of Hoa Lo Prison, the "Hanoi Hilton," where many (but not all) U.S. airmen shot down during the Vietnam War had been held. Most of Hoa Lo had been torn down and the Hanoi Towers Hotel built in its place, but the side we visited is now open as a historical site. Some of the rooms and cells have mannequins of prisoners in them for illustrative purposes.

This had not been a happy place for captured airmen, so it seemed strange to go there as a tourist. I at least have a better—though still cursory and superficial—idea than before of what the place was like.

In the *Los Angeles Times*, David Lamb quoted Do Muoi, Vietnam's Communist Party chief in 1991, as saying he, too, had been tortured in Hoa Lo, but by the French. This had been a prison for a long time. One room contained an old French guillotine, to which I suspect more political dissidents than common criminals had gone. Death Row had been near the guillotine, probably for good aural effect upon the condemned.

I thought about which uncomfortable concrete slab in a cell would have been partly mine if that Air Force Cessna had run out of fuel in the hills near Camp Evans 28 years earlier. But from what I've learned, a bamboo cage in Laos would have been more likely.

Against His Wishes

Not far from the prison, we left cameras on the bus and filed, two-by-two, into a large stone mausoleum. Around a corner inside, well lit, surrounded by military guards who stood motionless, was Ho Chi Minh. He was dead. Down his right side, around his feet, up along his left side, and back out into the sunlight we walked. I found interest in the expressionless faces of the guards who stood at attention around Ho. I doubt they felt as severe as they looked. Rather, they were young men doing their duty with pride, and they did it very well. They enhanced the image of Ho by setting a solemn tone.

Who keeps Ho at his best? Does he need care now and then? Hairs of his beard curl upwards. Are they waxed? Has he a curator? I've learned since that Ho had been taken to Russia yearly and kept looking well. But now the Vietnamese do this task themselves.

From the mausoleum we walked near the presidential palace in which Ho had refused to live. Too removed from the people, he had said. Instead, Ho lived in a small house nearby, elevated on pilings. It was a pleasant-looking place which had an open but screened-in section where he would write or study.

Ho would sometimes visit the schools. Afterward, he'd go to the homes of absent children to inquire why and to urge the value of education upon them in presidential tones. I don't remember Presidents Ford, Carter, Reagan, or Bush ever doing that when I taught high school.

Ho Chi Minh's will specified that his body be cremated, his ashes divided into three parts, and those parts buried on unmarked hilltops in the north, center, and south of Vietnam. Did that happen? No! The hardcore communists who then ran the country had a gigantic mausoleum built, similar to the one in Moscow that houses Lenin. That is where Ho is today. He would not be happy about it.

Literature and the One Pillar Pagoda

The Vietnamese value literature. That's partly expressed by the extensive Temple of Literature in Hanoi, which includes several buildings, arches, walkways, and large ponds with water plants. On the grounds, a small group played instruments that most resembled the xylophone; their music included a rendition of *Oh Susannah* for the Americans. Nearby was the One Pillar Pagoda where a shrine stands atop a single pillar that rises from another pond. Deliberately damaged by the French as their army withdrew, the pagoda was rebuilt by the Vietnamese.

Countryside and Rowboats

The plan was this: We'd go about 60 kilometers (km) south and a little west to the base of the mountains. Some would bicycle out, others would ride the bus. Once there, we'd board rowboats and go upstream on a broad, slow river. From a landing, we'd be able to walk uphill on a trail to the Perfume Pagoda. Then we'd all bus back. I rode the bus both ways, thinking there'd be plenty of cycling soon enough.

Our route required us to drive across the city through astounding traffic on streets where work was being done, and where the shoulders were very muddy although it wasn't raining. Somebody said a water main had broken and that caused the mud.

It's normally a passion with me to know my location, but on this day I didn't have my map. I knew only generally where we were. (Gail's notes say we went to the small village of My Duc.) Out in the country now, delayed by crews cutting down some trees, our guides and driver sometimes jumped out of the bus to help pull large branches to one side. There was no evidence of a that-isn't-my-job attitude. The trees were beautiful; some of us wondered why they needed to come down.

The bicyclists in our group were coming along, having somehow gotten through the mud and city madness. We arrived at a small village where commerce included capturing river creatures for food, the ever-present growing of rice, and rowing people upriver a couple of miles to the Perfume Pagoda trail.

There must have been over 100 identical rowboats in the village, all around 17 feet long, made of sheet steel. No doubt they were all cut from the same pattern and welded together either on the same jig or on jigs that were identical. Each had wooden oars, fastened with many turns of twine to steel posts that served as oarlocks. Our group filled several of these boats, and off we went upstream. The woman who rowed ours had a great deal of energy, which she used effectively.

In another boat, a member of our group tried the oars. He didn't do well for a time, but got things sorted out on the wide, slow river. I know how to row and wanted to try. But I thought that if I asked, the woman would feel put upon. She'd surely think, "Just another tourist who'll end up slowing us down." So I never asked her.

Limestone Caves

We went ashore at a well-worn landing and soon arrived at a religious building with a courtyard. A good rest stop, but this wasn't our destination. Forty-five more minutes of walking up a rough trail brought us to a steep descent down a broad set of stone stairs with bordering walls on both sides. Halfway down, the stairs turned sharply to the left and continued their descent into the earth. We entered a large cave chamber, partially open to the sky, used as a religious shrine. It must have been part of a larger limestone cave system.

These mountains were of limestone. I'd learn later that cave systems abound, as I suspected they must. Stalactites hung from the ceiling and a big stalagmite grew from the floor toward the far end of the room. These cave decorations are called flowstone, which results from a slow drip of water carrying a bit of dissolved limestone (calcite, or calcium carbonate) in saturated solution. When the water evaporates even a little bit, a small amount of calcite gets deposited and the cave formation grows.

A Plan That Worked, Another That Had Failed, and Unease

When we assembled bikes that first morning in Hanoi, everything of mine was there. Bike parts, panniers, shoes, tools, monopod, everything. This was good. Thank you, someone! One part of the plan was now complete. My bike was in Hanoi, assembled and ready to go.

My laundry plan had already failed. Wet clothing just doesn't dry fast in that humidity. I'd washed a few items in the sink as a test, and they were almost as wet that evening as in the morning when I first wrung them out. They were mostly dry by the end of our time in Hanoi, so my back-up plan went into effect. This called for me to wash clothes only on the evenings before our two layover days. Yes, there were laundries that served the hotels enroute. But electric dryers were scarce and laundries hung wet clothing to dry, too, so the time problem remained.

The unease I felt in Hanoi was because this was going to be a real adventure—me among real cyclists. How would this long trip go? My bicycle would surely perform just fine. I mostly worried about me, not the machine. What sort of experience had I gotten myself into?

Out of Hanoi to Thanh Hoa

The bikes were ready after a six o'clock breakfast. Our bags had been brought down and stacked, ready to go onto one of the V.Y.C buses. The obligatory group pictures were taken by a guide. He operated all the cameras placed near him for that purpose, though my camera was not among them. I'd be taking plenty of individual pictures in the next three weeks.

The Kim Lien Hotel had, as did many, a small courtyard in front. There, we'd assembled bikes and gathered for departure. We went out through the gate of the Kim Lien right at 7:30 a.m., rode a block, and turned south onto QL1, which goes down the Red River Valley toward the sea. It stays fairly near the coast and goes eventually to HCMC. We passed the hospital three of us had visited earlier.

In heavy traffic, we might be stopped at one of several Hanoi traffic lights beside live hogs or poultry strapped to bicycles. Four lanes finally became two. This compressed the remaining traffic, which didn't fully relax as we all had hoped it would.

On the Road South

Small villages lined the road almost continuously for several kilometers and with some frequency thereafter. As it would turn out, only short stretches of land facing QL1 all the way south weren't populated. Indeed, a majority of Vietnam's population lives within perhaps 20 kilometers of QL1. (20 kilometers x 0.62 = 12.4 miles)

Particularly in this part of Vietnam, settlements typically consisted of disproportionately tall, boxlike cement buildings with open fronts, deep but not wide. Most had metal grates that could be pulled closed at day's end. I've been told the shape of these lots, and hence the building design, arose from an old French system of taxation in which assessment was related to highway frontage.

Here, and all the way south, many small shops sold a wide variety of goods: Cam pho (a very common noodle soup), canned or bottled drinks, bottled drinking water, a surprising amount of photographic film, and decorative items made of flowstone from limestone caves. Some shops offered motorbike repair. Some were full of machine tools like drill presses or grinders. In cities, the variety of shops and the offerings within each of them multiplied greatly.

About 10 men wielded iron chisels and big hammers. They were working on the road—but not with great machines that rolled down new pavement. They were peeling up a strip of pavement along the side of the road, apparently to improve the edge. Later, we would see paving machines. Parts of QL1 had brand new asphalt. Much more had been paved fairly recently, and it appeared the entire length of it had been repaved within the last several years. There were rough sections, but most of the road was quite good.

Apprehension

Rick would ask at dinner that night who had just set a personal record. On this day, I rode a bicycle almost three times farther than I'd ever ridden in one day before. I did so without making significant stops, except for morning and afternoon water stops and lunch at a hotel restaurant in Ninh Binh. Why? I was riding in mild apprehension most of the time.

The strong bikers had already identified themselves by moving off ahead. We made no attempt to ride in one big group. I often rode near the middle or latter part of the group. A sweeper bus with a built-in bike rack would follow, but would it be there if needed? It turned out that it would, but I wasn't sure yet. I rode hard to keep other group members in sight. I didn't stop often for photographs, though normally I would have done that a lot throughout the day.

It was 40 km (25 miles) to the place where our first water and snack stop had been set up. Then I rode that far again, nearly nonstop, to lunch. It was the same procedure for quite a ways, since I didn't know this culture and didn't yet feel comfortable. I told myself I wasn't going to slow down and learn anything the hard way. Everywhere, swarms of kids converged immediately if anyone stopped even for a moment. The kids and their elders seemed quite friendly but I didn't want to be stuck by myself if, for example, I had to fix a flat tire.

Tire Repair

Gail experienced a flat tire early on and its repair was a story in itself. "No need to fix your own flats in Vietnam," Wilson explained. He looked around and spied a bicycle repair shop nearby. A young man, probably 15 years old or so, carefully patched the tube and tested it by immersion in a bowl of water. He gave Gail and Wilson seats inside the shop and tea to drink during the repair. The man worked on the tire for about 20 minutes.

It became apparent he did not intend to charge them, but Gail and Wilson insisted on leaving him with 10,000 dong (about 80 cents) for his labor and for several cups of tea. The young man was ecstatic, Gail reported. Before, he'd just been friendly and generous. I wish I'd heard this story earlier; I still had much to learn about the Vietnamese.

The large streams of bicycles we saw in Hanoi had decreased now, but were still plentiful. It was not easy riding with lots of truck traffic, pedestrians, and other moving obstacles. I was putting on the distance, but was I seeing much between breaks? The idea that I'd have time to stop, photograph, and look around was evaporating. But after lunch, Laurie, Jerry, and I hooked up as cycling companions and we stopped anyway.

We'd climbed a gentle hill into a long series of villages and made an abortive attempt to find cold Cokes or Pepsis at a small roadside eatery. These were readily available, but not cold ones! A few seconds of thought about the refrigeration situation here would have predicted this, but the inquiry increased our awareness.

We had already lost Jerry. She knew the culture quite well and kept disappearing into various shops along the way. We newcomers may have worried about her, but I doubt she was worried about herself. This was her fifth Cycle Vietnam ride.

Jerry's First Trip

Jerry Brown and her husband had been to Thailand where they'd hired a boat for a few days. About to board an airplane home, Jerry had noticed flights departing for Hanoi and had thought, "I didn't know you could go places like that!" Not long thereafter, Jerry's husband called her attention to Cycle Vietnam's first trip. So you really can go to Hanoi! Jerry joined that trip, though there was a problem to solve first—she didn't know anything about cycling! A knowledgeable friend told her to "buy what he said to buy and do what he said to do." It turned out well for Jerry.

On that trip, Jerry had gotten lost the first day out of Hanoi. She needed to turn right across train tracks but, not knowing that, she went straight. She ended up way out on the coast of Vietnam, walking her bike in the dark. The local authorities detained her and interrogated her "half the night," she told me, possibly thinking she worked for an American MIA (missing in action) group, then put her in jail. This wasn't particularly punitive; her captors just didn't know what to do with her. In the morning, she was reunited with the Cycle Vietnam group. Rick and others had looked for Jerry even longer than half the night, it turned out.

I rode with Laurie to the afternoon water stop, past a place where the road was cut into the side of a hill. After that, we actually went downhill a little bit! With about 30 km left to go, Laurie said she wanted to go for it. I did too, and we set off. Though the road was reasonably level, I said to Laurie I wouldn't be able to keep up her pace. She backed off a bit, but then I worried about holding her up. Later in the trip we'd each feel comfortable setting our own pace, but I certainly didn't feel so yet.

Approaching Darkness

Nearer the equator, there's less low-angle atmospheric scattering and diffraction of last light because the sun is higher in the sky. With a shorter twilight, darkness would come on quickly. We discussed briefly whether we should pick a "go" or "no-go" point, lest darkness overtake us before we got into Thanh Hoa. Should we get onto the sweeper bus or should we bicycle in?

Finally, with the bus in sight, I decided to get on while Laurie decided to continue. I'd cycled about 143 out of 151 km—a good beginning, though I'd pay for it over the next several days. Another rider had just gone ahead. Trip leader Rick, riding sweep, arrived just a few minutes thereafter. Learning of the two riders ahead, he sped after them. Soon, the three of them were riding together and indicated a desire to continue. We on the bus passed them twice more, stopping to let them get ahead again. Each time, they reconfirmed their decision to keep on cycling.

They cycled their last several kilometers well after dark, but Rick knew the way to the hotel. Laurie was much impressed with Vietnam at night, though not all favorably. She mentioned later that she'd wanted on the bus but had been talked out of it. Had I known then what I came to know later about the culture, I would have bicycled in, too.

Rick left Cycle Vietnam from Thanh Hoa that evening to go to Myanmar (Burma) where he'd work out the details of a new trip. He left Hung Luong in charge of our trip. It was the fifth Cycle Vietnam trip for Hung and his fourth as an employee. In Myanmar, travelers must have permission not just from the government, but from several minor rulers along the route. With such matters largely finalized, Rick would later rejoin our trip far south in Nha Trang.

Wakeup, Readiness, and Plumbing

Our wakeup call came 15 minutes late, at six o'clock. In general, wakeup calls often came late. Sometimes they didn't come at all, though their reliability increased the farther south we traveled. Roommate Lanny and I got out from under the mosquito nets that covered our beds. Most hotels had these. We generally used them, though mosquitoes didn't seem much of a problem during the dry season.

These nets came out of boxes about as wide as the bed, attached to the wall over the head of each bed. After the front opened, two arms would swing out to support the far end of the net. We'd tuck the bottom in around our mattresses. Encased then against bites and malaria, we'd be much safer for the next several hours.

Something ought to be said about the hotel showers in Vietnam, which clashed greatly with western experience. Mostly, they were just corners in the lavatory, certainly not the walk-in showers many of us know. We'd find a fixture with a valve that selected either a faucet or a showerhead on a hose. This could be hand-held, or placed on one of two holders—one high and one low.

Most hotels supplied slippers to wear, for good reason on those damp floors. Our towels normally would get wet unless put outside the door during showers. The plumbing worked as long as the water pressure stayed up, which wasn't always the case. Just a few places had bathtubs, looking very much like they'd been added later. A very few places even had an inexpensive touch of luxury—shower curtains!

A seemingly awful deficiency was the usual location of the drain—on the other side of the room so water ran across the sloping floor. Given the humidity there, the floor remained wet all night. But perhaps the drain location was purposeful in that water ran *away* from where we stood instead of *toward* us. Maybe the designers knew their business after all, worked well with what they had, and had brought forth fine facilities compared with certain other parts of the world.

I normally try to escape from excess luxury rather than participate in it. Though I appreciate and use technology, I often do things in a rather basic way. I was riding a bicycle through Vietnam, wasn't I? I'd rather live with primitive showers than go to an opposite, artificial extreme. However, I appreciated our hotel air conditioning in the oppressive humidity of the tropics. In fact, I appreciated it considerably more than Lanny did, so I usually got the bed nearest the unit.

Lanny got ready to leave faster than I did in the morning. He had less stuff to pack and mine wasn't organized very well that first morning on the road. The evening before, I'd spent time writing my daily notes, which would end up filling a thick spiral notebook.

At breakfast, I only had time to eat a couple of bananas (Vietnamese bananas are short and fat), two fried eggs, and a half loaf of bread with a generous amount of butter. These loaves are about eight inches long, a couple of inches thick, and good! The French controlled Vietnam for a long time and introduced a number of words—these loaves are called baguettes. I'd have eaten another, but I didn't want to cause delay.

Thanh Hoa to Vinh

There was no group start today; we departed over a range of several minutes. I got moving relatively soon, still not wanting to be near the end as the group spread out. Getting out of Thanh Hoa was easy compared with the capital city's frantic traffic.

Bicycling south, I perceived an aesthetic improvement in the villages, though Hanoi is a beautiful city. Early on, villages had seemed coarse in their appearance—concrete structures were drab and box-like, crowded together facing the street. The positive trend had probably begun with that village on the hill a day earlier. Settlements became more three-dimensional. Dwellings and other structures might be set back from the road, with paths going off between buildings toward farther ones.

Occasionally, I stopped and photographed people working in the paddies. There was a slight fog in the air that morning. At one place, a man was plowing in deep black mud and standing water. An ox drew the plow. Mark stopped and hurried down from the raised roadway to the field. There, he induced the farmer to let him try it, though with close guidance the whole time. Mud up to Mark's knees! I can't help but wonder what the rice farmer was thinking. Was he bemused by it all? What seemed exotic to us probably seemed less so to this person who did it every day. Do oxen think? If so, what thoughts came to this one?

William had two stories to tell at dinner that evening. First, he'd been invited to a family's house for lunch and he went. Second, and unrelatedly, his camera and notebook had fallen out of his bike bag, which had somehow been left open. He ended up paying a kid to get them back, after which the kids who had first told him his bike bag was open wanted to be paid, also. But the sweeper bus showed up just in time and carried him to safety after he experienced this introductory lesson in microeconomics.

Other Challenges

Our way south was improving, but was this fun? I was developing saddle sores so it helped to sit a little cross-wise on the seat. Even so, I couldn't sit still in the saddle for long. My knee was a bit sore, the soles of my feet hurt, and I didn't have the stamina I'd felt a day earlier.

I'd gotten partly over not wanting to be stranded alone in case of mechanical or other problems. I would set out alone, but I still endeavored not to be the last one in the group. By necessity, someone must always have been last, but I was uncomfortable with it being me. I rode for a while with John and Kathy, and then with Jerry who still kept disappearing into different shops along the way.

Riding alone through a village, I saw Heather stopped and surrounded by kids at a shop that sold woven mats. I stopped, too, but she was only trying to figure out how to carry a mat if she bought one. It wouldn't roll up. I thought briefly about buying one myself, but the same problem would have immediately arisen. We both departed without mats.

I began to resent the distances we needed to travel each day. No time to do much except keep up with the group; I would have made more photographs otherwise. I rode with Holly for a time, but we both decided to get on the bus at the upcoming lunch stop. I was tired and sore, paying now for the day before.

The average day on this ride was 132 km (82 miles), but three days were *centuries* of at least 100 miles (161 km). Distances were mostly determined by locations of cities large enough to accommodate our group. With a number of strong exceptions, our route wasn't hilly overall. Even Gail, a strong cyclist, said she wished distances were a little less. But she noted: Heat, traffic, and lack of privacy made the cycling more difficult. I would add humidity to Gail's list.

Hanoi traffic, on the streets and from our bus enroute to the Perfume Pagoda.

Top right, Jerry Brown

Top left, Kostas and Hung assemble a bike at the Kim Lien Hotel in Hanoi.

Left, Bach Mai hospital

Bottom, the former Hoa Lo Prison, the "Hanoi Hilton" A real hotel, the Hanoi Towers, has been built right behind. It replaces part of the old prison which is now open as a historical site.

V.Y.C provided a bag lunch this second day. It contained one of those good baguettes, a cucumber, a potato (small, cold, and baked—an idea I resolved to implement more often at home), and a piece of chicken which turned out to be mostly bone.

The bus took us through hilly country to a scheduled water stop. Down a hillside from the road, several small dwellings punctuated a valley floor covered with trees. Nearby were the tracks on which the Reunification Express passenger train would go rumbling northward toward Hanoi each morning. Looking at my map later, I saw that our road had been running close to the sea, though I'd seen no hint of it.

Into the City of Vinh

We'd been warned and it was true! Vinh was not a beautiful city, though it could be and will be again. Almost leveled during the Vietnam War, many apartment buildings had been erected afterward. They'd been designed and built by East Berliners, we were told. Functional, I suppose, but they looked like drab, blocky fortresses, and were very dilapidated. There

Top, the presidential palace in Hanoi where Ho Chi Minh wouldn't live because it was too removed from the people.
Middle, the smaller house nearby where Ho actually lived.
Bottom, school kids line up at the Ho Chi Minh mausoleum.

Top, one of the musicians at the Temple of Literature

Middle, bus drivers help clear trees as Joe cycles past on the road to the Perfume Pagoda.

Bottom, trees line that same road elsewhere.

is talk about removing that wretched housing, but the mayor of Vinh told David Lamb of the *Los Angeles Times* that to do so right away would leave many people homeless.

Getting to Vinh on the bus, I took an early shower and washed my cycling shorts. They'd dry by morning because of the fabric they're made of. I couldn't wash anything else for the opposite reason—it wouldn't dry in time.

Dinner at the hotel in Vinh: The meal itself was mostly fine. We sat at a long table eating the normal Vietnamese fare. But three women on a nearby platform continuously blasted out music at great volume. Additionally, my fingers were curled from holding the bicycle handgrips so long, and from the pressure on my palms. The fingers of both hands felt numb and no longer had their normal strength.

Controlling chopsticks became a problem. I hadn't used these for 28 years and not much then. Surprisingly,

Top, these steel rowboats carried us upriver to the Perfume Pagoda trail. This mother had brought her young son to work that day, and he'd probably ridden up the river many times in his life.

Left, a family gathers food from another steel boat.

Two houses along the way from Hanoi to Thanh Hoa

the technique had come back fairly well for the first couple of days, but now I was slipping again. I asked Hung how he held chopsticks. He answered, "I don't know—I just grew up with them!" Gail had a fine solution to the chopsticks problem; a set of flatware in her purse. "So I can eat," she told me.

One of the delicacies offered was dark and somewhat circular, each about an inch in diameter, with a shape I was trying to recognize. I realized it was a snail just in time not to put it into my mouth. I don't do snails. I'm not overly adventurous with food, and so be it if I don't eat blood-pudding or chopped intestines either (nothing like that was ever served on this trip).

Later, I sat writing notes in the hotel lobby. Joe came by and asked me to listen to a strange sound that emanated from the mechanism in one of his two medium-format camera bodies. He really just wanted a second opinion and had already resolved to use only the good one. I had a spare camera, too, though it came to no use in Vietnam. He and I talked briefly of photography, which he teaches at a school in Massachusetts, and of a canoe trip he'd done on the Green River in Utah. We shared impressions of that remote stretch, which we'd both floated. Others came walking by and stopped to talk for just a bit before they headed off to bed.

I absolutely had to write my notes each evening, or the trip would just be a blur in my memory. I was in the lobby writing because Lanny had gone to bed tired. I didn't want to keep him awake with my doings, but now I was tired, too. I went up to bed, though during the whole trip I don't think I got a decent night's sleep.

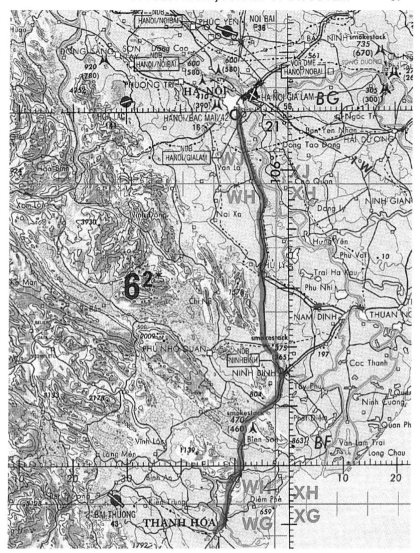

Hanoi to Thanh Hoa
From near QL1 Kilometer 176, 151 km total distance
1 km = 0.62 miles, 151 x 0.62 = 93.6 miles

No way did I feel like riding 171 km (106 miles) the next day, but that's how far it would be to dinner and bed. Maybe I could have done this ride another day, but not *that* day. Swift reevaluation arose about what I wanted from this trip. Jerry had said earlier, "The bike is a tool." I knew the bike was not an end in itself and was not my master. What had I come here for, anyway? I decided I'd rather see this country and not suffer for it. I would think of my bike just as Jerry did hers. I settled upon a strategy.

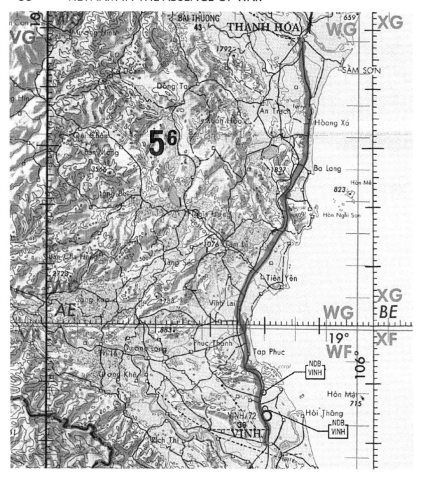

Thanh Hoa to Vinh
from QL1 Kilometer 326, 137 km total

Vinh to Bo Trach

There was a good way to avoid some of the distance. Cyclists who wanted to ride all the way left early. Hung suggested the rest of us bus to the first water stop and bicycle as far after that as we wanted to go. I got on the passenger bus after making sure my bike was on the other one. We referred to these vehicles as the red bus (a Daewoo) and the blue bus (a Hyundai) after the colors of their trim.

Leaving Vinh, the driver only slowed for three water buffalo who chose that moment to plod across QL1. We made the necessary 90-degree left turn at the south end of the city and proceeded out of town in a light rain. Then off we went through several more villages, rice paddies, and some sort of wetland that wasn't rice. Where "ferry" was marked on my map, there was in fact a bridge.

Many of us started biking at Kilometer 500, our first water stop. I moved along then at good speed, though I'd forgotten to make certain adjustments on my bike. I stopped along the road at a place where crowds of kids seemed less likely, got out the appropriate hex wrenches, and tilted the seat back a bit. At lunch, I'd undo about half this seat adjustment and raise the handlebars a bit. An experienced cyclist would have figured all this out much earlier.

Numbness I'd first noticed in Vinh had grown worse. I had hoped to relieve pressure on my hands by making those bike adjustments. The third and little fingers on each hand resembled hooks even more than before. I could straighten them manually but they wouldn't straighten themselves. They weren't good for much— chopsticks, flatware when we had it, or even soap in the shower. Lanny told me bikers call this palsy—though knowing the name didn't make it better. That it had a name only indicated I wasn't the only rider who had ever suffered from it. The numbness would last the trip and for a couple months thereafter.

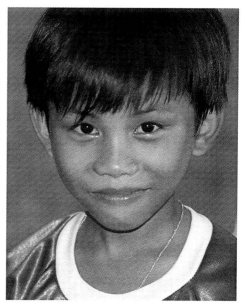

Top, kids like this boy often gathered around me.

Bottom, the boy here wasn't being obnoxious—just exhuberant.

Photos of Kids

We were immediately surrounded by multitudes of kids each time we stopped. One time, I wanted a certain photo but a kid stood right in the way. I don't think he was trying to be a pest since, when I pretended to be interested in a photo in a different direction, he didn't move. I often made the best of these situations by photographing the kids themselves.

Later, we passed through a larger village where another multitude of kids in white shirts had just gotten out of school for the day. Most were on bicycles; some were standing. They were gathered in front of a small shop that sold snacks of some sort. That's exactly how I'd spent parts of my youth during trips home from junior high school. Certain aspects of the world have remained universal. Mingling there, a couple of us realized that these students had been studying English, but theirs wasn't well developed. I was asked my name and where I lived. "America" was the best answer to the latter question. "Colorado" didn't evoke visible understanding.

Where I'd stopped to adjust my bicycle seat earlier, Laurie had asked a boy to hold my bike for me and he did. I shook his hand warmly upon leaving. Like most other kids I've known, they wanted to be friendly and helpful. I didn't notice much fundamental difference between these kids and ones I'd known elsewhere, though these young Vietnamese seemed considerably less jaded.

We crossed several bridges over water channels, usually raised just a little and located just outside villages. These became favorite places for me to stop and photograph. There'd be the village, people

Top, a heavily loaded bus goes around construction near a bridge south of Hanoi. Middle, road construction south of Hue. Bottom, the young man who repaired Gail's flat tire. Photo by Gail Lowenstine.

Vinh to Bo Trach
from QL1 Kilometer 463, 171 km total

on the bridge, and sometimes boat activity on the water below. In those villages, open shops of great variety continued to line the streets. One of them featured a centrally located sewing machine, so I assumed sewing was its business. In the United States, you know what a shop does mostly by its name. Here, we could see the whole inside of the shop from the street.

My saddle soreness was back, though not as badly as the day before. The second seat adjustment had improved things and the handlebar adjustment took a lot of pressure off my hands. Nevertheless, I ran out of personal fuel at about Kilometer 550. That wasn't very far, but I was still paying for that first day. Hung was there, and we both stopped to await the sweeper bus. It didn't come and we both wondered if it had already gone by. It would often go ahead a ways, wait there for bikers to pass, then drive ahead again. We biked for a couple of kilometers and I stopped for more photos. Then the bus came.

From top, the ferry near Bo Trach

The bridge under construction near the ferry

The dilapidated housing across from our hotel in Vinh—photo by Gail Lowenstine.

Bottom, a street corner in Vinh

Decreasing Latitude and a Beach

The real highlight on this day was a stop at a fine, sandy beach. It stretched off southward toward a headland where cliffs rose from the surf. The beach had shade trees and a thatched shelter, under which some of us talked while others took naps. I didn't swim because having wet clothes the rest of the day wasn't my wish. Nude swimming would have been better, but perhaps nobody wanted to be first! Also, it would be unwise to outrage the locals and most of us hardly knew their ways. Nudity, I would learn later, is very much against custom.

The headland we then drove up and over was Ngang Pass, which had served as a cultural divide in Vietnam over the centuries. Jerry said it resembled Hai Van Pass to the south, though it was nowhere near as high. She said we'd have several of these to get over.

My map showed our beach stop to be near the earth's 18th parallel. Our Hanoi hotel had been at the 21st parallel. Three degrees south on the earth's surface already! North and South Vietnam were formerly divided at the 17th and Ho Chi Minh City is just south of the 11th. Our whole trip would traverse nearly 10 degrees of latitude without much longitude change. Vietnam is tall and skinny, though gracefully curved.

Waterworthy?

A dilapidated old ferry crossed a wide river estuary near Tho Ngoa. We got off the bus and stood down by the water watching as our boat came and went several times. Finally, our bus drove aboard the ferry. Loading was done from a sloping, seriously cracked concrete ramp. There was no docking mechanism. A fixed steel ramp on the boat scraped and bumped up onto the concrete. A man took one end of a chain fastened to the ferry and linked it to another attached to the shore.

The bus caused the ferry to list considerably, but each additional vehicle on board provided better balance. A tugboat was tied to one side of the ferry, which in reality was just a barge. I truly hoped this contraption would make it across the estuary one more time this day, but nothing I saw filled me with optimism.

Finally seated on the flat-topped side railing with Holly and others, I acknowledge making certain unencouraging and caustic observations about the operation—the apparent lack of safety equipment, the several catastrophic ferry sinkings that had occurred recently in this part of the world, and my general conviction that this one would sink, too. I further noted that we might sink with it. No life preservers were in sight.

There were four similar ferries. Each set of two kept swapping positions on opposite sides of the river, using two sets of ramps. The chance of our own ferry sinking remained undiminished and excellent, plus there was quadruple the chance of sudden great disaster somewhere in the system. I like being pleasantly surprised—we made it across. Nearby, still under construction, a new high bridge arched gracefully across the estuary. With this new bridge coming soon, it became obvious why little attention was being paid the ferries. They were merely serving out their last days.

We proceeded probably less than 10 km to what would be our most pleasant hotel thus far. Not the nicest shower or anything like that, but the nicest setting we had yet seen. Wilson and Gail came rolling in. He said Gail rode the distance while he (not feeling well and on the bus part of the time) had "just survived." The only others who rode that whole day were the three who would cycle the entire trip.

Geckos, Negativity, and Germs

Geckos are my friends! These house-lizards, wall-climbers because of adhesive pads on their toes, became a common sight. They help hold down the insect population and I'm happy to share the earth with them. Writing notes in the hotel lobby that night in Bo Trach, I could see the first of them up above, near a fluorescent light. Almost every hotel and restaurant thereafter had geckos on the walls.

After dinner at the hotel, I showed my maps to Joe who wanted to double-check our position on his own map. Then I spent time alone again, writing. Nearby, several men who worked at the hotel spread two blankets on the floor, sat, and played cards. I ended the day feeling a bit negative about long bike trips. Saddle sore, tired, unable to ride the entire distances, and having hooks for fingers. Was bicycling worth the effort?

Revisiting Vietnam had reminded me of its extreme humidity. Things mildew quickly if left undisturbed. Not only do cloth and leather mildew in this climate—people rot too! Where were those bacteria that caused what we called jungle rot when I was here before? Everywhere, probably! The jungle rot bacteria would affect areas of skin, mostly on the hands. That skin would perish and slough off. The unit medic would pass out ointment that helped, but which seldom helped enough.

Personal hygiene was considerably better on this visit than on my earlier one. We showered daily instead of perhaps monthly. When I was just cannon fodder to the Army, they didn't need me clean. But cleanliness felt good now. Soap is a fine antibiotic. Death to germs! To the particularly harmful ones, anyway.

Bo Trach to Dong Ha

The geography had become more interesting. Our hotel-against-the-hill was on the inland side of the highway, across from a narrow grove of evergreens that separated QL1 from the Gulf of Tonkin. We were near where the Gulf, if it could be seen overall, opened to the East Sea.

The large body of water south of Hong Kong, and between Vietnam and the Philippines, is the South China Sea. Regionally, that name seems best and I'll usually call it that. But the Vietnamese call it the East Sea, because there is so little love for China in Vietnam. I don't think a particular nation gets to determine the name of an adjacent ocean; that's an international function. But still, the East Sea is what they call it.

I walked about 100 yards to a small bridge where a stream channel passed under QL1. A *blue line* with clear water flowing? No, it was dry. A streambed in Vietnam dry? This was the winter of 1997–98 during which El Niño, that occasional warming of Pacific waters, was associated with massive storms in the United States. But I'd read that in Asia, El Niño was associated with dryness. On the other hand, Hung thought we were having a comparatively wet trip. Wet or dry? The point was unsettled.

Along QL1, in addition to the helpful and well-done kilometer stones, stood tall red and white posts with numbers on them to indicate flood depth. The thought of water even at the base of those poles was impressive since, in some places, QL1 was already elevated on earthwork several meters above the general level of the land. In this dry season, we encountered no flooding anywhere.

I didn't feel well enough to bike this day. More than just tired, I felt depleted. Long distance bicycling wasn't working. Or was it the necessity of having to get up early to bike all day in a horribly humid climate, not having much time along the way, and finally getting in near dinnertime? I was already tiring of the food—I was ready for steak, not snails (though no more of those had been forthcoming). Cycling seemed to involve far too much labor per mile, but I really thought I should try it under more favorable conditions, and when I felt good, before making that judgment.

Bicycling and Rafting

Bicycling has obvious differences from river rafting, which I'd done a fair amount of. A less obvious difference: Bicycling is a continuous effort whereas rafting usually isn't. Sometimes, you have to pull really hard on the oars to move around an obstacle, trying to reach a slot that leads safely into and through a rapid. You'd darn well better get to these slots and that can be tense. But after you do, you'll pass among the rocks and holes, and soon come bobbing out on the tailwaves of the rapid. You'll be upright and undestroyed. After this, you can often relax and row along easily with the current.

I like planning my route through rapids by scouting them. That means going ashore above big ones and walking down the bank, planning exactly where to go, seeing *what* moves must be made to get there, and exactly *when* each move needs to occur. Then it's back to the raft in silent contemplation, feeling the adrenaline, and rowing into the current to carry out the plan with utter precision. Bicycle touring, I far as I could see, was not nearly so punctuated with must-do moments. Nor did it have the relaxation that usually follows.

Re-evaluation

I'd come to Vietnam mostly to gather writing material, and that was happening. How could I *keep* it happening? Just because I wasn't going to ride that day didn't mean I wasn't going to see anything. I could see things fine from the bus, though it was a quick look and I couldn't photograph. But looking around too much while biking was a good way to collide with the backs of carts, slam into heavily laden bicycles that had perhaps begun their careers on the Ho Chi Minh Trail, hit water buffalo, ox-dung, an occasional big rock, or crash head-on into a truck.

I made yet another quick re-evaluation: The trip was going to continue and I'd ride the bike only as much as it was fun. Then I wouldn't. Either way, I'd keep my eyes open. I wasn't in this just for the bicycling distance, winning any sort of contest, or for amazing displays of athleticism. As Jerry had suggested, the bicycle was a tool that could help me experience what I'd come here for.

Off we went up a hill, through another village, past fishing boats, sand dunes, and what must have been an old French pillbox with gun-ports. What a hot, miserable enclosure that would have been. France is known for having built fortifications that failed. Along QL1 were geese, ducks, and rice paddies with people working in them.

A Pleasant City

The city of Dong Hoi looked prosperous, especially in comparison with areas just to the north. Up there, as Rick pointed out, items stocked for sale in shops (bottled drinking water, canned soda, and other things) had looked to be considerably less plentiful.

Kids were playing in a Dong Hoi schoolyard as we passed, all wearing blue pants, white shirts, and red ties. There's a large soccer stadium—a game so popular and such a source of national pride that it was pictured on a Vietnamese 6,000 dong postage stamp. On the other side of the highway, what looked like a large theater was being built. The hammer and sickle was displayed prominently on a multistory building, set back behind a courtyard in Dong Hoi. During hard-core communist days, those in charge of Vietnam revered the Soviet Union, which then collapsed. Russia still appeared to have a presence in Vietnam, though the Vietnamese remain wary of foreign domination.

Billboards here and there showed various kinds of workers standing shoulder to shoulder in solidarity, gazing together into the far-off. This must please the folks for whom togetherness is a mantra. I suspect you need to feel like that to be a communist. These signs might very well make a specific group feel better, but I don't know what effect they may have on the general population in Vietnam.

In one of these cities, Wilson, Gail, Joe, and I talked for about an hour with a man who had once been an interrogator with the South Vietnamese military. He'd also worked with United States Marine and Army units in military intelligence. Ho Chi Minh had died six years before North Vietnam won the conflict and hard-core communists held power. Our friend had been arrested after 1975, imprisoned, and made to fill in B-52 bomb craters, though he had contracted malaria by then. Many were sent to reeducation camps—a term that really meant concentration camps for possible political dissenters. Wilson asked him mostly about prison conditions, while I was interested in a certain geograhical area. The man sketched out a rough map to illustrate what he was telling me. Discussion continued about that area, and about Vietnam in general since 1975.

Collectivism and Repression

After 1975, the rulers attempted to reorganize Vietnam along the lines of Marx and Lenin. Farms were collectivized (brought from private to government control) and the farmers didn't like it. According to historian Stanley Karnow, even the barbers were collectivized. Hardly anyone liked it, plus they were starving. The economy had collapsed.

Thousands of people escaped from Vietnam on small boats in those years—the *boat people.* Many of those escapees were among their best and brightest citizens who could have helped Vietnam rebuild itself had they not been driven off. We talked to another man, now a lawyer, who had tried to escape but had been captured. He and his whole family were put in prison.

A Turning Point

In 1988, what wasn't working began to change. Much debate occurred between the old guard and the "new thinkers." The government adopted

Doi Moi (fundamental renovation) as a policy and a process of liberalization. Vietnam had been receiving aid from the Soviet Union and other countries of the still-intact eastern block, but then the Soviet Union collapsed. Aid would stop, but foreign dependence hadn't been getting the job done for Vietnam anyway.

Time was short for the Vietnamese, who faced many problems along the way. Something had to happen quickly. Let us note that Vietnam was one of few countries to jettison near-total collectivism in the light of necessity without an overthrow of the government.

By 1990, much change had been accomplished. Small business was once again encouraged and has proliferated. Roadside shops are numerous. The doctrinaire idea of collective-everything was scrapped. Land still belonged to the government, but was leased cheaply to farmers for fees that cover various projects like flood control. Personal freedom increased markedly. People were free to travel or relocate. Our friend was again permitted to talk with foreigners like us. He owns a business now. At the same time, the Vietnamese struggled with how, and to what extent, to attract foreign capital for larger enterprises.

A communist country? The Vietnamese would be insulted if it were suggested otherwise, but they certainly practice a pragmatic version of communism. At least on a certain level—that of small, individual entrepreneurship—much capitalism was evident. The country also seemed open and free. Visits by foreigners were encouraged. Vietnamese sometimes leave their country on tours, though travel is far beyond the means of most.

Authority may not have been too far beneath the surface. That map our friend had drawn for me? He rolled it up, lit it on fire, and burned it. I'd drawn a map, too. Noticing what he'd done, I offered to burn mine. But he quickly said mine didn't make any difference—just his. Was his fear grounded or was it paranoia? Were there watchers about as we talked in Vietnam? Maybe so.

An analogy: While there's plenty of irrational paranoia at home in the United States among certain groups, it remains true that the U.S. went through the very real Joseph McCarthy and J. Edgar Hoover years of extreme and politically-motivated spying on citizens. Should we expect differently of other nations?

To what extent had our route been sanitized? Why had there been no prostitutes soliciting around our hotels? The website of an earlier Cycle Vietnam rider said his group's hotel had been switched on short notice once and they had been plagued at the new one. Speaking of prostitutes, officialdom during hard-core days had assured historian Karnow that the ancient practice, "resulting from the presence of Americans," had ended in Vietnam. Perhaps the girls who pestered Karnow outside his hotel had much to learn about the new order!

A River, Dunes, and Tunnels

Just south of Dong Hoi, there was a narrow bridge over another river. Cyclists and the small van fit, but the bus had to take another ferry. Out came the heavy boards it carried to smooth transitions from docks onto boats, and we drove aboard. Probably, there was little wrong with yesterday's ferry that wasn't wrong with this one, too. But I was in a much better mood and didn't notice.

Sand dunes stretched along the coast here, between QL1 and the sea. The sand had been there since we left Dong Hoi and I knew it would continue for some distance now. We were approaching the part of Vietnam I'd known years earlier. I had general knowledge of the geography now, but I would see changes as we went south. Kilometer Stone 672 said Hue was another 158 km away.

We were now very near the former border that had divided the nation, and also near the Vinh Moc tunnels where civilians spent much of the Vietnam War living underground because of U.S. bombing. I almost put my bike on the passenger bus so I'd be able to make the afternoon loop out to the tunnels near the coast. I didn't know in time that I could have gone out there in the Toyota van.

But I had a touch of several ailments and in combination I still felt down. I wasn't up to doing the 25 km loop regardless of vehicle—van or bicycle. The bus moved along QL1 to the end of the tunnels loop where, in time, Cycle Vietnam riders began to appear.

Delegation of Photographic Authority

While waiting, I spent time reviewing all the functions on my fairly new camera. I'd been making photographs for a long time, but this Nikon was so computerized and automated that photography seemed like a new adventure! I'd never owned an autofocus camera before. If used in accordance with what I already knew about lenses, it would be fine.

I'd been a Zone System photographer for over 30 years, in color or black and white, whenever I wanted to be slow and careful. I'm usually not one for photographic haste. Sometimes I'd been quite rigorous about this, but even when not, Zone System principles guided most of my photography. I want to previsualize photographs. If an important brightness value falls on zone VI, this ought to have been because I had *placed* it there—not because it fell there accidentally. Zone VI means one step above middle gray on a scale from zone I to zone X. (I know, many practitioners consider zone VIII to be white.) The point is that photographs, in my view, should be made deliberately, not by accident.

Shouldn't I feel inconsequential and embarrassed now, letting an automatic camera make decisions for me? Could I claim good photographs as my own? Would it have been creativity or merely a fluke? Accidents may be fortunate but are hardly the result of skill or intent.

What if I concentrated photographic creativity upon what I alone could decide? This mostly meant pointing the camera in the right direction, from the right place, at the right time, and adjusting the focal length appropriately. Could I allow the Nikon to control what it controls so well, which meant focusing and letting in the right amount of light? Could a Zone System photographer delegate such authority without shame? I was working on it. Anyway, time was too short on this trip for much else.

Past the Monument and Across the Bridge to Dong Ha

We arrived at the 17th Parallel—the former dividing line between North and South Vietnams—where an old, narrow bridge crossed the Ben Hai River and a new one was being built next to it. We all got out. A monument stood near the north bank with these dates on it: *20.7.1954*, which is when the country was divided, and *30.4.1975*, which is when North Vietnam overran Saigon. Reunification of their country had been of overriding importance to the Vietnamese. On that latter day, they had achieved it.

Not long after, we turned inland through Dong Ha, and then up to our hotel on a hill. Had we continued west, we'd have been on QL9, the road that crosses the mountains toward Savannakhet, Laos. This had been the route of Rick's Cycle Laos trip.

Tourist Hotels and the Populace

This tourist hotel reminded me of something. When I was here before, out in the *beaten zone,* we'd set up night defensive positions as described earlier. Our purpose was to detect and forcefully repel unwanted visitors, though none ever came. Now, we stayed each night in one of these tourist hotels, on the grounds of which the general population did not appear welcome. I'm sure this meant freedom from peddlers and prostitutes, but the analogy between hotels and night defensive positions was a striking one. Both were arguably better than their alternatives, given each set of immediate circumstances.

Our group was separated from the populace in many ways. For example, did any of us think the full Vietnamese dinners we ate every night were like the ones being eaten in those houses we'd biked by? One was not necessarily better than the other. Strong similarities must have been rice and soup but there must have been significant differences, too. I know there's a difference between what I eat at home and what I eat while traveling. To be sure, as in many countries including my own, not everyone has enough to eat in Vietnam.

Dong Ha to Hue

To our west was Khe Sanh, that well-known 1968 battleground. In the morning, the V.Y.C Toyota van would take a few up there on QL9. I'd have gone too, except had I gone to Khe Sanh, my bicycle would have gone to Hue on the bus. I wanted to bicycle past Camp Evans where the Army had based me for a year. I also wanted to bicycle from there down QL1 into Hue, since I'd driven that road a few times back then and was curious about what had changed.

We coasted down the hill from the hotel and turned east toward QL1. We made our way through city streets, past a huge market we'd passed the evening before, and turned south through Quang Tri and beyond.

I'd expected to be familiar with this part of Vietnam, but in many ways I found I wasn't. The population seemed to have multipied quite graphically. As I recalled, this was mostly open country 28 years earlier, when there'd been the village of Phong Dien, the Army's Camp Evans, and then not much until the city of Hue. Had I known I'd be returning, I'd have kept better records then, both written and photographic, for comparison. Now, this part of QL1 is much more a segment of the Hanoi-to-HCMC strip village, though major parts of it do remain unpopulated or agricultural.

White sand increased and, for a time, there wasn't much population. I knew the sea was farther away now. A large bay was there on which a fishing industry must still prosper. Beyond that bay was a narrow strip of land with rice paddies, a small village, then white sand dunes facing the ocean. I'd visited there in 1970 as an Army photographer. Village by the Dunes, I've called it earlier in this book.

On the extremely small chance I could have gotten out there, I had with me two photographs of kids I'd taken then. They'd be 40 to 45 years old now and it would have been most interesting to find them again. I'd have given them those photos from the past. (See page 39.)

A little farther south was the former Eagle Beach where military units took occasional seaside relaxation. I'd like to walk that beach again, only much farther. But it wouldn't happen this day. At one point, we crossed a river that must have been the one I waded across once, upstream toward the mountains. We passed through Phong Dien. There, I'm sure I spotted a certain building where I'd once taken photographs. It was now a school. A few places were familiar. Many others weren't. On down the highway, could I find the former entrance to Camp Evans? This used to be open country with low vegetation only. Now I saw tall trees, some apparently planted in rows.

Not a Stereotypical Veteran

I never located the former Camp Evans entrance for sure. I thought there were at least two possibilities for it. At the more likely of these, a dirt road left QL1 in approximately the proper configuration. Camp Evans had been very close to Highway One, but caution, please, when referencing QL1 as a landmark. The highway may have been relocated! I would have ridden up and over the small hill to look, but others were moving on. Besides, the place had been made a small dump, with loose dirt.

I was not looking for any sort of closure or therapy and I strongly dislike being cast as a veteran who returned in search of those things—though that media stereotype has been popular. Other vets do find they need closure. Some still have nightmares and other manifestations that apparently stem from the Vietnam War. Speaking personally and mostly through good fortune, I haven't experienced any of those things. I haven't gone wild and

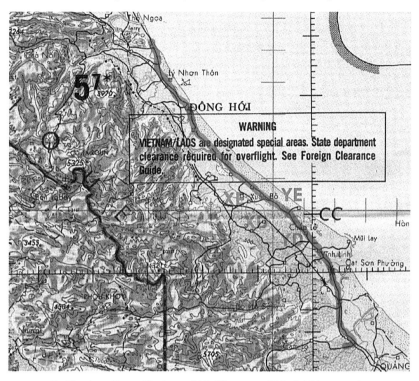

Bo Trach to Dong Ha from QL1 Kilometer 636, 146 km total

William runs along a fine, sandy beach.

Buildings in Dong Hoi: From top, a Russian facility, the main highway (QL1) through the city, and a sports arena

Bottom, A kilometer stone is found every kilometer. This one is 672 km south of China on QL1. It announces that it's 158 km to Hue, and on the other side was the distance back to Vinh. The next stone would show distances to different cities. A farmer works nearby.

sprayed crowds with gunfire. Being calmly in control of myself is absolutely necessary in much that I do. I returned from Vietnam addicted only to books, but I'd arrived there that way.

My interests in life haven't always matched the norm, but they didn't before the Army got me. Indeed, I'm more rational now because I know more. I'd knocked around a little right after Army days, but ended up in a teaching career. I taught in one place for a heck of a long time.

Past Informs Future

I'm aware that some veterans would never go back to Vietnam and maybe I wouldn't have either if I'd had their experiences. But for me, the past must inform the future while not being allowed to interfere with it. That is, we should incorporate the past into our future.

I see experiences as learning opportunities; *not* learning is very much like being dead. I'll keep at it as long as I can. This trip was part of that.

I certainly hadn't come here to relive the Vietnam War, but that experience had shown me what an exotic, beautiful place Vietnam is. I was far more interested in Vietnam the place, and in Vietnam the nation, than I was in former U.S. military bases and battle strategy. I now had the opportunity to explore more of it. I would glide along freely, without worrying about my immediate future as I had to do 28 years earlier.

The stupidity of the past was not going to take my goal of exploration away from me. If I allowed that, my 1968 draft notice would have been for life, not just for two years. Many soldiers had that choice made for them because they'd been drafted and killed near here. My good fortune in sharing only the first part of that fate would only be as meaningful as I made it. I had come here to experience a beautiful land again, to see what the Vietnamese had done with their independent, united country, and to share that through writing and photographs.

Top, a farmer works his field.

Bottom, QL1 just north of Hue— sugar beet slices dry beside the road.

But I knew I was turning the tables on those who had sent me here the first time. They hoped I'd do their evil bidding and think no more about it—wrong! Returning to Vietnam had been, in small part anyway, an act of defiance. At home, people who hike or cross country ski into the mountain wilderness near my home defy the people who hate wilderness and would destroy it if they could. An acquaintance of mine had been a career Air Force man, but he visited Vietnam again and says some of his former fellows no longer speak to him. They thought he had defied them. For me, bicycling past the former Camp Evans was an act of defiance.

All this said, a quick tour of the old Camp Evans would have been interesting. I was curious to see the place, though it wasn't essential. But if I'd ridden up that road through the dump and found the old base, it wouldn't have been just a quick

Top right, vegetables, dwellings, and dunes south of Dong Hoi

Top left, a Vietnamese soldier is depicted on the monument at the Ben Hai River.

Bottom left, a pole that measures flood depth stands beside the highway.

Bottom right, Mark wields the plow.

look. I'd have poked around, taken lots of photographs, and spent a while there. By then, I would have turned up missing at the hotel in Hue.

The Vietnamese military had taken over some U.S. bases. The former big one at Chu Lai is an example, but Camp Evans apparently was not among these. I stopped looking for it and biked on toward Hue. The QL1 strip village continued, and presently I saw a landmark—the water tower that stands across the Perfume River near the city. But shouldn't I be seeing the citadel wall to my left? QL1 passes right along it, on the western side.

The citadel in Hue resembles a gigantic fortress. I'd driven that road in Army vehicles and I'd seen it from helicopters. The outer wall is high with large buttresses, and there's a moat around it. Two more walls and moats are concentrically arranged inside the outer one; from the air I'd seen a small runway within.

Finally, I realized the citadel was right there. I just had to look between blocky buildings to see it. Twenty-eight years earlier, there'd been buildings here, but not such high ones and not so close together. The citadel wall and the moat had been plainly visible alongside Highway One. Had there been a population explosion? Yeah, I think so!

A Street, The Citadel, and the A Shau Valley

We made the left turn around the southwest corner of the citadel to bicycle east between it and the Perfume River. I don't recall large trees along that street in 1970 but trees overhung it in 1998. This is possibly the most beautiful street in all Vietnam now; I may have seen it when those trees were still unplanted. The wall and moat were fully visible here, through trees and greenery. Hung and I were riding together now. We bypassed one bridge over the river, took the second, and found the hotel by a back route though the city.

I'd never been inside the citadel, but we toured it after lunch. What an ornate and beautiful world within! Off the bus, we walked through one of the main gates facing the river. It's a huge place and we'd only see a tiny bit. A fierce battle was fought on these grounds in 1968. Considerable work was underway during our visit, but I don't know how much was ongoing maintenance and how much was restoration from war damage. It wasn't long until we stood before the glorious throne of former emperors, though the most recent ones had been mere puppets of the French.

Bob and Holly were the only ones of our group to take a scheduled boat ride up the Perfume River to a pagoda. I would rather have seen this river closer to its source in the mountains, as I had from Army helicopters. There's whitewater up there, small streams, steep slopes, lush growth, birds that almost sing scales, and more than a few monkeys. What else? Tigers? *One-step* snakes? That's a snake so venomous that a person gets just one more step after its bite. That may be an exaggeration, but the truth is sufficiently awful. Unexploded ordnance? I know roughly where there's an unexploded hand grenade and I doubt it was the only one.

Exactly once, I'd stood squarely on the flat floor of the A Shau Valley near its center, and I wanted to stand there again. Back then, we had spent quite a few days patrolling around the periphery, but the actual valley floor seemed one of the earth's powerful places—a hidden valley, isolated. I'm sorry I only learned of it because of war. It had looked as though there might be a chance to get out there, which was another reason I hadn't gone to Khe Sanh in the V.Y.C van. My resolution to visit a peaceful Vietnam included the A Shau. But as it turned out, a visit to the valley wasn't going to happen. I toured the citadel and took rest time at the hotel instead.

The Hue electrical power, judging by the lights in and near our hotel, went off, back on, and finally off again for an hour or more. During that time, we bused to a restaurant for dinner where cooking was done using propane from tanks. The Vietnamese tend to be independent people; an individual's control over propane is greater than control over city utilities.

Salesmanship?

Peddlers had been particularly numerous outside the Temple of Literature in Hanoi and again here in front of the Hue citadel. Some were boys, but most peddlers seemed to be girls in their middle teens. They competed with each other for our attention and business. I bought post cards, though I could have purchased other items: note paper with envelopes, tee shirts, hats, and banners.

I'd already decided I wanted some post cards, but didn't want to carry them around with me. I somehow made it clear I'd buy them from the same girl when we came back to the bus. I remembered what she looked like, or what she was wearing, and bought as promised. In fact, I wish I'd bought more to have taken home.

Other girls would still pursue me with their wares, but their sales technique was poor. They all knew I'd just bought some cards, but they gave the impression that I should buy because they wanted to sell, not because I needed the goods. The sales pitch was exactly the same in both cities. Each seller would clearly demonstrate that a package really did contain 10 postcards. "One, two, three," and up to 10, while physically counting them out before me with great emphasis.

I wish I'd taken these girls aside and shared with them what factors I would find important about a set of postcards—that this one illustrated the One Pillar Pagoda, this one the citadel wall, this one the Perfume River, or this one the emperor's throne. By then, I was quite satisfied that each package contained the stated number of cards. But if I hadn't bought yet, their technique only included additional recounts with increasing fervor—as if numerical fraud were my only concern.

Selling things to tourists, Hung had indicated, was more a way of supplementing family income than a livelihood unto itself. These were energetic girls doing what they needed to do. They tried to beat the competition to each customer, but didn't realize their basic spiel wasn't working.

It would be easy to consider these sellers pests; indeed we often felt that way. But what's it really like, selling postcards for part of a family's living? What were their lives like after day's end?

An Intelligent Girl's Story

A few Cycle Vietnam trips earlier at a beach farther down the coast, Hung had noticed one girl among many peddlers. Not trying very hard to sell, she stood off to one side by herself. She was, in fact, crying a little. Why? Talking with the girl, he learned she just wasn't a seller and felt herself a failure at it. But Thuy was intelligent, well-spoken, and wanted to finish high school.

High school in Vietnam is not free. Sending children to school can cost too much for many families, though they can support themselves otherwise. Besides direct costs, there may be an indirect loss of income or labor when a family member is occupied elsewhere, like at school. Do you suppose this partly explains why the several schools we'd see along the way got out for the day at lunchtime? I'll bet it does.

Hung felt a strong connection to the people of Vietnam. His country needed help. He couldn't help them all, but he could help that one girl and that's exactly what he's doing. It's "one human being helping another," he told me.

He sent her money so she could finish high school. Very importantly, Hung considers her a sister. College is now coming, with details to be decided. What she does in life will be up to her, of course. But whatever she does, it will help Vietnam considerably more than hawking postcards and souvenirs. Thuy would join our group for dinner in Hoi An. She is a worthy person. By helping Thuy, Hung can help many, since the effect of intellect is multiplied many times over.

How could an educated Vietnamese person help that nation? One way, though certainly not the only one, would be through medicine, which is expensive and not always available in some areas. If a truck breaks down in Vietnam, it'll probably be running again shortly. But suffer injury or fall ill, and the outcome could be much different. Building a nation is a complex business, and medicine is but one example. The Vietnamese are helping themselves, and Hung is helping them through Thuy.

Who is Hung?

Hung Luong is a native of Vietnam. He grew up along the coast, east of then-Saigon, and was about two years old the first time I came to his country. When hard-core communists ran Vietnam, things became bad even for a 13-year old boy. Luong Thanh Hung escaped Vietnam then as a boat person in 1980. His mother made the decision; she had, in fact, organized the exit on fishing boats. Hung was picked up by an Exxon tanker and taken to Hong Kong where he spent almost four months in a relocation camp. He finally ended up in Oregon, went to school at Portland State, and then to work nearby.

He'd been on all the Cycle Vietnam trips since their inception, after Vietnam reopened its culture to the world. On Rick's first trip, Hung was a client and became an employee after that. When he married, he and his Vietnamese wife had two ceremonies—first in the United States and once more in Phan Thiet, Vietnam. They've done Cycle Vietnam on a tandem bike. This time, Hung would leave our trip at Phan Rang, go down the coast to be helpful to his mother at home, and rejoin us in HCMC.

Gail asked Hung how the Vietnamese people react to him when they see him in his cycling clothes riding with Americans. He responded with this analogy: Suppose a spaceship arrives from afar and lands in the United States. The aliens climb down—and the last one is an American dressed like an alien!

Hue to Hoi An

Could I leave some post cards to be mailed, I asked the man at the hotel desk in Hue? Certainly, but he noticed that I'd put 6,000 dong stamps on them. That was right for Hanoi, but from Hue it costs 6,400 dong (around 55 cents) to the United States or Canada. Postage is different from different parts of Vietnam? Yep!

The helpful man at the desk said if I left him the appropriate amount of money, he'd add the extra stamps and mail them for me. He did, too. Those cards from Hue arrived at recipients' houses after about three weeks, which was normal. But they did arrive, and I appreciated the man's extra effort on my behalf.

Rain, usually light but intermittently heavy, fell this morning. Bicycling didn't look like fun, so I got on the bus for the ride out of Hue. The route was about the same as I occasionally used to drive from Camp Evans down to either Phu Bai or Camp Eagle. I looked for the Catholic cathedral I'd seen then, but I didn't see it this time. I don't know what happened to it or whether it was still there. Hue seemed to have expanded southward and swallowed up many things, as growing cities do. An Army errand had once taken me to the south part of Hue, but on this trip, once across the Perfume River by bicycle, I saw nothing I recognized.

Hue is one of several cities with a fine airport, "courtesy of the U.S. tax-payer," as Wilson put it. It's a former U.S. airfield just south of the city at Phu Bai. The runway looked to be in good condition. Something seemed familiar about a road that left QL1 approximately opposite the Hue-Phu Bai airport. It may have been the former entrance to Camp Eagle, the main base of the 101st Airborne Division during later war years. Near there, QL1 entered open country again, leaving the city.

On the Bike Again

I started biking near our first water stop at Kilometer 861. Rain had relented, though it soon began again, lightly at first, and then harder. I got out my lightweight breathable waterproof shell and was glad I'd brought it. I wrapped my glasses, put them in a pannier, and the rain was fine. When the precipitation intensified, water ran down my neck so I put the hood up over my helmet. That worked.

I could have taken an entirely different approach to rain—the approach we took in the Army. I would still have put my glasses away (I see fine at a distance without them and didn't wear them at all until recent years) and not done anything else. Had I just allowed myself to get thoroughly wet, it would have worked as well. As Rick had said, "Once south a ways, the rain isn't cold. It's just wet." This was Vietnam where it's supposed to rain. But that rain did not contribute to photography. I didn't want my Nikon wet, nor did I expect to find any dry places where I could clean the lens or change film. I left it safe in its camera bag inside one pannier.

At lunch, we went under a roof to eat. The restaurant right at the water was open front and back, and we parked the bikes just in under the edge of the roof. I spread my shell over the seat for it to dry as much as possible, which wouldn't be much. Excellent lunch! The rain fell very lightly afterwards. I biked on, but I left my shell unzipped this time.

Just down the road, a bridge crossed a bay that opened to the sea nearby and a small village lay just beyond. Fishing boats were moored there and I managed a few photos in the drizzle. A Reunification Express train was stopped at the village where the track briefly paralleled the road. The tracks go out around the large headland there, close to the sea, while the road begins its ascent to Hai Van Pass.

Mystique of Hai Van Pass

There was another reason why I got on the bike where I did. Hai Van Pass retains a particular mystique for me. The name means sea and clouds. I'd previously seen the area from the north and I'd seen it from Da Nang. Army shuttle helicopter pilots wouldn't fly over it, of course. Better to go home alive than in a box. They'd always fly out around the headland and over the sea between Da Nang and Phu Bai. I had no doubt the pass was rather dangerous to cross then, by land or by air. But it fascinated me then and it still does. The day had come to bicycle over it.

I had bicycled through the village where the Reunification Express was stopped. QL1 turned seaward near the base of the big headland it would cross soon. It went over the railroad tracks and ramped up toward Hai Van from the end of the village. Rain had stopped and shafts of bright sunlight shone through clouds along the coast. But I passed up an excellent photograph of the bay's inlet from the sea. Kids were selling things there and I heard something in their tone I didn't like. I kept moving. Almost everyone in Vietnam had been very friendly; I wasn't looking for exceptions.

Exotic Adventure

I was surprised how far seaward the road went. I stopped, walked over, and photographed down onto the surf and the tracks below. QL1 turned back inland, climbing through forest. This was a journey I'd wanted to make. Crossing this pass would turn out to be an outstandingly exotic experience in an exotic land.

Notched into a steep slope, the rock along the highway was dark and reddish with a plutonic (once-molten) look about it. Most rock looked quite weathered in this warm, moist climate, but occasionally I'd spot a freshly broken face. For a petrologist (rock geologist), that's like looking into a rock's soul—the crystals, colors, and cleavage faces—seeing the ancient material for what it is and maybe for how it got there. Though I'm not a petrologist, I still appreciated such petrologic soul-baring.

On the outside, the highway was bordered with a low wall only about 2½ feet high, which had an upper row of alternating red and white blocks, making drivers less likely to crash over the cliff. Vietnamese road crews had done a good job marking this highway.

On steep, mountainous roads like this one, on the outside-ends of particularly sharp switchbacks, stood round, convex mirrors on poles. Drivers used these large mirrors to see oncoming traffic around the curves. In the United States, such mirrors might soon be stolen, though a truly dreadful penalty should be laid against that theft. But mirror-theft did not seem a problem in Vietnam where a sense of community apparently suffices to prevent it.

Almost everything except the road cut, the road itself, and the outside wall, was verdant green. What a color contrast! Here was "the bare Vietnam," without hordes of people and the inescapable kids. It would be a total of 15 km from lunch to the top and there was no population for about the last 10.

This was mountain forest, and I was nearly alone in it. Though the trees didn't have huge trunks, some were tall. There was low vegetation and lots of shrubbery, as I remembered from hills around the A Shau. I'm not subject to jungle flashbacks, but if I were, I'd have experienced one here for sure! As it was, the place seemed a bit spooky, as in: "Here's something I'm familiar with." I looked off into the forest to see if there were any trails, but the bank was too steep and I saw none. On this day, I was free to enjoy Vietnam's wildness.

Several streams came steeply down the mountainside. QL1 would sometimes curve into a small canyon a stream had cut. There'd be a bridge across the stream and the road would curve back out the other side. Water tumbled down a rocky channel, pouring from one pool to another. It was tempting to fill my water bottle from one of these. Though I had halozone tablets to disinfect water, I didn't fill up there.

Some of the road must have had about a 10% slope and I couldn't sustain this climb on the bike. So I just walked the steepest parts—several kilometers in all. I would learn something later about going up hills, but that didn't help now. Still, this pass was one of the places I'd come to Vietnam to experience.

Up toward the summit, ragged cloud forms whipped by from north to south, up and over the ridge. Visibility in those clouds decreased to about twice the width of the road, but the steepness lessened. I got back on the bike and rode to the top at Kilometer 905. Out of the mist, our sweeper bus appeared, parked at the summit.

The Summit and Down

The top of Hai Van didn't seem overly dramatic, but getting there had been another episode in this journey of discovery. Crossing the pass mostly by bike, partly on foot, had been another gratuitous act—something one does just for its own sake. This was not what many people would fly overseas to do.

Thai wanted me to put my bike on the bus, but I hadn't humped up Hai Van for that! Though he warned of a slippery road, it turned out just fine. I broke out into sunshine a few kilometers down and the road became dry. As I suspected, the clouds at the summit had been orographic (influenced by the terrain) and would dissipate down the Da Nang side of the pass, which was shorter than the Hue side. I stopped once or twice for photographs on the way down, but the smooth highway made for a really great rush to the bottom.

QL1 leveled off rather abruptly, just where a purple house stood among green rice paddies. I'd visited a powerful place and felt no need to ride farther that day. Three of us waited there; presently the sweeper bus picked us up. On we went just past Da Nang, then eastward off QL1 toward the sea for 10 km, to spend a layover day in Hoi An.

Marble Mountains and Two Beaches

A long, broad staircase ascended the Marble Mountains, close by the sea near Da Nang. Steps of stone, finely made with low walls along both sides, went higher and higher. At one point, there was an opportunity to descend into a chamber resembling the one at the Perfume Pagoda near Hanoi. The high point of the pathway was a saddle between two of the peaks. The rock type here looked to be marble, in accordance with the mountains' name.

Aboard one of our buses, several of us had started a tour of the Da Nang area, only a few kilometers north of our Hoi An layover city.

Wilson led the way through an opening in the wall. This passageway got smaller and darker. It went radically upward. No finely made steps here! Wilson, Gail, and I clamored up over large stones that had probably broken down from the walls.

The Grim Crawl of Death was a cave adventure I'd read an article about once. It was somewhere in the eastern United States. There, the account said, cavers had to creep through narrow passages, inching along, able to make only small movements. I surmised that if a body part itched, that was too bad; scratching may not have been possible. This continued for a long way. Some enjoy exploration of such passages and I respect that, but one thing that keeps me out is the horrible thought of being stuck—unable to go forward or back.

The cleft up through the core of Water Mountain wasn't really like that. Though dark and slippery, it was just a steep scramble up over some rocks, not long by cave standards. It wasn't overly constrictive. Yet, with emphasis on certain real or imagined similarities, the comparison with the Grim Crawl is what came to mind.

Upward we climbed until we popped out through a small opening on the summit of Water Mountain. Three other peaks stood close together and shared a common base. Their names were Air, Earth, and Fire—all elements in a particular philosophy of matter. The sea was near. A new beach resort right below us was being called China Beach. This was surprising, since the Vietnamese tend not to name things after China. Wilson said the historical China Beach of war (and then television show) fame had actually been several kilometers north. To the west and northwest was the city of Da Nang.

Water Mountain was a good place from which to orient ourselves to the area. Then back down we went into the hole, finding footholds, slowly descending through the dark passageway we'd climbed. A very ornate Buddhist shrine was down near the base of the mountain.

Reboarding our bus, which had come around the mountain to meet us, we drove out to the new China Beach resort. Some of us sat outside relaxing. We watched the surf and various fishing craft, which included little round boats, half-spherical, shaped like the brassy bottom of a kettle-drum. They were the right size to be sculled by one person, using one oar in front. Others were motorized and had propeller shafts extending through the hull. These boats would go right out through the surf into the water beyond and move parallel to the shore, their occupants in search of fish. Larger fishing boats were farther out. Much Vietnamese food comes from the sea because so much of Vietnam is seacoast.

A Fried Fish

We bused up to the original China Beach. During the Vietnam War, this had been an in-country R&R site on yet another fine beach. Now cafés line the sand, with eating areas out on stilts toward the sea. We chose the nearest one. My companions ordered seafood like oysters or shrimp. I saw exactly what I wanted and I ordered it. A fried fish. Time passed. The others had been served their meals and had nearly finished eating. Mine hadn't come yet. Had miscommunication occurred? But the waiter gestured that mine was still in preparation.

Finally it came: a whole fish, probably 10 inches long, lightly covered with sauce, with slices on each side at a slight angle to the spine. I had chopsticks, asked for a fork, and was given a ceramic soup spoon. Not best, but it would help me do the job. I scraped loose each section of sliced fish with the spoon and ate the pieces with chopsticks (my use of which seemed to be mending a bit). Was this meat-fix ever good! I turned the fish over and ate the other side—along with cucumber slices and another cola.

For most Vietnamese meals, it was best to be seated at tables of four. Lanny the former restaurateur later made what he called a "professional comment." He noted it was easy for these establishments to prepare food for us as they usually did, where we'd sit in groups and have bowls placed among us. An individual meal like my delicious fried fish at China Beach was a fine exception.

Afternoon's End

Lots of cola to drink that day. Most trip meals were provided, though not this meal at China Beach because it was on a layover day. But we normally had to buy our own drinks. Soft drinks cost 7,000 or 8,000 dong, yielding change from a 10,000-dong bill. There was not always exactitude about this. If a U.S. dollar bill were offered, it would be gladly accepted and usually treated the same as its nearest Vietnamese equivalent, a 10,000-dong bill, though the dollar was worth around 11,000 dong. Oh well.

We visited a shop in Da Nang where skilled artisans were carving decorative lions out of large marble blocks. They used no patterns, yet lions would emerge from the stone. Safety glasses, usually worn while using a hammer and chisel to carve marble, probably were unheard of and certainly not used by these sculptors.

Going back to Hoi An that afternoon, Wilson photographed the Da Nang airport, which he'd known during war years. His unit used to fly there sometimes, since they made lots of personnel-transportation flights. Large hangars still stood, left from those days. He also described other missions on which Chinook helicopters carried sling loads. Occasionally, a load had to be dropped just to save the helicopter. One of these was a rather costly and secret USAF electronics Jeep that had to go crashing down—to the extreme displeasure of the Air Force.

Wilson's unit occasionally delivered ice cream to soldiers in the field from the ice cream manufacturing plant the U.S. had built at Qui Nhon. I wished a helicopter would bring us ice cream right then (as once happened) but helicopters weren't part of the plan that day.

Hoi An to Quang Ngai

The 10 km ride from Hoi An back to QL1 was one of the most enjoyable of the trip for me. Under a bright morning sun, we left the city and cycled through rural villages beside a broad river where new houses were being built. Smoke poured from one building where bricks, freshly made, were drying. I biked alone most of the way, setting my own pace. This made me more efficient and I maintained a good speed. My body was feeling much better now, plus I was much more secure about being alone on the road.

Soon I came to an intersection with a much busier road. This was QL1 and HCMC was south. One of our riders turned north and biked 10 km in that direction, but things didn't look right! She was one of the stronger bikers on the trip, so I doubt the extra 20 kilometers had much physical effect on her. She did not, however, appear to be pleased about it.

Five kilometers south on QL1 was a house with two haystacks. These can be things of beauty in themselves. I've long suspected that different regions of the world have unique ways of storing hay, and these fell into the broad category of hay fastened to a pole, gracefully hanging. This was right near our first water stop.

I biked past Kilometer 1000 near noon—at 12:02 to be precise. Kilometers are measured from far in the north, near the border with China. Our Hanoi starting point had been at Kilometer 176. We were going to pass our halfway point before long.

This area was heavily agricultural, like most, though it included the usual string of villages along QL1. I was finding the population density too high. I wanted to see more of the geography of Vietnam, without this constant veil of humanity in front of it.

"But," someone may protest, "don't you know Vietnam is the people? It's those cities, towns, hamlets, schools, kids, water buffalo, rice paddies, gardens, and cafés that serve cam pho. It's those squeaky bicycles, motorbikes, buses, and trucks with air horns! It's those geese and chickens! It's those people, their lives and their problems! That's Vietnam."

I understand those sentiments, but I'm as much a rock-person as a people-person. Civilization exists only by the whim of geology, a wise person noted, and that whim is revocable. If not for the rock Vietnam is made of, there'd be nothing else. Geology has been going on for nearly five billion years; civilizations showed up only several thousand years ago. The rock will outlast them, as is the case worldwide.

Piles of stones had been assembled for building purposes along the road from Hoi An. The stones were granite. I use that term loosely because it refers to a range of rock types that share a preponderance of light-colored minerals, though dark ones are present, too. Salt and pepper rock, it's sometimes called. Granite has fairly course grains and a molten history—a large, underground molten mass that cooled slowly and solidified, making a pluton. Some was later uplifted. I could discern the rock's characteristics even from my bicycle that morning, and more of this granite would appear as we traveled south.

In the north, the rock had been mostly limestone. Its watery history involved calcite sedimentation on the sea floor. Marble of the Marble Mountains must have come from the metamorphism of limestone—a process that may have involved deep burial under high heat and pressure, though heat may also have come from a near-by pluton. I wasn't sure. In any case, calcite had been recrystallized.

I wanted to know several things: What heat source melted the plutonic rock? Where and when did it intrude and then cool? How extensive is it? What forces lifted that rock to its present position of prominence? How much of it erupted as still-molten lava onto the surface? How, when, and why did basins develop to collect the limestone? Did heat from the igneous bodies cause metamorphism of nearby rock? Why does a cordillera run down the spine of Vietnam and Laos, making a steep range of mountains almost to HCMC and the delta? How, when, why? I could see that I had much to learn!

What fascinate me most about North America are the great landforms—rivers, mountains, canyons, prairies, coasts, and dunes. The deserts, outpourings of lava, a great cordillera that runs the length of it, and other ranges with their own stories. Europe has the Alps, the Black Forest, and the River Rhine—that splendid setting of legends. Australia has the outback, jungles of the north, Ayers Rock, and the Great Barrier Reef. Siberia, that great unknown, that terror of Stalin, must be a land of wonder and awe, with glaciers, tarns, moraines, deltas, tundra, and peaks.

Africa seems so varied, from burning deserts of sand in the north, through equatorial tropics in the center, to beauty in the south. It is being torn apart geologically in the east. All of Africa was earlier severed from South America, which looks to be a fine example of a westward-moving continent overriding oceanic crust. The result has been the Andes, which rise along its west coast. What's going on under the ice of Antarctica? Under the Pacific Ocean lie deep trenches where seafloor is being swallowed into the mantle of the earth. Subducted material may appear again as clouds of volcanic ash that occasionally choke cities of the Pacific Rim.

Asia rises southward from deserts to the Himalayas. Great rivers like the Mekong and the Yangtse, whose headwaters are but a few miles apart, drain the mountains and lowlands. In Vietnam, it's the Northern and Southern Truong Son, that rugged chain of mountains. Headlands project out from the mountains into the sea, across a narrow, discontinuous coastal plain.

Vietnam has harbors like Cam Ranh Bay, beaches as at Nha Trang, and islands like Con Son. East of Hanoi, the limestone towers of Ha Long Bay rise from the sea. Broad river valleys carve the mountains. As I'd noticed years earlier, peaks seemed to have a particular shape in central Vietnam where those huge trees are still visible in silhouette on the ridges. Windwhipped clouds blow across the Hai Van. Hidden, verdant valleys like the A Shau exist among the mountains where drainage runs west into Laos. I've seen the green forest there and I've seen the cacti near Phan Rang. I've seen sandy coves and great dunes along the coast. Vietnam is a geography not easily forgotten.

On Past Chu Lai

When we stopped for lunch at a café in a town, we went through a gate and back into a courtyard, leaving the bikes out front. No need to worry about them. As usual, I didn't eat that much. Mostly rice and soup, but not enough greenery or fiber.

After lunch, we biked past the large base at Chu Lai. Formerly a United States facility, it's now used by the Vietnamese military. The base must have been even larger once. Such things tend to fade into the earth, but it looked like a former perimeter had extended along QL1, a long way out from the present gate.

The government strongly disapproves of photos around military facilities. Near Chu Lai, I realized my camera was around my neck and shoulder but I just left it there, unused. Several uniformed soldiers passed on motorbikes, but no problems arose. On his previous Cycle Vietnam trip, Wilson had inadvertently made a photograph of something forbidden. Soldiers appeared and he had to give up all his film. He commented that soldiers sometimes just wanted to procure bribes by hassling photographers. I can't imagine how any photograph I could have taken would imperil Vietnamese military security.

Our afternoon water stop was just beyond the military base, and I still felt fairly good. I was just beginning to notice my sore knee. I had put away the gel seat cover I'd been using and that was a change for the better. Saddle sores were no longer a factor. The soles of my feet didn't hurt and I felt I was getting stronger as the days passed. So I'd continue feeling good, I stopped riding for the day.

I'd pulled up to the water stop in strong fashion, parked the bike to await the sweeper bus, and tried to answer questions from Vietnamese people who had gathered there. One man on a motorbike asked me to photograph him and his small daughter, so I did. I'd have sent him one, but I didn't think to get an address.

Another reason for boarding the bus near Chu Lai was to make sure I'd be at the hotel in time for our afternoon bus ride out to the My Lai Memorial at 3:30. We crossed the Tra Khuc River to our hotel in Quang Ngai. A little later, we backtracked just across the river and drove 9 km east to the site of the My Lai massacre.

This Was My Country

Those who carried out the My Lai massacre weren't Nazis, crusaders, Spanish inquisitors, the soldiers of Ghengis Khan or of Attila the Hun. It wasn't the North Vietnamese—who had murdered about 2,000 people in Hue during their 1968 Tet offensive from a list prepared months ahead of time. Those responsible for the My Lai massacre had been sent here by the United States of America. "This was *my* country…" noted Lanny. That's why, for thinking Americans, My Lai differs so profoundly from history's long series of such events.

Was it the fault of low-level soldiers or did the blame lie with unit-level or higher officers? Joe, who had been an Army lieutenant in Vietnam, commented that in Officer Candidate School he'd known "lots of Rusty Calleys; young, gung-ho, and not well educated." Requirements for officer trainees were being stretched considerably in those years, Joe added.

The enlisted men I'd been with in my infantry company years earlier were mostly younger than I by about five years. Most were fine youths who found themselves caught up in the whole thing, as I had been. But others considered the military and the Vietnam War a rite of passage into adulthood. Take a bunch of 19-year-old kids of the latter sort—whose sensibilities were rather primitive, who were far less educated than their officers (and less, too, than many of their countrymen), for whom a very early job out of high school was to go to Vietnam and kill people! What should we have supposed would happen, given that set-up?

It is my personal belief that massacres of various degree and size happened all over Vietnam, not just at My Lai. Clearly, the U.S. military tortured prisoners in the Quang Ngai area, perhaps even more severely than they did elsewhere. Some call My Lai unique, but that doesn't square with all the stories soldiers have told.

In a conversation with a former U.S. government employee who had been in Vietnam early on, I learned this: There was an Army unit operating among villages. Its commanding officer would ride around haughtily, standing up in his Jeep. Told he ought not do that, he continued until he took a sniper's bullet in the forehead. In response, the United States of America called in napalm and other air strikes on the nearest village, killing about 2,000 civilians of all ages and both sexes.

Philip Caputo writes how a Marine colonel wanted to carpet-bomb and B-52 a small village near Da Nang and kill everyone in it. To his immense credit, then-Lieutenant Caputo talked this monster out of it. How many other colonels weren't talked out of it? My Lai was the only massacre my country carried out? Some think so, but I continue to hold strong doubts.

We came to know about My Lai largely through the heroism of an Army photographer there at the time. I, like Ronald Haeberle, had been an Army photographer during the second half of my Vietnam tour. I did not see any massacres. But if I'd photographed one, would I have had the foresight and courage to withhold the photos from the Army? And then, after I was out, to have brought the matter forward against the absolute lies of the commanders? I can only hope so.

There was also heroism on the part of Hugh Thompson, the Army helicopter pilot who prevented further murders at My Lai by landing between the perpetrators and other villagers. By forcing so many men into military service through an all-points draft to fight their immoral war, those in charge got exactly what they wanted in many cases. They also got some soldiers who would murder civilians and boast about it. But in other soldiers, they got more than they bargained for. Haeberle and Thompson were examples, and these men came from my country, too.

Has the My Lai massacre been politicized? Sure. Were our soldiers frustrated because they couldn't distinguish the enemy? No doubt. Were there Viet Cong among the villagers? Probably. Maybe they all were VC, except the babies. But even if the My Lai massacre could be understood in those terms, the question remains, why were Americans there at all, involved in that nation's civil war?

Quang Ngai to Qui Nhon

Lanny and I ended up in a real morning rush because we couldn't get a wakeup call in Quang Ngai. It was almost six o'clock, breakfast time, and we hurriedly packed. I had no time to get ready properly. Still, I rose with good biking expectations for the day and got my luggage downstairs to be loaded onto the bus.

I carried my bike panniers and helmet with me to the dining room so I could eat and go. But there, I immediately discovered I just couldn't handle the smell of food! With this the case, I probably couldn't bike, either. Lanny, who had said earlier he didn't feel well and wasn't going to ride that day, got his stuff together and biked off. "Not for very far," he said. Yet, he biked quite a distance that day, as I recall.

The Song Tra Hotel in Quang Ngai had a sunken front courtyard where vehicles could go down a short ramp from QL1 and park. I walked into that courtyard and sat for a few minutes near the large fishpond, contemplating. From that level, I could see the city moving about its morning business. Horns blared along QL1 as the highway came north and crossed the river on a long bridge. Electric poles had primitive wiring on them. A tall red and white tower tapered upward, with a group of antennae at the top. Some were parabolic microwave communication antennae pointed south toward Qui Nhon. The populace continued to rumble, creak, and honk past this bit of technology.

My sudden sickness at the smell of food was totally unexpected and discouraging. How did this trip compare with my first one over here? As I recall, I felt fairly good for most of that year except for some jungle rot and tripping over something that loosened my big toenail. On this trip, which would last less than three weeks, I'd felt a general malaise much of the time. After our first day of cycling, I hadn't felt good. I had felt much better approaching Hue, with slow but steady improvement thereafter. Sickness here in Quang Ngai was a setback.

The bus passed slowly through Quang Ngai, which had many shops of the now-familiar open-front configuration. As elsewhere, some shops repaired motorbikes while others sold machine tools, electronic equipment, coffee, bottled water, rice, or candle holders. They sold whatever anyone in this city might need and much that a visitor might want. On the way out of the city, Hung gave me a tangerine, though it was more like what we'd call a tangelo. It was my first food of the day. I also ate one of my blueberry breakfast bars. At the first water stop, I had a couple of pineapple slices—another of our snack foods that I enjoyed.

How many ways are there to get water from one ditch into another, or from a ditch onto a field? Earlier, I'd seen one device made from a bicycle. Other times, water was moved by traditional manual methods, scoop by scoop. One motorized pump was throwing a stream of water, but what an exception! Lanny and I talked with Thai, our V.Y.C guide, about the lives of people *out in the provinces,* as he called it. They may work 12 to 14 hours a day in their fields. In addition, they may raise a few cattle or do some crafts to earn a little more money, of which there is seldom enough.

What a fine beach we enjoyed near Tam Quan! Small surf right then, though waves were breaking farther out as though moving over shallows. We ate lunch there. Some in our group wanted to bike ahead, but the rest spent several hours at this idyllic place with palms and other trees. More palm trees appeared in the countryside now—not tall, but broad on top. At the beach, others of us reclined on chairs in the shade, took chairs out onto the sand, or went into the water.

I didn't bike that afternoon, either. I didn't feel ill anymore but I wasn't energetic. Yet, I wanted a productive day. I wrote in my notes and photographed where I could. I felt less like a dedicated cyclist while on the bus, but reality mattered, not how I felt about it. This day's bus time was made to suit my purposes and (unfortunately) my body.

Wilson and Gail had come this way the previous evening. They wanted to get ahead of the group so they could spend more time in the area where he'd been during the Vietnam War. He planned to deliver photographs to a Vietnamese friend he'd met during his previous Cycle Vietnam trip. With that friend, Wilson had possibly exchanged shots during the war.

What is the Third World?

Our hotel in Quang Ngai hadn't been horrible, as Jerry and others with previous experience had suggested it would be. In fact, our rooms were quite livable on a basic level. The bathrooms were a sadder story: They were unattractive to customers, though a department of public health would have found interest.

Perhaps this bathroom in Quang Ngai had been upgraded recently. It even had bathtubs in place of the now-familiar wet floor, and ours had a flow/temperature control lever on the shower. I don't recall having the luxury of a shower curtain. Something leaked and water seeped constantly around the toilet from above. There was a plastic rack near the basin but it was awash, too.

Why did our expectations about cleanliness and hygiene take a real dive after just a few days? Maybe it's because standards of sanitation required a certain support structure that just wasn't there. Among other things, the plumbing has to work. Clean, sanitary water must come from it. But the truth was, we were strongly advised on pain of illness not to drink the tap water. Our buses carried a large supply of bottled drinking water.

We figured out ways to deal with these things. Most hotels provided a pair of sandals for standing on wet floors, for example. In the end, it wasn't as much unhygienic as inconvenient. Our own way of life would probably seem artificial to many Vietnamese. Would they laugh at us?

Many trip members told me they had come partly to see this country before improvements progressed too far. Plush resorts were not generally our style or we wouldn't have been here. Some toilets were much more primitive than the ones in hotels—ceramic slits in the floor, maybe with wet bits of paper in a basket and a small cistern from which one poured water as needed with a plastic pitcher provided.

What is "third worldliness?" Is it the lack of infrastructure? Lack of what? I didn't know it yet, but experiences and observations the following year would retire the term "third world" from my vocabulary about Vietnam.

Qui Nhon to Tuy Hoa

I felt much better today, ready for the 10 km ride back inland to QL1, then south. Out on the divided street, I stopped to photograph the Seagull Hotel in Qui Nhon, our nicest lodging so far. But my lens and filter had fogged over.

I knew what had happened. Warm, moist air inside the camera had been cooled by the air conditioning inside the hotel. Cool air can't hold as much water vapor as warm air, so the excess could do nothing but condense as liquid inside my camera. I missed several more photos. I could have cleaned the front of the lens, but the problem probably was not just that. While I flew along on a good ride, the camera returned to equilibrium on its own, as I suspected it would. The fogged surfaces cleared.

I rode at a speed of 15 to 17 mph for a ways. That ended as we reached another headland to the south. It was about one third as high as Hai Van Pass. The approach was even more isolated, forested for a ways, and steep. Once again, this was the Vietnam I'd come to see. I couldn't bike it all the way, so I walked. Exposed rock again looked plutonic. Near the top, I got back on and rode to our water stop.

Wilson knew this pass from his previous bicycle trip. He also knew it because his unit had sprayed Agent Orange here during the Vietnam War. The Army covered the area near the road and the Air Force sprayed the more remote hills. All this is now mostly low growth, not trees as it should be. This particular forest was wantonly destroyed; I hope it will be beautiful again in several decades. Vietnam now buys timber from Laos.

It was a fun coast down off the pass! Lunch had been changed from Kilometer 1280 to a closer place at Kilometer 1261, which suited me.

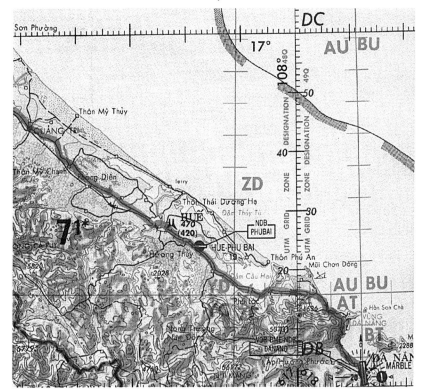

Dong Ha to Da Nang/Hoi An
east to QL1 at Kilometer 759, 71 km total to Hue
from QL1 Kilometer 826 at Hue, 136 total to Hoi An

After lunch, we came to rolling hills. A couple of these hills were rather steep, with a 10% grade posted. Again, I walked up. Vietnam's complex coastline included many islands and harbors. Fishing fleets were moored and large ponds formed by dikes near the shore were filled with water for growing seafood.

QL1 was a blacktopped highway, warm in the sun—why not use it? Local people were drying small shrimp along the side of the pavement, just as slices of sugar cane had been drying up near Hue. Rows of small rocks lined the traffic lanes on both sides to encourage drivers to stay off the shrimp. More rocks anchored long rolls of green cheesecloth. When dry, the shrimp were swept up with brooms.

I was told the shrimp were destined for animal feed, but which animals? I hope none ended up in our soup. That possibility aside, what an efficient and picturesque shrimp-drying this was! Later, hay was drying on QL1's multiple-use pavement. In a labor-intensive land, the people seize on simple solutions.

Top, an entrance to the citadel, from inside

Middle, ornate walkways, waterways, and buildings within

I'd noticed a definite and progressive change in the aesthetic quality of villages since those first kilometers out of Hanoi. It was more pronounced south of Hue and even more so down here. Villages had increasingly more character and open space. Vietnam is a land of saturated colors—houses might be painted bright blue or yellow. Rows of flowers or palm trees might line the path to a house, which was often surrounded by growing things. This region had a homier feel about it than farther north.

Our day included hills, villages, seacoast, and even a tailwind for a while. After lunch, I biked down to our final water stop at Kilometer 1300. There, I got on the bus though I was still feeling fine. I didn't want to drag in. The

Below, Tran Hung Dao, the street between the citadel and the Perfume River

Thuy, the girl Hung Luong is helping.

hotel near the south end of Tuy Hoa was at a large intersection. That evening, I photographed kids who had gathered around me at the hotel gate. Motorbikes poured through the intersection as the city ended its day.

Tuy Hoa to Nha Trang

A new day had started. Cyclists got around the divider that runs down the middle of QL1 in Tuy Hoa, then headed south. Most others with our group rode ahead of me, pulling away slowly. Two others had stopped, but they passed me and went on. I hadn't started last, but apparently I was the last one then.

Before riding, I'd tried to pump up a low rear tire, but the floor pump provided didn't fit my Schraeder stem. Hung looked around, borrowed Jerry's pump which was better than my own, and stroked my tire up hard by feel. I cycled south. But was that tire low again, a few kilometers south of Tuy Hoa? I stopped and gave it a few strokes with my small pump, which I'd been blaming for not being good enough. Looking back, it was my numb hands that weren't good enough, but I didn't recognize the problem at that time.

After another kilometer or so, my tire was softening again. I thought to pump it, still denying the obvious, but there didn't appear to be much future in the situation. I got my tools out, took off the rear wheel, and set about changing the tube. An older Vietnamese man, also on a bicycle, had stopped and held my bike for me earlier as I'd pumped up the tire. He soon arrived, stopped again, and started helping me.

I had my tire levers out by then, and we both worked around the wheel, getting the tire off on one side. The old tube came out, the new one went in, and my helper had the tire back on quickly, save one place where we soon popped it over the rim with the levers. But could I pump it adequately? The man took my short pump, set the wheel against the ground, and went to work. Very soon, he had it inflated as hard as I thought it could be using my pump. By this time, a small crowd had gathered around us to watch.

Some of the men looked at my unrolled tool kit, especially the combination tool, with great interest. One man picked up that tool, examined it, and put it back. I had absolutely no feeling that anyone intended to steal anything. Only in Ho Chi Minh City later would we be warned about theft, and only in HCMC would there be much reason for concern. In the present situation, I soon felt quite comfortable. What a giant advance for me! Just days earlier, I'd zoomed through villages

Top left, a watercourse over the rock on Hai Van Pass.

Bottom left, a worker doing restoration inside the Hue citadel.

Top right, previous page, a convex mirror stands at the end of a sharp curve. This one is on Ca Pass to the south. The idea seems to be catching on in the United States, where I've now seen several.

Bottom right, previous page, Luong Quoc Thai, our head V.Y.C guide

Top, this page, these red and yellow buses were numerous throughout northern and central Vietnam. As we cycled farther south, they tended to be blue instead of yellow.

Middle, a northbound truck comes over Hai Van Pass.

Bottom, brickmaking along the way from Hoi An back to the highway.

Opposite page, a child and a statue on the grounds of the My Lai Memorial

Right, this smaller statue was also on the My Lai Memorial grounds. There were several of this size in addition to the larger, more centrally located one pictured. There was a small building with photographs and other displays.

feeling apprehension about being there alone.

Later, I realized I'd forgotten something very basic during this period of social discovery. I hadn't checked around inside the tire to see why the tube had leaked. The rest of the day, I'd hope whatever it was had broken off, fallen out, or whatever. Maybe it was the valve itself. I didn't need a repeat of all this. I was lucky—months later, that tire was still holding air.

Just about the time we were getting the bike back together, the sweeper bus appeared. I motioned to the man who had helped me. Away from the crowd, I gave him a 2,000 dong bill I happened to have. But that's only about 20 cents, so I also found a U.S. dollar bill to give him. A dollar has considerably more meaning in Vietnam than it does at home.

I Hope Not

If he lived closer to me now, I'd invite him to dinner. Not just because he helped me fix my tire that day, but because he seemed the sort of man I'm proud to know. I don't think he helped because he hoped I'd pay him, as had certainly been the case with certain kids elsewhere. I was beginning to realize that these people are just plain friendly. I've wondered since about the effect of tourists giving these people money for their helpfulness, since I know there's satisfaction just in helping. On one hand, most people needed money and this man had certainly rendered

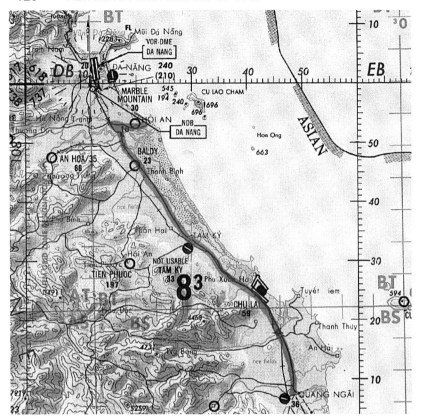

Hoi An to Quang Ngai
west to QL1 at Kilometer 949, 116 km total

a service. On the other hand, did I somehow denigrate what he'd freely offered? I hope not.

Thai and I agreed—I should ride the bus because I was now far behind everyone else. Besides, we had a pass to cross. My bike was loaded aboard and off we went, but it was a ways before we started catching up with the other bikers. We saw Holly steaming up the hill, then others. Laurie hadn't felt well that morning and was already on the bus.

Over the top we went, then stopped at a scenic spot overlooking the sea. This was Ca Pass, the second highest on QL1 after Hai Van to the north. Instead of testing my tire repair on a steep downhill along with the truck traffic, I bused on to the fishing village at the bottom.

Missed Photograph

By not biking down off the pass, I had missed a fine photograph of the inlet. There was a long, gently curved beach of white sand set between two headlands north and south, with a fleet of fishing boats moored at the northern end near the village. The missed photograph would bother me. It may well have been the place I'd seen years earlier from the window of an Air Force C-130. Just that one scene had played a large role in my wanting to return to this beautiful land.

After our water stop there, I biked on through rice country in the company of William and Heather. Rick had promised a strong tailwind and it was there! On we went at good speed. But I felt tired; in due time, the bike and I got on the passenger bus. Refreshed, I got back off at our afternoon water stop to bike into Nha Trang.

Gail was biking again. She'd been sick for a day and a half, but didn't know why. She hadn't partaken of local water, a prime cause of distress, though she later suspected some ice she'd had. Ice! A very likely suspect indeed. Made from what water?

Easy progress in the tailwind toward Nha Trang! At one point Gail, Wilson, and I stopped at an overlook beside the highway. There, I photographed some fishing boats moored close in and a man swimming in the water among them. Simple pleasure! Our speed was encouraging, even while ascending the gentle hill before our turnoff just past Kilometer 1445. A V.Y.C bus was parked at the turn so nobody in our group would ride on by. The climb would be quite steep for about a kilometer, then we'd coast down easily into the city.

Gail and Wilson, right ahead of me, rode up the hill. I dismounted to walk up. My best walking speed exactly matched their slow biking speed. There was a lesson in this, but it wouldn't sink in for a few more days. I stopped for more photographs as a pickup truck full of men passed in the opposite direction. The ones riding in the back waved and smiled as they sped on down.

Hung waited at the top, in front of another ramada in the shade. We talked briefly, then headed downhill together into the city. He led a swift ride, but we stopped on a long bridge to photograph the fleet of brightly colored fishing boats moored there. Rick had said we'd see a red and white antenna tower, and our hotel would be right beside it. Hung and I wheeled south, turned east with the tower in sight, and angled to the right again. We were soon at home for two nights in one of Vietnam's most visited cities, Nha Trang.

A Foreign City at Night

I wanted to send e-mails to friends in the United States. I also had an arrangement with my sister in which I'd e-mail her if I could and she'd pass on the trip's progress to a list of e-mail addresses I'd given her.

A Vietnamese man helping with the trip said he knew where to do this: "Oh, the Buu Dien!" There was a big post office right across from our hotel; in Vietnam these often have phones and fax. E-mail too, he believed. But first I'd have to change some United States currency into Vietnamese dong. Where to do that? My companion said he knew.

Off we walked into the utter depths of a dark, foreign city at night. Past a market where preparations were underway for the upcoming Tet celebration (the Vietnamese new year), we turned right and walked some more.

Finally, my friend slipped through a partially opened grate into a shop that seemed to sell things made of gold and other precious substances. There, I changed 30 U.S. dollars, which made me feel quite wealthy in dong! We walked back toward the hotel; I had about 300,000 dong in my pocket. I also had my GPS receiver in another pocket, having tried that day to make it lock on and assure me I was really in Nha Trang. I wasn't into being robbed, and my experience in other dark cities at night, though purposefully limited, made me wary.

My friend would take my arm from time to time, guiding me this way or that. He wanted to keep me out of the paths of bicycles and pedicabs that zip all over. Other times, his purpose was to steer me down a different street. We walked in the midst of chaos and bustle. Several times, I heard comments I thought were directed at me; someone touched my shoulder and offered me something before fading back into the humanity and darkness. The Vietnamese were a friendly people, but why should I push the margins?

I felt alert rather than scared and was operating in the *yellow zone*. On that scale, green would mean relaxed and red would call for action. But what action would I take if it came to that? I'd be vastly outnumbered in this strange place! We both walked fast, my friend still guiding me this way or that, as needed.

We got back to the post office and entered. No e-mail! Only fax, and I didn't know anyone's fax number. I was out of luck. My friend said, "I'm sorry" and meant it. I said it was ok, which it was. But here I was, rich in dong. Was I going to take it home with me? I said good night to my friend, went inside to the hotel desk, and spent most of those dong on phone calls to the United States. I did bring home one crisp, new 50,000-dong bill. I don't know whether this was legal, but I certainly left some dollars in trade.

Beach Chair Capitalism

On the morning of our layover day, we were drawn to the sea about a hundred yards from our Nha Trang hotel. The beach was steep. I didn't go out very far, but each breaking wave that tried to knock me over felt wonderful. After that, I sat in a beach chair to dry off and talk with Laurie.

Afterward, two women demanded money from us because we sat in their beach chairs. My chair had broken, dumping me on the ground, and I was left sitting on the stones. The owner of the chair apologized, and I assured her I was fine. I didn't understand the capitalistic beach chair arrangement and didn't know I was going to be charged for sitting there or I might have hobbled off right then!

More seriously, though I wasn't rich for a westerner, I was fabulously wealthy compared to most of these people. Why should I complain about paying to sit in a chair? A privately owned chair, too, I would realize. It wasn't a proud thing to be overly cheap when the modest amount of cash I had on the trip was more than they'd see in months. I had no money with me at the beach, but Laurie paid 5,000 dong (about 45 cents) on my behalf. Thank you, Laurie!

I also note this: In the United States, an apology for a collapsing chair would have been a self-serving one—an effort to forestall litigation, stave off receiving a safety violation from the beach chair police, or help ensure license renewal as a concessionaire. There was freedom from this in Nha Trang and it felt welcome. I wish now I could buy the woman a new chair for a couple of bucks; her old ones were well used.

Seeing a photograph at one point, I walked back to the hotel to get my camera. It was fogged again, as at Qui Nhon. Front and back of the filter, front and rear lens elements, and somewhere else as well. An internal lens element fogged? How did the moisture get inside my lens? Perhaps it was on the mirror or the ground glass, and I wasn't about to start wiping those parts. Mirrors in single lens reflex cameras are silvered on the front surface; if you wipe, you'll be buying a new one later. The ground glass was too close to the mirror.

I went back to the hotel to clean the lens, then back to the beach to take the photograph I wanted. The other internal fog had vanished by then, but every exposed surface including my glasses collected a film very quickly. Ocean spray and vapor? An onshore breeze was blowing.

That afternoon, a few of us walked to a small restaurant a few blocks into the city. The eating place was another open-front concrete building with a big metal grate in front that could be pulled shut from each side and locked in the middle. I've eaten better spaghetti, but you won't find that in most Vietnamese restaurants at all. It was no longer a scary walk, at least in daylight. Maybe these cities, like villages and countryside, were becoming a little more familiar.

Nha Trang to Phan Rang

I rechecked my tire pressure as we were about to leave Nha Trang, It was still up, but needed a little more air. Cycle Vietnam's floor pump only fit the smaller (Presta) valve stems, whereas mine and just a few others were the larger diameter (Schraeder) stems, like those on automobile wheels. Later, I'd learn that Presta valves make it easier to get air into a bike tire. William borrowed my little pump for his tires and offered to pump mine, too. Numbness, that unwelcome effect of bicycling, continued and I didn't have much arm or hand strength left. William got lots more air into the tire than I could have.

We started cycling through Nha Trang. My experiences had made it easier to get through these cities! We had about 10 km to go, back to the open highway. I was following a group I hoped knew the way. Holly's bike computer no longer functioned; when she worked with it, the device fell into pieces on the street. She stopped, picked up those pieces, and went on. A bike computer is a small electronic device, usually mounted on the handlebar, that displays time, speed, and distance.

At one point, we turned in a direction that felt like north to me, though shadows made it more northwest. But soon we turned onto our friend QL1 in the proper direction—south, toward Phan Rang. Numbers on kilometer stones would increase. This was just the third day of the whole trip on which I felt really good. Keeping up with the group ahead of me didn't matter, now that navigation in the city wasn't an issue.

Holly told me the strap holding a small tool bag under my bike seat had worked loose. Instead of fiddling with the strap, I just took the bag off and put it in a pannier. Behind the others now, we took turns leading a steady pace to our first water stop. I didn't want to stop for photographs or I'd be far behind. But I stopped a few times anyway.

Rick had promised a roaring tailwind today and drinks on him for anyone who made it all the way. After lunch, several riders got on the bus but I still felt fine. I'd decided not to attempt the ride up the mountain to Dalat the next day, but today I would have that free cola!

Across some water was the site of the former MACV (Military Assistance Command Vietnam) reception center at Cam Ranh Bay. There, I'd flopped onto the sand one night 28½ years earlier and listened on my radio as Apollo 11 settled onto the lunar surface. I couldn't see much over there except the top of what appeared to be an airport control tower. My map (the same aeronautical chart segment used in this book) showed this as an active airfield. Wilson took a side road up a small hill. From there, he could look down on the harbor facilities.

School Boys on Bikes

We ate just beyond the village of Cam Ranh at the most picturesque restaurant on our trip. As I departed from there, a nearby school had just ended its day. A large crowd of kids in their white shirts and red ties were headed south on bikes, many with books in their bike baskets.

I really didn't want to be in the midst of a crowd, so I pedaled faster. I easily bypassed the ones who weren't hurrying, but one boy was pacing me. Then there were two. Finally, there were about five alongside me. They were curious, having fun, and probably challenged to keep up with me. I set a good pace and they matched it.

At first, I felt uncomfortable being paced by these boys, but they clearly weren't malicious. They didn't impede me at all as I moved left once to pass a slower group. Indeed, they seemed to anticipate what I'd need to do and gave me room to do it. They just stayed with me as I rode ahead. Occasionally, one would even reach over and touch me. I wasn't very comfortable with that at the time, though I'd soon realize these kids simply held me in awe. How many times in life have I been held in awe? I still set a good pace, but I was no longer racing them, as before.

Sometimes, one of them would attempt a question, though language was a barrier. I didn't want to pretend I didn't notice them. Thinking good will would be better served, I tried a few questions of my own. I asked one boy how old he was, but he didn't understand. Each had a bike basket on his handlebars, with several paperback books or notebooks. I pointed to one basket and asked what it was. Not much response, but I could tell they liked my talking to them.

My pacers and I moved on southward; we soon became leaders of the after-school crowd. I'd done enough school teaching to have a rough idea how kids behave. Though younger than those I'd taught, kids here no longer seemed different from ones at home. Having had a foreigner to bike home with must have changed their day!

I was the foreigner in their lives then. For me, it changed more days than just that one. I know teachers can learn more than their students and I'm convinced I learned more about these boys than they did about me. Teaching and learning go both ways, but they did most of the teaching without even intending it. I learned how interesting these kids found me. Their good will was obviously genuine, and I felt no apprehension. Indeed, I learned that I should feel honored. I was probably a subject of conversation in several homes that evening. We must soon reach the village where these kids live, I thought, and that's what happened. The boys bade their goodbyes and I mine with a sincere wave. I rode alone again.

A Collision and Protagonists

A little farther on, Lanny was riding just ahead of me and a different boy on a bike was ahead of him. That boy turned sharply left across the width of QL1, probably to go back the other way. Lanny tried to turn, too, but couldn't do it sharply enough. He almost made it, then they collided. Lanny went off his bike onto the opposite shoulder of the road, flying through the air and landing on all fours in the dirt. It didn't take him long to get up and see if the boy was ok. But this boy didn't appear to want further dealings with foreigners and departed quickly!

Lanny straightened his handlebars and rode on. He commented later that if he'd been Vietnamese, there would have been no collision. As the boy turned left, Lanny said, he should have just slowed and swung over to the right to pass behind the other bike. On the bridge out of Tuy Hoa, I'd momentarily hooked handlebars with a woman, but neither of us had gone over. I'd almost run into slow bicycles or carts, and I'm sure others had similar experiences. Had one of us been injured, what then?

Not everyone along QL1 was nice, as Gail and Wilson would later relate. A guy and girl on a motorbike first tried to run Gail off the road, then approached Wilson from behind in an isolated place with no other traffic nearby. Gail and Wilson both had small rear view mirrors mounted on their helmets. Wilson, looking back, had seen what the guy on the motorbike had tried to do to Gail. When the motorbiker tried the same trick with him, Wilson said he'd launched a "major booger" and his aim was true.

The protagonists motored ahead, then stopped and waited, probably thirsting for unwarranted vengeance. I suspect the whole thing was a case of macho showmanship on the man's part. Gail and Wilson got there, stopped, straddled their bikes, and picked up rocks. Both of them are medium-sized westerners who must have seemed like angry giants to the would-be thugs. Wilson told us it was like saying, "Come on, guy, let's go! Any way you want it!"

Thus confronted, the guy and girl departed toward the north. But they came back from behind, possibly thinking to try the same assault again. When Gail and Wilson saw them coming, they stopped. The motorbike kept on going. If the miscreant happened to have an old hand grenade that somebody had kept from 30 years ago, there might be trouble if he went home to get it. But Gail and Wilson never saw them again. These motorbikers were not a credit to their country, though most citizens of Vietnam were and are.

At Kilometer 1551 is a large war memorial. Arriving there, we turned off QL1 onto a road toward the beach near Phan Rang. It was 7 km from there to our hotel. What an immediate change! No more trucks, honking of horns, or exhaust to breathe. These had been almost constant along heavily used QL1. Here, we rode quietly through Vietnam's grape country. The climate in this part of Vietnam is more favorable to grapes, and we'd also pass cactus patches.

Into a labeled "tourist area" we turned. Here, the hotel was built at the site of a former South Vietnamese presidential retreat not far from Phan Rang. Showers followed, then relaxation among trees near the beach upon which gentle waves broke. We took our meals on an open-air porch on the hotel's ground floor. The next day would be the hardest of all. We'd leave the sea and climb to Dalat in the Central Highlands.

Phan Rang to Dalat

It would be a tough ride on QL27. Cyclists would climb gently up a valley for about 45 km, then steeply up a mountainside for 18 km more. Lunch would be atop Ngoan Muc Pass, 980 meters (2714 feet) high. After that, we'd have a choice of two routes to Dalat. The more adventurous could turn off QL27 onto QL20 at Don Duong (pronounced don-oong), do some serious climbing, then cross high country directly west to Dalat. This route was labeled in the Cycle Vietnam map book as "steep, rough, remote, wonderful!"

The more southerly route would be to remain on QL27 and ride gentle terrain to another intersection with QL20, where that highway comes north toward Dalat from the direction of HCMC. Then it would be a steep climb. Note: I've seen one map of the region on which the highway numbers QL27 and QL20 differ from my description in places, but I'll go by the numbers I believe I saw on kilometer stones there.

I didn't think I was cyclist enough to do the high route and certainly not the first climb to lunch. Neither did some others, so eight of us got on the bus intending to start bicycling from our lunch stop at the pass.

A set of Cham towers was our first stop by bus. These works of a former civilization stood just inland from Phan Rang. Lanny and I had stopped at a Cham tower just the day before, but that one had deteriorated seriously in the last several hundred years. These near Phan Rang were in excellent condition. I don't know what degree of restoration had been done here or what upkeep continued. There were two in the set, close together and rising from the same base atop a small hill. Steps went up the hill under a pointed archway. The two brick towers on their hilltop in the morning sun were magnificent from the road below. I'd learn more later about the history of the Cham people in Vietnam.

Not a Great Ride

The first stretch, though slightly uphill for a long ways and a bit rough, would not have been overly difficult on a bike. Bob did note that "It hadn't been a great ride." This part of QL27 sloped northwest up a river valley to the village of Song Pha at the very beginning of the steep climb. On the way, we passed tobacco fields and hills forested with tall trees. We crossed a river that would have been raftable though strewn with rocks. Hills here were generally brown, not a lush green. Sheep, cattle, and goats were keeping down the height of grass in the low country.

Joe got to Song Pha a different way. One of the small, local buses stopped right in front of ours, which was parked in the village awaiting the bikers. Joe got off and someone helped retrieve his bike from on top. Because of a sore ankle, he'd caught a ride on this small bus that took a very circuitous, and probably interesting, route here. He intended to bicycle up the mountain if his ankle felt better.

Photos All Around

In photography courses, one exercise calls for remaining within a few feet of a place and seeing how many photographs you can find in your surroundings. I'd done it once, with amazing results. Our stopping place in Song Pha was truly magical in that way.

We parked in Song Pha long enough to observe the comings and goings of people, and I made several photographs. Westerners are accustomed to broad streets off the main road that go into neighborhoods of houses. But that wasn't the case in these villages; only footpaths went off into the trees. The nearest path was well-worn, about four feet wide, and within that was a narrower path. It was lined with tall slender palms, other trees, and lots of low vegetation. Melons were stacked near dwellings.

One older man wearing shorts and sandals came walking out the path to the road. He talked for a few minutes with a boy on a bike, then turned and walked back along the same path. On the way, he raised his arm about 40 degrees from his side several times to make gestures of greeting toward friends. I saw him take a coconut from a large pile and go into a house carrying it.

Big water pipes came down the hill from above. They were penstocks from a reservoir high up, built years earlier by a Japanese company to supply water for hydroelectric generation. We'd pass right under them later on the highway. Rick had warned us to avoid photographing there since the Vietnamese are as sensitive about such installations as they are about military facilities. Why were these never attacked during the Vietnam War? Possibly the North Vietnamese and Viet Cong knew they were going to win and they would need those penstocks intact afterward.

Up the Hill

Rolling again, we negotiated the many switchbacks on the steep, narrow uphill through lush greenery. More convex mirrors were mounted on poles at the ends of switchbacks, as on other passes. The valley where we'd started grew increasingly distant in the haze.

While busing up, we passed bikers one by one who seemed to be suffering as I had determined not to do. They labored up the big hill as if tormented for sins unpardonable. I didn't change my mind then about busing. I felt glad for those who could ride up the hill, but I wasn't among them. I'd helped pay for the presence of this bus and now I was going to use it. My bicycle was a tool. I wasn't there for a contest. We had each chosen our own way to Dalat that day.

Then the bus broke down.

Quantities of smoke poured from the center console. Opening that to investigate, it became apparent the power steering fluid was worse than low. It had been freely escaping. The drivers announced they'd obtain more fluid, fix the leak, and the bus would soon be underway. I was unconvinced.

Off came the bikes. I took my panniers with my camera and notebook. I was going to use the camera, and I wasn't going to leave my trip notes on a smoking bus that looked apt to burn. I had no choice about all my exposed film in the cargo bay.

I wasn't good at climbing and it didn't look like it was going to work this time, either. I struggled along for about a mile, my energy running steadily lower. It wasn't so steep that I had to walk; rather, I had to stop frequently, and there was less left of me each time. At least I made photographs. Heather came up the hill as I was resting and admonished me to take it easy.

What had I been missing about climbing hills? What would have helped earlier on that hill into Nha Trang? I'd just noticed how starting out from a stop had been fairly easy, but once up to speed, it got tougher.

Speed? A revelation came then, about 40 years late. I'd been trying to climb too fast, so I tried riding just fast enough to remain upright on the bike. Doing this, I was able to keep going with only an ordinary number of rest or photographic stops.

Momentum

Momentum means the tendency of an object to continue moving in the direction it's already moving. Momentum increases with the mass of the moving object and with its speed. It's part of rowing a raft through big whitewater, flying, plowing cars through snow, and driving heavy trucks. All my life I'd been concerned with having and using momentum, but here I realized it had little to do with getting a bicycle up a long hill.

I'd spent a few months driving a big truck and learned to use momentum on rolling hills, trying to come off downslopes with momentum enough to get up the next with minimal downshifting. A car driver who makes a trucker slow down while pulling a hill will be called unimaginably bad names inside the tractor. Deservedly, too. The car driver made the trucker lose momentum.

Driving a car through deep snow, don't stop! Don't speed either, but it's easier to keep moving to break through those snowdrifts. Once stopped, it's much tougher to get moving again. Momentum!

Aircraft have momentum. The bigger and faster the aircraft, the more important this becomes. Best to make flight a thing of beauty in its control and smooth transitions, using momentum advantageously and not letting it push the aircraft here or there. Thus, the flight instructor's admonition: "Fly the airplane, don't let the airplane fly you!"

Rowing a small raft through big rapids on rivers can be a study in using momentum. In some rapids you just aim and go, but in others, you must enter precisely, at a spot you've selected, pointed in a certain direction, with maximum momentum in the direction you need to move.

For example, in the Grand Canyon's Hermit Rapid, we needed left-momentum as we entered. But I had to straighten out to miss a rock I hadn't adequately scouted, lost momentum, and we just managed to miss the train of giant, breaking waves. We got *hammered,* as rafters say, and it wasn't a good moment because my satisfaction comes from making a plan and executing it exactly. Yeah, we made it, but maybe this was a wakeup call. Crystal Rapid was next, in which momentum is an order of magnitude more important. We nailed that one!

Steady Power on a Bike

If you stop pedaling while going uphill, a bicycle will stop very quickly. It's less a matter of building up a head of steam, so to speak, and more a matter of your body putting out a sustainable, steady amount of power to keep you climbing. That power relates to your rate of altitude gain, the weight of you and your bike, plus whatever power would have been required just to keep moving on level ground overcoming friction, wind drag, and so forth. From the standpoint of physics, raising a certain mass a certain distance (raising you and your bike up the hill) represents a certain amount of work. It is a fixed quantity for a particular bike and rider on a particular hill. Power is a measure of how fast that work is done; how fast the work is done is the only variable a bicycle rider can easily adjust.

The less quickly a cyclist gains altitude, the less power is needed because the same work is being done more slowly (though slower takes longer). It's like walking up a hill rather than running up. I'd thought I should gear down and pedal fast, but what worked was to gear down and pedal slowly. Even if you had a gear so low you could just spin the pedals, you'd have to spin them very fast. Your body's power output to go the same speed would need to be about the same. There's a pedaling cadence that's best for your body to put out the required work; achieving that cadence is the purpose of bicycle gearing. Changing gears doesn't change the amount of work to be done or the power required. The latter quantity is adjusted by the bicycle's speed.

Certainly, well-trained bicycle racers would be able to climb that hill very quickly because their bodies are capable of putting out considerably more power than mine. "Well-trained bicycle racers" didn't describe many of us, but I certainly developed new insights about the whole matter. My skills had improved in the process.

Into Dalat

It was about 6 km from the bus breakdown to lunch. A relaxed lunch it was at a small open-air shelter atop that first summit. I got back on my bike for a downhill stretch that passed the turn onto QL20 (the high route to Dalat). Rick had wanted to know which of us were going that shorter, steeper way, since Cycle Vietnam wouldn't be able to support us there. A few of us followed that high road; it became one of my regrets that I chose the more southerly, less scenic route.

I saw nobody I knew all the way from lunch until I had turned north at the next junction with QL20. I loved feeling alone and independent as I biked over small hills, through village after village. Being alone felt comfortable and normal now.

QL20 became steep after the junction. I had stopped to eat an energy bar when our passenger bus came along—I don't know how or where it had been repaired. I signaled a "thumbs down" and was taken aboard. Three other bikers turned up within the next 2 km and we all bused up the really steep 10 km or so into Dalat. There, it was around 5000 feet above sea level and relatively cool. Houses had glass in the windows, unlike down along the warmer coast!

Later, I turned down a bus tour to a pagoda. Pagodas were not atop my list, but I would have gone on a tour of the many waterfalls near Dalat or on any other tour that would have increased my knowledge of the area's unique geography. Instead, I used the time to collect my thoughts and write my notes.

We spent that night inside another tourist enclave: The Lavy Hotel in Dalat belongs to V.Y.C. This one not only had a bathtub in the bathroom but a shower curtain and a bathmat. No wet floor here!

Dalat to Bao Loc

It was a lazy morning in Dalat, with breakfast served over a range of time. Nobody was rushing anywhere that day, but Bob commented that, in general, it would be better to organize this trip around having more time in different places and less emphasis on point-to-point rushes for hard-core cyclists. I agreed, but I believe Rick does that very thing on his less ambitious Vietnam Sampler trips, not all of which attract enough riders to go.

I felt no desire to ride into the city. Our hotel was about a mile east of Dalat. From there, it was a pleasant ride along a shaded street overlooking the city's large lake and the city itself. Many dwellings seemed very out of place in Vietnam because of their splendor. Dalat as a whole seemed out of place in Vietnam for the same reason.

The shaded street (which was QL20) went to a traffic circle above the city. I rode with several others, some of whom said they were going to turn left toward HCMC. I really wanted to be on my way south, but everyone turned right toward Dalat and I turned with them. In a few minutes, I caught up with Gail and said I was going back the other way.

That meant I had to climb back up toward the junction again, but I had another project in mind. I backtracked about half a kilometer east to make photographs out across the lake, and of one large house I'd seen along QL20. Satisfied, I rode back to negotiate the same traffic circle for the third time in just a few minutes and started south.

From the circle, QL20 passed through the margins of Dalat and wound steeply down the mountain for about 10 kilometers toward Bao Loc and HCMC. The road swept down the hill through one curve after another, probably descending through a couple of life zones in the forest. The pavement had "just enough texture," as Rick commented, that I couldn't let my speed build unchecked. But still, what a ride!

On the way up that same hill the day before, close to Dalat, there had been an elephant whose keeper would take people for short rides. Holly was quite taken by that possibility and an elephant ride quickly became a goal of hers. How many of us have done that? I found Holly and Lanny at that place but not the elephant, who may not have been an early riser.

Near the bottom of the hill, several others detoured to a place called the Chicken Village. The name related somehow to a large likeness of a chicken right there in the village. Yes, I heard a story about how the chicken got there and why the village is so named, but it sounded a bit artificial to me. People in the village sold various sorts of woven fabric and (with little doubt) many other items as well.

Where Did the Water Come From?

Far down the road, Lanny and I stopped at a roadside café where he ate soup and we each drank a Pepsi. The Pepsi bottles were placed in ice soon after we got there and were cool, but not cold, when we drank them. Canned or bottled drinks were safe, but I didn't know the water source for other foods readily available along our way. The soup at this café was kept hot in a large, metal container, heated with propane from a cylinder. It was probably free of disease vectors, though I have no idea if the same could be said for the bowl and spoon. Again the question—where did water come from? The answer might provoke discomfort.

Someone might say, "Aw, it doesn't matter! It's all part of the local color!" I beg their pardon. It certainly does matter whether I ingest bacteria that can make me sick or dead. Rationality must override sentiment. Those who live there surely develop a resistance to many things. Others beware!

While Lanny and I sat with our Pepsis, two men riding a motorbike crashed right in front of us. I don't know why they went over, but they sure did. The bike skidded on its side for tens of feet, southbound down one of Vietnam's main highways. The two young men rolled over and over after it, but both jumped up running as though they wanted off the road before the next truck came along. They straightened their clothing and perhaps felt a bruise or two. But one walked back to get his sandals while the other stood the bike upright. It started and off they went.

Lanny and I reached our lunch stop at a fairly early hour. It was another picnic-style lunch where foods off our bus were spread on a table at a place that served only drinks. We sat squeezed into what looked like little toy plastic chairs with arm rests. "This is like snack time in the fifth grade!" someone remarked. These chairs, widespread throughout Vietnam, hardly fit the western body. My chair kept getting up with me each time I rose.

Twenty-eight years earlier, I'd noticed how blades of "devil grass" in Vietnam looked similar to the same plants in Southern California, only significantly bigger. This trip, more in contact with the people, emphasized the opposite difference in body size. Since Vietnamese tend to be smaller, chairs and other things tended to be smaller, too. It was a hint of Gulliver's storied visit to Lilliput.

Sugar Mills

Rick had told us about the sugar mills we'd see and one was across from our lunch stop. Trailer loads of sugar cane were taken to these small mills. Each had a tall smokestack because a fire heated the sugar cane in a vat, after which sugar was pressed out. Further processing included additional application of heat. Once pressed, the sugar cane was dried in piles, then used to feed the fires that refine more sugar. This efficiency was admirable.

Wilson beckoned me over to a nearby trailer. He asked if I recognized the material from which the trailer was built. It was runway revetment steel. During the Vietnam War, the United States had used interlocking sections of steel to cover runways and helipads. Here was that steel, still at work, hauling sugar cane.

My plan was to bus to the afternoon water stop, then bicycle into Bao Loc from there. Several others had the same plan and bikes filled the aisle of the passenger bus—something that would be highly illegal in the United States where bus drivers are required by law to keep aisles clear and passable. In this bus, we could move forward or back by climbing over seats, though some walked along using armrests as footing. An emergency requiring quick exit would not have been good.

At the water stop, the bikes remained on the bus. Instead of riding, their owners transferred to the Toyota van. I didn't wish to be so ugly as to demand that all the bikes be unloaded to reach mine, so I got into the van myself. What would be the difference? I was soon unhappy to be stuck in the van because fine photography was all around me. Plantations swept up and over steep hills. There were views down valleys where rice paddies wound along the bottoms. I had my camera, but it would have been a waste of film to photograph from a moving van—even though I was in the front seat with the window open. We got into Bao Loc about two in the afternoon. The city of Bao Loc had a rather striking skyline late in the day so I photographed it.

Last Evening on the Road

Our hotel had two elevators. Earlier, I'd had gotten on one of them and pushed the number 1, thinking to reach room 109. But I found I needed to push 2 instead. Next trip up, with my bags from the bus, I got on the *other* elevator and pushed 2. The result was that I walked into room 209 where I apologized to Anne. On the *same* elevator again, I pushed 1, which got me to my own floor. Button numbering is among the many seemingly mundane details to be worked out in a developing country. Though there are certainly elevators in these countries, I suspect most of the people who live there have never seen one.

I was more tired than I thought; now it felt good to have taken the van to Bao Loc. I flopped onto the bed to write notes. But two ball point pens quit working within a few minutes of each other and I couldn't find another in my bag. This was serious. I needed to keep notes each day, without fail.

I went down to the hotel desk with one of the deceased pens to see if I could buy another. After sufficient gesturing and a demonstration of the pen's demise, the woman got a key, went to another display case, opened it, and found a container of pens for sale. All of them had rose-colored ink, but I wasn't complaining. I'd be out of business without one. It cost 15,000 dong, which is roughly a buck and a half. I finished the trip using that pen and I used it at home for a long time, too.

Then, at the desk, I saw bags of M&M chocolate candies for sale. One bag, please! It had been three weeks now, and were they ever good! All 40 grams of them, packaged in Jakarta, Indonesia. Pens and M&Ms! Truly—the closer one gets to HCMC, the closer one is to the west.

Before dinner at Bao Loc, Rick went over the "Saigon-arrival proce-dure." Traffic would increase radically when we rejoined QL1 as it came from Phan Rang through Phan Thiet along the coast and headed straight west toward HCMC. It would really get wild upon reaching the city, he said. We'd assemble just this side of the Saigon River and ride across the bridge as a tight group with V.Y.C vehicles in front of us and behind. Then we'd take a quick tour of the city before riding to our hotel.

We'd clear everything off the buses and have a *lost-and-found* session. There'd be a list passed around on which to write our e-mail addresses. There'd be jars handy in which to leave tips for V.Y.C drivers and guides. We'd take the bikes apart and box them during our day in HCMC. I under-stood there were eating places in HCMC besides Vietnamese, so I planned a western meal. Though that never happened, I was ready.

I made my own plan. From Bao Loc, I'd bike to the lunch stop and bus to the rendezvous point. I wasn't going to fight the QL1 noise, traffic, and pollution. Maybe I'd ride into HCMC after that, or maybe I wouldn't.

Down the Hill!

It was still early in the morning, 6:30 or so, when Holly, Lanny, and I left the hotel. There were some short uphills until we reached Kilometer 108 on QL20. Then came one of the most wonderful parts of this whole Vietnam exploration! Ten kilometers of steep, winding downhill.

What we photographers call *enveloping light* swept across the hills and defined their shapes. Great white tree trunks glowed in the morning sun. Thick forest covered the hills from the valley floors to the summits. The terrain was, in the geologic sense, rapidly being incised by stream courses. The rock looked volcanic in places but granitic farther down the road. Before, I'd resented that if I stopped for photographs I'd soon be the last rider. Well, on this day I'd made several stops and was already last. It didn't matter—I was going to enjoy this wild area.

Again, this was the Vietnam I'd come to see! A beautiful country, parts of which still seemed remote. The road was good, with a bump here or there. Like the descent from Dalat, this wasn't a place to let ourselves go—both for reasons of safety and because I liked being there. I didn't want to just zip down the hill and have it all end too soon.

I came upon Lanny. He'd just fixed a blown rear inner tube and said he'd been lucky not to have "lost the bike." He said to go on, that he was ok now. On I went. I saw one small group of buildings with grass roofs. Just beyond, I photographed a particularly well framed portion of the road, where tall trees overhung it.

Down and down! I made a new plan right there on the hill; I'd go to the bottom, not far off now, and get on the bus that I knew would be waiting there. Physically I felt fine, but I had absolutely no desire to plow through the sea of humanity I knew was coming. I'd just seen Vietnam with very little superimposed in front of it. I wasn't ready for more crowds, various kinds of carts, trucks, buses, air horns, exhaust gases, or the associated particulates. No more being wheel to wheel with a river of traffic. I couldn't contemplate more of that. I'd done what I came to do.

At the bottom of the hill was the sweeper bus, which I boarded. I wasn't driving it so I didn't mind the congestion as much. The culture is interesting, to be sure, and many individuals had been extraordinary. But I prefer fewer people at a time, if not solitude.

Down the road, QL20 crossed one arm of a large reservoir, the same one that had been visible from the airliner departing HCMC days earlier. On that reservoir were many houseboats; one of them was disassembled. I could see that it consisted of a large metal hull, like a big pan, on which a bamboo and straw house would be built. If I lived in this climate, such a house would be just fine. If it floated on a lake, so much the better!

Our bus stopped right beside Tri An Reservoir, no doubt to check on other bikers' progress. A girl in a blue dress who lived on a near-shore houseboat stepped off her home onto smaller boats. She walked along them to the shore, then up the steep bank to the bus. Apparently, she had no motives other than curiosity, and to greet us.

Lunch was just beyond that point. Some of the strong bikers were still there, though they were starting to move off toward HCMC. Farther on, banana plantations stretched up and down over the hills. Rubber plantations appeared near the junction of QL20 and QL1. Wilson and I walked among the groves of rubber trees there.

Highway Into Congestion

Vietnam's major highway wasn't the same anymore! I wrote in my notes there was "no way I'd bicycle that stretch" of QL1 from the QL20 junction into HCMC. Traffic moved like an organism, full of big trucks, little trucks, many cars, and lots of buses. The shoulder was a pathway, often down off the edge of the pavement and strewn with rocks. In fairness to the highway planners, this shoulder was slated for work. In addition to smoke, noise, and heavy traffic (with its associated risk of violence), the temperature on that January afternoon was a very humid 105 degrees.

Which is more riveting, I asked myself? The sound of a bullet whipping by, as happened to me years earlier in this same country, or the sound of a truck's air horn immediately behind while biking on a narrow highway? I concluded only that the two are very different: The sharp "snap" of a bullet passing means it has already missed and can do no harm, though its clones may be enroute. But there is nothing final about a truck's air horn close behind. That particular truck continues to advance.

The bus ride to our meeting place near the Saigon River passed increasing levels of light industry, which certainly must increase truck traffic in this southern end of Vietnam. Some trucks were probably heading toward places not far off, like Phan Thiet. Others might have been bound for Hanoi, but they all would pass here. The area near the former large U.S. military base at Bien Hoa is now full of commercial enterprise. As with any city, much activity seemed related to food distribution. I specifically remember seeing a sweater manufacturer and a Coca Cola bottling plant. Both Coke and Pepsi had established themselves in Vietnam soon after President Clinton wisely ended trade restrictions.

Down the four-lane highway built by the United States, we arrived at our rendezvous near the river, across from the city. We snacked at a semi-outdoor restaurant under a shady arbor of foliage, waiting for other riders to come in. Rick arrived at 3:30, as he said he would.

Why Did I Agree to This?

I didn't think I was going to make the short ride into Ho Chi Minh City, but Rick considered it important and was having all the bikes unloaded off the bus. A plan unfolded. The Toyota van would precede our group of bicycles and one of the buses would follow. The ride would be about three kilometers. Off we went—across the bridge into chaos.

Nobody wore bicycle helmets in Vietnam but us, and this had served as a means of identification during the whole trip. I did my best to follow helmets and yellow Cycle Vietnam tee shirts up ahead. We negotiated several traffic circles, turning left 270 degrees (three quarters of the way around) at one of them. I almost, but not quite, got run over by a truck.

I did nothing on this ride except avoid about a thousand more opportunities for a violent end. Vehicles were even more numerous here than in Hanoi and were mostly motorized. Some were huge. There were slow bicycles, but motorbikes dominated in HCMC together with a generous mix of cars and trucks. There was no stopping! The idea was to make no sudden directional changes so traffic could swarm around and past. Fortunately, drivers appeared to go about their business quite sanely.

Our tour would include certain landmarks from the days of the defunct South Vietnamese government. We'd pass the former U.S. embassy and the presidential palace. I hardly saw them—I just saw traffic. Some HCMC streets have separate traffic lanes for bicycles and motorbikes, to the right of the major traffic lanes and separated from them by narrow islands. What a wonderful thing this was! Once we reached those, cycling in the city got much easier.

We all stopped across from the former palace beside a green park with many trees. There, people laid their cameras in a row on the sidewalk and

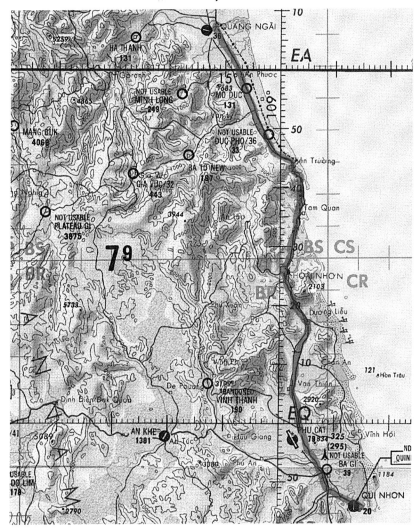

Quang Ngai to Qui Nhon
from QL1 Kilometer 1055, 175 km total

grouped together so one of the V.Y.C staff could take the same photo of our group with each camera. I had plenty of photographs, so I left my own camera on the bus.

I'd noticed a one-per-revolution drag on my rear wheel during the ride into HCMC, and sure enough, the wheel was out of true because of a broken spoke. "Rick, I've got a broken spoke. Suppose it'll get me there?" He predicted it would get me home. I hoped so.

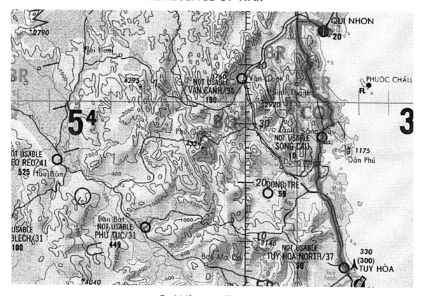

Qui Nhon to Tuy Hoa
west to QL1 at Kilometer 1230, 112 km total
Nine km were missing from the numbers on the kilometer stones—the stone
preceding the turn had been Kilometer 1221.

Tuy Hoa to Nha Trang
from QL1 Kilometer 1333, 115 km total

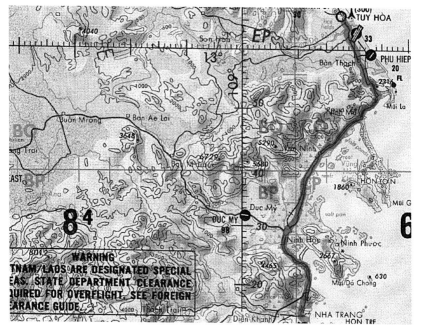

We made a few more turns, rode just a little ways in a bicycle lane, and arrived at the Metropole Hotel. Our group had not remained tight, as planned, because some tended to shoot on ahead and leave the rest of us. Two riders did get separated and lost enroute, but everyone somehow turned up at the final destination.

All in all, bicycling into HCMC may have been the dumbest thing I'd ever done. I was mostly glad to survive—perhaps even more so than the first time I was about to leave Vietnam. But I must say, this city ride was an adventure. Life is about that.

Relaxation, Ice Cream, and Darkness

The cycling was over! Sirens and traffic streamed by the hotel outside, but Lanny and I just crashed in our room. I wouldn't have much to do for the next several months, I imagined, except write. That was a situation I'd been aiming toward, but does it ever work that way? Ha! It had been a fine goal.

One adventure still waited, and it was a priority—finding the rumored Baskin Robbins ice cream place in HCMC. We bused to dinner that night at a restaurant. Afterward, sentiment was strong among us to go to the ice cream place,

Top, shrimp drying beside QL1.

Bottom, a house along QL1 in central Vietnam

about a kilometer from our hotel. Our V.Y.C bus driver said he'd take us, but that we'd have to walk back to the hotel. Thai pointed and said it would just be a straight walk along a major street. No problem.

Top, the seacoast in central Vietnam

Middle, Nha Trang beach near our hotel

Bottom, a fleet of fishing boats moored at Nha Trang

My two scoops of rocky road ice cream were exceptionally good and a credit to ice cream in general.

Our navigational abilities were surely up to the challenge of walking straight down a street to the hotel. A group of us started back together, but most began looking at items for sale along the sidewalk there. We were soon split up. I made the choice to walk with Gail and Wilson because I calculated this would maximize my chances of finding the hotel.

But soon, our "straight shot" involved a close choice between two streets at one of several traffic circles. We took what appeared to be the straightest, but we apparently got onto one that ran about 30 degrees right of our proper course. In hindsight, it would have been wiser to have returned to the intersection

and found the correct street. But we didn't realize there was a problem and walked on.

Our street became increasingly dark and spooky. HCMC was as crowded in darkness as in daylight, but this particular street wasn't crowded anymore. It got narrower and darker. I recall light glowing out of dwellings where robbers and murderers probably lived. No one else appeared to be around, though I'm sure we were seen by people we didn't particularly want to meet right then.

Down that dark street we walked, the three of us. To our left, we saw a long, fenced-off construction project that

Top, a house near the edge of Song Pha

Right, men relaxing in Song Pha.

Bottom left, our lunch stop at Cam Ranh

Lanny takes a break on the long hill above Song Pha.

Looking back down the hill toward the coast near Phan Rang

apparently had to do with reworking the street itself. On the far side of it were several hotels. Ours must have been near, but if so, none of us recognized it. Finally, we came to a way around the end of the construction.

Wilson said we needed to find out where we were. Truth lay in that statement, and we headed toward one of the hotels to ask. We hadn't the slightest idea where we were and this ignorance was trashing our simple plan.

On the way, near the middle of a block, we had to cross a street swarming with motorbikes. But now we knew how. We just stepped off the curb and walked slowly across the street without stopping. The results were magical! All that traffic just flowed around us. It's good to make eye contact with oncoming motorbike riders, but I believe that had we just closed our eyes and walked, the result would have been the same. This works

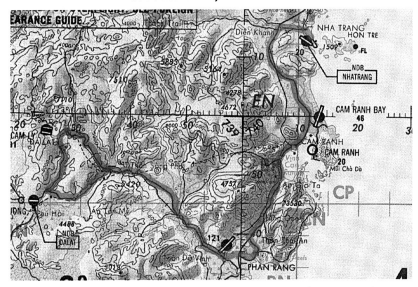

*Nha Trang to Phan Rang, through city to QL1 at Kilometer 1463,
then off QL1 at km 1550, 104 km total*

*Phan Rang to Dalat, cross QL1 at Kilometer 1557,
116 km by the shortest route*

A sugar cane press in Song Pha

with bicycles and motor-bikes—not with cars or trucks! Best we not misapply our recently learned, powerful, street-crossing technique.

With gestures and the drawing of a map, people at the hotel desk instructed us to turn left, then left again. Fine, but how far between turns I wondered? I think we turned too soon the second time, and that's why we ended up on another rather small street, this one much more crowded than the dark one earlier. It looked like a *cul-de-sac*, so we backtracked to the larger thoroughfare.

Top, a house along QL20 near Dalat—only there did we see dwellings like this one.

Middle, view across the lake at Dalat

Bottom, pine trees just south of Dalat

Thus defeated in this unknown maze of streets and humanity, we invoked an extreme solution. We hired three cyclos. It was a pleasant ride, and not really so extreme except that it emphasized our navigational failure.

A cyclo (or pedicab) is a hybrid vehicle with a seat in front between two bicycle wheels. The rear is that of a bicycle, including the pedals. The front passenger seat essentially replaces the bicycle's front wheel. These serve as taxicabs in HCMC where they go everywhere. (I've learned their numbers may decrease in the future as the city moves toward motorized transport.)

The cyclo drivers were skillful and brazen in their negotiation of traffic. But though the proper direction wasn't known for sure, I thought we only had a few blocks to go. Our cyclo ride was growing a bit long. It became increasingly clear the drivers didn't have the first notion where to go! They often gestured, pointed, and spoke among themselves in Vietnamese. None of us knew more than a couple words in their language, but their confusion was evident.

At first, they took us to the wrong hotel, but sufficient communication came from Wilson that we started moving again. I sensed that our route was circuitous at best, going for a ways on streets where I thought we'd bicycled earlier. I hoped we weren't being taken somewhere to be robbed, but we suddenly appeared before the Metropole Hotel. Though the agreed-upon price had mysteriously increased, I was so happy to be there that I just paid and went in.

As I wrote my notes for the day, I could still taste that ice cream. Never had I endured so much aggravation over just two scoops of the wonderful substance, but it was worth it. Also, I could live for years, yet never experience another hour of learning like this one in HCMC.

HCMC is unlike the rest of Vietnam in the behavior of certain of its citizenry. Holly told us about her costly ride that same evening, returning from the same ice cream place with Bob in two cyclos. Someone had paced Holly's cyclo and snatched a necklace she was wearing. We'd been warned about this very sort of thing, yet it happened. Holly and Bob chased the thief. They caught him, too, but only for a second

A sugar mill, and the sweet pleasure of sugar cane!

There were a number of signs similar to this one throughout Vietnam.

before he escaped through a fence. Later, Bob told vivid, blood-curdling details about what he'd have done to him, had they been able to hold on. I can only comment that murderers are punished less in most parts of the world than what this thief had in store!

The point is, in large cities anywhere, don't give the bad guys a shot at you! Following Rick's advice, I'd tucked my fanny pack inside my shirt along with the money and passport pouch that I'd worn around my neck throughout the trip.

Expectations, Results, Discomfort, and Home

During bad moments, I still suffer confusion about the International Date Line. But we knew Super Bowl XXXII would be played in San Diego, California, that weekend and we also knew which teams would play. Rick commented that the "real Super Bowl" had been played earlier, when the National Football League Packers had beaten the Forty Niners for their divisional championship. His opinion was shared generally: The Green Bay Packers would destroy the Denver Broncos.

The Super Bowl was broadcast in HCMC, live, at six o'clock Monday morning. We thought we could watch outside near a rooftop swimming pool at the Metropole Hotel. But perhaps the Vietnamese were less in tune with football than we Americans; nobody came to turn that TV on, nor could we make it operate. I went back to my room and watched it there instead. HCMC hotel rooms had televisions! The Packers scored first and easily, but the unfavored Broncos won. It confirmed what I'd long known; if we always knew the outcome of a thing, we'd never have to try it and life would be dull.

We packed up our bikes. Most of us used the cardboard boxes that new bikes come in, though a few had plastic bike cases. I skipped the city tour

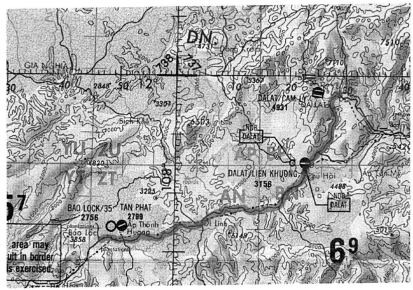

Dalat to Bao Loc
from QL20 Kilometer 235, 115 km total

that was offered, having had my own little tour the evening before. A final dinner, a night of rest, and we'd be off in the morning.

It wasn't quite this good for Mike, one of the strong cyclists on the trip. Seems that on our final bicycling day, he'd stopped with others at a roadside café for a cool drink—and had allowed them to put ice in it! Again the question: What was the water source?

On the day we left, Mike could barely get to the airplane. At Ton Son Nhat, with bikes and baggage checked, we all went upstairs to await our flight. With departure imminent, we went down other steps to board a bus that delivered us to the aircraft. We cleared space for Mike to lie down across the seats in the rear of the bus. Somebody took his carry-on aboard. Mike managed to climb the roll-up steps and slump into his seat. Then Vietnam Airlines departed Ho Chi Minh City for Singapore.

At a clinic in the huge Singapore terminal, Mike was given a liquid to drink containing powdered activated charcoal. This material is very porous and has a huge absorbent surface area far greater than would be expected for its volume. In chemical preparations during college years, we used it to absorb unwanted side-reaction products. In Mike's case, it would absorb nasty toxins resulting from whatever had been in that ice cube. Perhaps the clinic personnel had seen this very situation before!

By the time we taxied up to the gate in San Francisco, Mike felt fine again! He and I shared a motel room near the airport the night of our arrival. He left in good health for his flight home.

Girl in blue stepping ashore

Bao Loc to Ho Chi Minh City from QL20 Kilometer 121, 172 km total

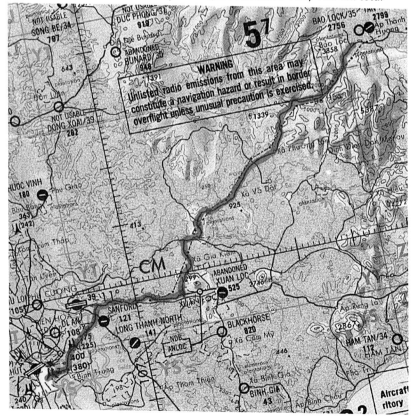

Bao Loc skyline

I flew home in the morning and ran my air conditioner while driving across a 9000-foot high, snowy plateau in the Rocky Mountains! It was as though I couldn't get cool enough on that winter day. Temperature, like so many things in life, seems relative.

Small statue, shrine at the foot of Marble Mountain, Da Nang

Drawing by My. She exhibits at the Cham Museum in Da Nang.

Further Discoveries in a Land Less Strange
What Was This?

I had left Vietnam twice, with only the vaguest thoughts about a possible return. But hey! Wasn't this the Kim Lien Hotel in Hanoi? Weren't we assembling bikes out here in the courtyard, and wasn't one of them mine? Wasn't that the same mad traffic honking and moving by on the street? What was going on here? It was 25 January 1999.

I'd actually been planning this trip for three months. I wanted to do the trip again, and do it better. I also knew I could write better if I experienced Vietnam again. Specifically, there were simple things I wished I'd kept better track of, like noting the kilometer stones nearest each starting and stopping place along the way. I would photograph a kilometer stone with each roll of film so I could more positively identify the photographs (I only forgot to do that once). A serious matter was that I'd missed some key photographs in 1998.

I'd improved my bicycle by adding proper pedals, different inner tubes with a more favorable (presta) type of air valve, a saddle better designed for the anatomy, and a more adjustable seatpost with a bolt I trusted not to strip. I had restored my original handlebar headset so I'd be able to position the bar better and avoid the "biker's palsy" that resulted from pressure on a nerve in the outside part of each palm. I'd upgraded my bicycling clothing and now had cycling jerseys that I could wash and wring out, with increased hope of having them dry by morning. I'd adopted Gail's 1998 laundry plan, which was to take a few hangars on which to dry clothing in the bus if need be. I'd bought a better helmet. In general, though, I'd pack less stuff.

I wasn't particularly satisfied with my physical performance the year before; I hadn't felt good much of the time and had only bicycled 47 percent of the distance. This year, I was in better physical condition than last. I still didn't consider myself a real cyclist, but I was a whole lot closer than I'd been before.

Jerry Brown told me that making another trip was like seeing the country with new eyes. She'd been on several. Hung Luong predicted I'd enjoy it more because I'd know what to expect. I knew what needed to be done. Plans to repeat this ride came together in the autumn after that first trip.

These tools and methods would help me do the job; the job was to replace first impressions with more lasting ones. It was to solidify and add to what I'd already learned, nail down details, make more photographs, and see what trends I could discern. I wanted to bicycle most parts of the trip I hadn't bicycled the year before. So off I went again to Vietnam.

To Hanoi

Singapore Airlines flew us across the sea again. After an overnight stop at that big retail mall that is Changi Airport (which includes hotel rooms for travelers), another Singapore Airlines flight took us right to the capital of Vietnam. There was no stop in Ho Chi Minh City for customs.

During our approach into Hanoi, a French businessman (who dealt in lubrication products and engine oils) told me Vietnam had been much less affected by Asia's economic recession than other countries in the region had been. A big new terminal and a hangar were under construction at Hanoi's Noi Bai airport. This should have served as early notice that Vietnam was on the move economically.

Customs booths had been built in the already-small, older terminal at Noi Bai. Some of us needed two more passport pictures, which a customs agent quickly took for only two dollars. Bikes and baggage went through X-ray machines that said "film-safe." Outside into the Vietnamese sunlight we walked. The smiling girl who greeted us turned out to be Hanh (*hun*), an apprentice guide with V.Y.C. She showed us where to put things, then it was into Hanoi by bus.

The road into the city was lined with billboards, and I got a much better look this year because it was daytime. One billboard advertised "American technology." Others advertised Pentax, Fuji, and Kodak photographic products. Others directed attention to Mazda, Samsung, Isuzu, and Ford automobiles. Also represented were Seimens, Vinaphone, Vietnam Telecom, a Chinese petroleum company, a beer, and the Hanoi Opera. Hotels urged travelers to "Stay with us!" You can learn much about a place by observing the advertising and at whom the advertising is directed; these billboards were all in English.

Shops and Patterns

Thousands of Hanoi shops still sold nearly everything: dresses displayed on plastic models, coats, watches, motorbike helmets (though nobody on cycles seemed to wear them), tiles, magazines, rope, aluminum and steel stock, pipe, chimney duct, and a display of water hoses.

All this was ordinary merchandise, found in any city. But something looked odd: Shops tended to be grouped together by type. I noticed, for example, a whole city block of shops that sold furniture made of wood. Other rows of shops might sell wooden carvings, or brass objects. Dealers of particular commodities would be grouped together. Near one city far down the road, there would be a whole row of stalls that sold caged birds—a trade in wild animals I regret, but they were there.

Suppose a resident of Hanoi goes shopping for wooden furniture and the first shop doesn't have the desired piece. Another shop selling the same sort of furniture would be right next door, with more after that. The pattern of personal transportation isn't the same in Hanoi as in the United States, where shoppers may think nothing of (wastefully) driving to another shop way across town. Devoting parts of certain Hanoi streets to a single purpose is very traditional, I learned, and it makes much sense. Strikingly apparent in the capital city, this practice would continue all the way south though Vietnam.

Around the City

Our city tour was similar to the one a year earlier, except this time I didn't walk past Ho Chi Minh in his mausoleum for two reasons. First, I had decided to photograph some things around the mausoleum instead and, second, I'd spilled soup all over my only pair of (required) long pants the evening before. They were still wet from being washed in the basin. Of these, the first reason was controlling and the second sealed the matter.

I was interested in the little screened house near the palace where Ho Chi Minh had actually lived. It's across a small lake near the palace. Now there's a platform with steps so people can easily walk by and look into Ho's living and workspace. Soldiers who must feel honored to serve there guarded both the house and mausoleum.

This year, we toured the Hanoi Opera House. Modeled after the Paris Opera, it's very traditional and ornate. At that time, the Philadelphia Orchestra was scheduled. Verdi's *Rigoletto* had been performed recently. There had been ballet.

The Hanoi Hilton now had a scale model of the former prison showing how it looked

Top, tripmember Chris with one of the guards at Ho's small house

Bottom, a Hanoi intersection in front of the opera house.

before most of it was demolished for an adjacent high-rise hotel. Gaunt-eyed mannequins occupied some of the cells. Visiting the prison this year, I felt much more detached than I had a year earlier because I'd been there before. I felt less struck by the entire reality; I was looking more at the details this time.

The grounds of the Temple of Literature were calm and peaceful with greenery, trees, and large ponds. There was a place within that sold books. I bought one that described the geography of Vietnam and would have bought a book on geology if I'd seen it. I have a weakness for books, and I certainly didn't buy enough of them. Somewhere in Hanoi is the Science and Technology Publishing House, which I believe would have just what I wanted about the geology of Vietnam.

Because dinner would follow, I went again with the group to the water puppet theater. I fought jet lag there and lost that battle a couple of times, without intending disrespect for the puppeteers. We ate upstairs at a small restaurant. Nice, but very loud under the nonacoustical ceiling. Conversation would have to wait. Cyclists this year turned out to be as varied as they were a year earlier, yet this group felt different. Not better or worse, but different, which is probably true on every Cycle Vietnam trip.

From Hanoi, we'd make that initial bike ride out to the Perfume Pagoda. I did most of the ride this year, though I took the bus through most city traffic to the turn south. Just because I had learned

Top, a mannequin in a cell at the old Hanoi Hilton

Bottom, walkway through an arch at the Temple of Literature

Left, work proceeds on a new wing at the Kim Lien Hotel.

Right, this girl ran the book shop on the grounds of the Temple of Literature.

the previous year how to bicycle through Hanoi doesn't mean I was brave enough to go there and do it!

Getting up the river involved the same ride in those steel rowboats to an improved trail up the hill. It was much more commercialized this year, and still populated with swarms of overly friendly kids who offered all manner of help and soft drinks. But Rick had warned that such friendship would come at a price! A new friend would soon ask us to buy him a cold soda and also one for each of his several friends, who all seemed to be there. If we did, then watched carefully, the sodas we had bought "for the friends" would be put back into the container to be sold again. These little sons of communism (if indeed they were that) understood certain tricks of capitalism rather well.

From top, road worker in central Vietnam

Second, ferry boats rusting on the shore because the new bridge was complete in 1999.

Third, new bridge near Cam Ranh

Bottom, new bridge over the Ben Hai River at the former DMZ, under construction in 1999 beside the older, historical one.

Change, Repaving, and New Bridges

When we first got to the Kim Lien Hotel, a new wing was being built—a second clue that Vietnam was on the move. Later, during the bicycle trip, improvement appeared everywhere. New houses were being built, as were other buildings that looked like light industrial facilities of various kinds. I noticed several new brick factories from which product must have been going out the gates very quickly. All the change in just a year's time was remarkable. I had come here again hoping to spot trends and it wasn't difficult!

A road as long as QL1 requires much ongoing maintenance and several stretches

of this national highway were being repaved. The long, graceful arching bridge over the estuary where the old ferry operated had been finished; the ferryboats lay rusting on the shore. Many smaller bridges were being replaced, including the one across the river near the former DMZ. The new bridge was being built alongside the old one and it will bring major traffic improvement.

There is local opinion in the Dong Ha area, according to David Lamb of the *Los Angeles Times*, that the old bridge there should be kept as a part of history. It surely played its part in the battle against the Saigon regime. Did the tank that finally crashed through the palace gate cross this bridge enroute south, or did it go another way? I don't know.

In general, I thought the pavement was rougher than it had been the year before. QL1 runs almost the length of Vietnam and is two-lane in most places. There is considerable medium-sized truck traffic. I saw truck escape ramps near Hai Van Pass and elsewhere, but I saw no weigh stations. The highway looked to have taken a real physical beating.

Thirty years or more of change in Vietnam really came home to two of our trip-members. Tommy had

Two more houses go up.

Top, a four-room living unit at our unexpectedly luxurious Nha Trang hotel in 1999

Middle, the semi-open hotel lobby

Bottom, our Qui Nhon hotel

been in the U.S. Army northeast of Saigon in 1965-66, and had traveled the road past Bien Hoa into the city several times. There'd been nothing there at all, he said, but now the city extends far in that direction. Peter had been a medical doctor at a hospital near Saigon, and he wanted to stop there and possibly visit. I was on the bus, too, when we stopped. The place was still a hospital, but the buildings had all been replaced. We drove on.

Vietnamese Trucking

Having been a trucker for a short while, I was interested in Vietnamese trucking. There, black-on-white license plates means a vehicle is owned privately. White-on-blue indicates a government vehicle. "White-on-red, army!" said Hung. Most of the trucks looked to be owned privately, either by an individual or by a company. The V.Y.C buses had black-on-white plates, though V.Y.C is a government enterprise. So vehicles belonging to companies, even if the government owns the company, are evidently licensed as though privately owned.

Hotels at Phan Rang and at Bo Trach, where trip members prepare for another day.

Third from top, sugar beet slicing near Hue—the slices will be spread on the shoulder of the road to dry.

Bottom, boats like these carried us up the Perfume River to the Thien Mu Pagoda.

It is my understanding that many truckers are analogous to *owner-operators* in the United States who own their own trucks. They either hire out as individual contractors seeking loads, or they lease their trucks to a company for which they drive. What an adventure trucking would be in Vietnam! A driver leaving HCMC for Hanoi (with the required assistant driver) would be starting a long, varied, challenging, and very scenic road. The journey would have strong elements of an odyssey.

Hotel Improvements

Again, what change! In 1998, many of our hotels were in need, shall we say, of improvements. In 1999, we stayed in four hotels that were new to Cycle Vietnam. Either brand new or freshly renovated, these were in Vinh, Hue, Quang Ngai, and Nha Trang.

Cycle Vietnam 2000, Rick told me a few months later, would be staying in "good hotels" the whole way. I

rather dislike being pampered and waited on, but I do like it when basic things work. Rick probably referred to that old hotel the East Germans had inflicted upon Dong Ha; by the time of this writing, it was to have been replaced. Sturdily built as a domicile for Russians when their activity in Vietnam was high, it seemed a bit dark, formal and somber inside. Its plumbing and wiring were in serious decay by 1999.

Vinh had been part of a depressed region, but in 1999, this whole area was alive with new construction. We cycled a few blocks past our 1998 hotel and stayed at another that had either been renovated or was brand new. Though nicer, it lacked the glorious view of those charming old East German apartment buildings across the street!

Just across the Perfume River from the citadel in Hue, the Morin Hotel was being renovated during our 1998 trip and we'd stayed at another a few blocks south. In 1999, the Morin was ready. Reviewing my 1970 aerial photograph of Hue for use in this book, I could see the Morin Hotel building, recognizable not only by its location near the river bridge,

Top, a young monk washes dishes at the Thien Mu Pagoda near Hue.
Bottom, the Perfume River in the evening, flowing from the mountains
past the pagoda

but also by the courtyard within the large building. I must have passed right by several times in those days, but little did I know...

The new hotel at Quang Ngai was just north of the city, across the river, on the corner where the road east to My Lai leaves QL1. Rick said about the old one, "Just be glad you're not there tonight!" That's where I'd suddenly felt sick that morning in 1998.

Again on this trip, several participants told me they'd wanted to see Vietnam before the country became too developed. A worthy sentiment indeed, but I heard nothing more about it after our layover at a luxurious new beachfront hotel in Nha Trang (www.soneva-pavilion.com/ana-mandara).

Vietnam is exploding with growth—and not just its hotels. I didn't see this in 1998, but it became obvious in 1999. I've wondered about negative effects on ordinary Vietnamese people who work at luxurious places like the Ana Mandara in Nha Trang. Financially, I'm sure it's good for them. Culturally, I don't know. But good or bad, change is coming quickly. I no longer think of Vietnam as a third world country, mired in the past and the past much like the future. Instead, it is a vigorously developing nation.

Top, a beggar in central Vietnam
Bottom, a load of rice goes to be planted.

Kilometer 1000, north of Quang Ngai, which felt like halfway for me.

Near Hue

Nearing Hue, I again couldn't find the old Camp Evans, but I'd seen plenty of it in the past. I believe the site of Camp Evans is where a large new building was under construction and almost finished. Language difficulties prevented me from reading the signs, but I was told it might be a concrete plant. It hadn't been there at all the year before, when the same place had looked like a landfill.

I cycled this stretch of QL1 a bit more carefully than other parts. It would be ironic, would it not, to perish on the road past my old army base, having come back here twice voluntarily? I had survived for a year near here once; I would survive the highway now.

Farther toward Hue, young men were feeding and cranking a sugar beet slicing machine. They spread the slices along the shoulders of QL1 to dry in the sun. If this system ever changes, I hope it changes in a way that benefits those beet growers.

The Reunification Express train approached a crossing north of Hue where QL1 swings across the tracks. Out of a small building came uniformed personnel who pushed barricades across the highway on both sides of the tracks. The train roared on north toward Hanoi, the gates were pushed open again, and the two agents returned to their building. Clearly, Vietnam is a labor-intensive country. The barricades rolled on lengths of ordinary railroad track, possibly to simplify procurement of parts. Many things work in practical, common-sense ways. The Vietnamese are resourceful people and use what's available. Near Hanoi, for example, long bamboo poles hold many television antennas aloft.

Boating to a Pagoda

In Hue, I decided to skip the citadel tour in 1999. But most of us boarded our scheduled late afternoon boat ride up the river to a Buddhist pagoda. What a fine view from there, across the broad Perfume River toward the mountains! We met some of the monks.

Top, this lion guards the Cham Museum in Da Nang.

Bottom, My, the artist who created the two drawings in this book.

*Top right, grapes growing near
Phan Rang. Top left, a woman
and daughter in Song Pha.*

*Our guides in 1999 were
Tran Xuan Hung, above, and
Nguyen Thi My Hanh, left.
Family names come first in Vietnam.*

Top, the junction in Don Duong where both forks lead to Dalat. QL20 as it climbs the steep hill toward the high country.

The high route, QL20, ascends to the right.

Bottom, a hillside near QL20

Though it can't be the only motivation, if it is motivation at all, Xuan Hung noted that if young men in Vietnam become monks, they "don't have to go to [the] Army!"

From this same pagoda, in 1963, came that first monk who publicly burned himself in then-Saigon to protest the Diem regime's anti-Buddhist repression. The car he used to get to Saigon was parked in a small garage, as if to be driven in the morning. The Thien Mu Pagoda had not always

Top, the high country on the way to Dalat, just where the road stops climbing.

Carrots and cabbages

been so peaceful a place as it was the day I visited, as told well by Susan Brownmiller in *Seeing Vietnam*. She traveled Vietnam in late 1992 and described this car. I don't think the Austin automobile had changed much in the six years since she saw it. A relative timelessness is surely one of its qualities; it had probably been right there when I drove near this pagoda in 1970.

Beggars

There are beggars in Vietnam as elsewhere, but I got a different feeling about them than I do about those we often see at highway off-ramps in the U.S. I know nothing about the presence of any social services, "safety nets," or other programs of that sort. I do think their need was a great deal more genuine and their situations less hopeful, than I've seen elsewhere.

Somewhere in central Vietnam, there was a woman beg-

Top, on toward Dalat on QL20
Bottom, a Bao Loc cemetary in the morning, at the end of my cycling
due to another broken spoke.

ging at our lunch stop. I know nothing about her, except that she was old and had a deformed foot. A mother was begging near our Phan Rang hotel. Maybe she wasn't supposed to be on the grounds, but she was; I don't know her story either. Numbers of kids along our way did a little half-hearted begging, but I don't think they were in need.

I gave small amounts of money to the first two. I'm glad I did and I'd do it again. But I gave none to the kids; doing so would only help establish unfortunate social patterns. Instead, those kids should grow to adulthood and contribute to their country as so many young Vietnamese are obviously doing.

Keith Famie, the video maker

The big hill near Bao Loc

Nina at a beach stop in central Vietnam

Feeling Like Halfway

The stone at Kilometer 1000 felt like the halfway point for me, though it was actually a few kilometers short. It's a peaceful area with small rural farms, rice fields, and lots of foliage. I stopped, photographed, and thought about the trip thus far.

I'd felt stronger on the bicycle this year. Not a single day had I felt sick, nor would I. On both trips, a few people had rolled around on the floor of the bus or had slumped in seats—looking unwell and drained of color. Their early demise must have seemed likely to them, but they evidenced no concern about it. Perhaps there was a rotation among them, since a new group performed the same ritual each day.

My hands hadn't been numb. Saddle soreness was very minimal. The food had been satisfying. I'd been photographing and seeing more. I didn't feel like I was cycling in an unfamiliar culture this year, though of course I still was. On our first day of cycling, it occurred to me that my cultural adjustment had been rapid; I felt no impulse to hurry as I had a year earlier. Cultural ease felt good.

Far down the road, a man on a motorbike stopped and spoke with me. His English was good, I thought. Turned out he'd just returned to his homeland from living in Minnesota. We wished each other well.

I left without breakfast at Tuy Hoa because service never happened and I'd waited as long as I could. But down the road several kilometers, I felt hungry—and a man appeared who was taking freshly baked baguettes (those small loaves of bread) somewhere to sell. Repaving was in progress along that stretch of QL1, and I was walking my bike at the time.

Mostly with gestures, I indicated I'd like to be his first customer of the day. If I understood him correctly after that, he offered me a price on a dozen baguettes, but I held up a finger to indicate I only wanted one. Was it ever good! I couldn't have carried a dozen anyway, but why did I not buy two or three? If I ever meet that man again under remotely similar circumstances, that's exactly what I'll do.

Multidimensional Traffic

The highway was effectively a three-dimensional space, but not the usual three. QL1 dimensions were forward and back along the highway, left and right across it, and time. In that space-time, everything moved: pedestrians, bicycles, motorbikes, minivans, small buses, large buses, trucks, oxen, and the occasional car. What a mix of speed and weight!

In Hanoi, I'd known what needed to be done but didn't feel up to the challenge except to make that right turn onto the highway south. In cities where traffic crossed, we coped as best we could. Successful outcomes were always amazing. Traffic could come from all sides, daunting in its complexity. Traffic lights in Hanoi and HCMC made the dimension of time less important there. Elsewhere, strong intuition about who would be where—and exactly when—helped greatly.

In the city of Quang Ngai, I finally experienced psychological "flow." In that state, I felt the master of my situation. It seemed I could "feel" the intentions of other drivers and cyclists, and I acted intuitively. Signaling my intentions was important, and now I could do it with a mere shift of my eyes or shoulders. I'd immediately see others adjust—and could then time and manage my passage through conflicting traffic. So that's how to do it! Cycling in traffic felt much easier.

This said, I did almost get run over by a truck leaving Quang Ngai. I'd joked at breakfast about the grim possibility of meeting one truck passing another on a narrow bridge, and a similar thing happened on the bridge south of the city. The two trucks, traveling in opposite directions, didn't have much room. I only saw three full-sized trucks in Vietnam, including the one going my way right then. Most trucks in Vietnam were "straight trucks" and didn't pull trailers. But this big one did. As it started to pass, I was trapped between it and the concrete railing of the bridge, beyond which was a drop into murky water where I wished not to go.

Closer and closer the truck moved, angling in my direction to avoid a northbound truck. In truth, the driver probably knew his width down to the decimeter and planned accordingly. Almost at the end of the bridge now, those big wheels went pounding by and I turned my shoulders just a little to help the end of the trailer miss me.

For a cyclist, QL1 along the greater part of its way is calm and peaceful; the bicycling was good. Nevertheless, there were opportunities for a violent end. But dealing with the traffic in cities felt much better after Quang Ngai in 1999. The danger didn't go away. It just became a great deal more fun!

The High Road—Cactus, Veggies, Pines, and Flowers

Something had been left undone in 1998, and I would correct it on this trip. I wanted to follow that high road to Dalat. I knew I'd have to bus up that first hill to the pass, so that's what I did. Ellen, a strong cyclist who topped 1100 miles (1771 km) on the trip, biked the first hill and could thereafter bike no more. My objective was that second hill.

From Phan Rang on QL27, we drove inland past a cotton research station, cotton and tomato fields, and grape arbors. Into a rural countryside with a few houses and villages we went—a gentle, hilly terrain where a variety of non-rice crops grew.

On we went to a village where our bus stopped to keep track of passing bikers and where I photographed town scenes. Xuan Hung lent me some Vietnamese money so I could walk down to the buu dien (post office, no foreign currency accepted) and send some post cards. I repaid him in U.S. dollars when I got back. Then we drove on to Song Pha, that photogenic village at the base of the mountain. I made photographs again this year while the bikers started one by one up the big hill.

A young woman with her daughter came walking out a curved path among trees. They went their way along the road. Across from us was an open-front barbershop made of poles that must have been bamboo. Woven material (as would be used to make baskets) formed the walls of the shop. The roof was of corrugated metal. On our side of the road, a small establishment sold snacks and drinks. In front was a bright yellow sugar cane press.

The people appeared to go about simple chores in a relaxed manner, on foot or on bicycles. In this village, I'd watched a man disappear into his house with a coconut a year earlier. Lots of motorbikes passed. Not many trucks use QL27, but a number of buses went that way, probably on tourist-oriented missions.

The big hill was wooded and very green. Tiny flowers grew by the road. Several watercourses came down over the granite. Rick upheld a personal tradition by jogging the 19 km steady climb, as he had Hai Van Pass. The (newer) bus did not break down this year! Atop the pass, V.Y.C provided a good lunch, but I ate lightly.

Then I quietly got my bike off the bus and started for Dalat. A bit apprehensive—I'd recently had two broken spokes—I didn't know how remote it might be up there or how rough the road. How long would it take if I ended up walking to Dalat? I'd put a pair of sandals in a pannier in case it came to that, since bicycle shoes with metal cleats make for clattery walking. Importantly, my injured ankle agreed with cycling but not with long hikes. Rick didn't think V.Y.C would be able to support us up there. What was this, anyway—a footpath? No, though rough and narrow at first, it would be the paved QL20.

As it turned out, the V.Y.C van would be able to support us. Small local buses ran in any case. The road was better than I expected. Once up the hill, it was quite good. It turned out to be a real look into a much different Vietnam, and I'd come to Vietnam again for new perspectives.

From lunch, it was mostly downhill or level for 7 km to Don Duong. Then there was that right turn onto QL20, followed by 10 unrelenting kilometers of steep uphill—up and up. I had determined not to walk my bike up hills this year, so I rode up. I stopped often, shall we say, to photograph! Hard, but I had committed myself months earlier to make this ride. I used the technique I'd learned a year earlier.

Nina went by, riding the trip's entire distance. As we shall see, she'd cycle the whole trip and then more. Jo went by, too. Ward went by, denouncing his malfunctioning derailleur. I'd see him later fixing his umpteenth flat of the trip, and still later fixing another. By then, he remarked that he wasn't angry anymore, just philosophical. Ward was a strong cyclist but, mechanically and pneumatically, his bike and tires challenged him in Vietnam.

Summits can be like fool's gold. It looks like you're reaching the top when in fact there's yet another hill to climb. There were several such places, but the road topped out suddenly. Steepness gave way to rolling terrain and a series of villages. This was Vietnamese high country, populated yet remote, and considerably more serene than the madness down along the coast. For the most part, I biked alone atop Vietnam and felt good about it.

Vegetables! I stopped and photographed men loading a big pile of carrots into a truck. One of them joked with me a little. The jesting felt fine, and we both parted in good spirits. That man lives in a fine part of his country. While crossing what looked like the veggie capital of the nation, I later photographed a stack of large cabbages.

Soon, I was within walking distance of Dalat, though walking remained unnecessary. My bike was performing well. The V.Y.C van drove by in the other direction so I told the driver which kilometer stone I'd last seen Ward near with his latest flat tire. My topo map showed the road climbing to over 5,000 feet twice and the second high point was very near Dalat. A few more ups and downs, a longer uphill, and there was Vietnam's resort region below in the afternoon light. The city itself was still hidden behind low hills. Descent was swift, and there I was bicycling among those luxurious villas.

V.Y.C's van was parked at the turn from QL20 toward the Lavy Hotel on the east side of the city. But after that, the map we'd been given made it appear I should turn right past a school. Besides, straight ahead looked more like a marketplace than a street so I turned right and rode past residences, along a curving way. This ended near a gate to a small military facility where the guard was quite pleasant though dutiful. Where he pointed didn't seem right, so I rode back to the school and tried what had been the left turn. It obviously was wrong, too, so I rode back out to QL20 to see if the V.Y.C van was still there. It wasn't.

I crossed the highway for a better view and thought I could see where I needed to go. Just then, a man who spoke English approached me and gave directions. "Thank you!" I started, but stopped for something on the other side of the road. The man crossed QL20 himself and said he had a hotel where he could fix me up for the evening. I thanked him again, but said I was settled. This time, I rode through that little marketplace and sure enough, the hotel appeared. Our maps were not always helpful if the route to the hotel was complex. Or was I the one who had made it complex this time?

In morning light, the city shimmered from across the lake during that beautiful bike ride out to the junction. I didn't need to see city detail, so I turned south toward Bao Loc. How different Dalat was from the coastal plain around Phan Rang that we'd left! Down there had been cacti and heat; up here, pine forests and coolness.

Soon came that long rush downhill through the pines! I enjoyed an uninterrupted descent; no photos came home from there.

Farther down, bright fields of flowers surrounded many houses where people were working the land on which they lived. No need for greenhouses on this broad, rolling terrain south of Dalat. A fortunate combination of climate, humidity and altitude (around 3,000 feet) seemed to work very well together.

Across more rolling country (which I understand was forested at one time) near Di Linh and then up a final hill into Bao Loc we cycled. I was riding mostly alone, enjoying and photographing what I'd missed the previous year. It had been an easy ride this day. The street from QL20 past the hotel had been in the turmoil of construction a year earlier. Now it was newly paved, divided, with islands of green foliage down the middle. Bao Loc would be our last night on the road.

Another Broken Spoke

No flat tires for me on the whole trip, but I'd had those two broken spokes: The first happened while entering Tuy Hoa, with the hotel nearly in sight. Another was next morning on the road south, not long after I bought that baguette. I was climbing Ca Pass enroute to Nha Trang, but I ended up in the van for one of the most beautiful stretches of highway in Vietnam. QL1 goes up over the pass and down again to the sea. Hanh knew what I wanted, communicated with our driver, and we stopped twice so I could make photographs. Thank you, Hanh!

Rick fixed those spokes later, both times, but something systematic was going on. At least my wheels had gotten me across the high country to Dalat, then down to Bao Loc. But cycling out of that city, I noticed a wobble in the rear wheel. Just a kilometer ahead was another photograph I'd missed the year before, of monuments in a cemetery just outside the city. I wanted that photograph and I got it.

I toyed with the idea of riding down the steep hill from Bao Loc toward HCMC even with the broken spoke, but thought better of it. I waited there by the cemetery and signaled a thumbs-down to our sweep van that I needed a ride. I expected to pay a creative penalty for it because partway down that hill was another photograph I wanted.

But Hanh was in the van this time, too, and I told her I'd sure like to stop. A wide place appeared in just the right spot and we stopped! I walked over and made several photographs across the valley—a beautiful place and the last of its kind on our trip. I'd photographed from there a year earlier, but this year, I applied some improvements and they worked. Hanh photographed, too, in the opposite direction.

Congestion and Mistrust

I sure missed a good ride down the hill. But I'd planned to get aboard the bus at the bottom anyway, as I'd done the year before. Little beyond that point made me want to be on a bicycle. Congestion would increase all the way to HCMC. I must confess that I went to sleep on the bus (to which I'd transferred) and missed the junction of QL20 with QL1. On down QL1 toward HCMC was our lunch stop.

A long wall ran beside an ordinary-looking house nearby. Along the top of that wall, many shards of broken glass were set into the concrete to discourage wall-climbers. We were getting closer to HCMC where such unfriendly gestures (and any need for them) are much more common.

Also at lunch, I first noticed my sunburn, so I made an effort to walk in the shadows as much as possible. The sunburned areas on each thigh, starting exactly where bicycle shorts end, would last for several months.

Ho Chi Minh City

About that final ride into HCMC, I made grim and unfavorable comparisons with other dumb things I'd done throughout life and possibly convinced others on the bus that it wasn't such a great plan. I wasn't going to make the same error two years in a row, and I watched my bike carefully to make sure Rick didn't fix that spoke! Partly because of a little rain, most of us didn't make that final ride into the city.

I'd skipped the Ho Chi Minh City tour the previous year, so I jumped on the bus this time. The former South Vietnamese presidential palace, after all, must have represented American tax dollars at work during early war years; it was rebuilt in 1962. Its former map room, with the maps still in place, was fascinating. Now the building is called the Reunification Palace.

Nina was the only bicyclist among us in 1999 who rode the entire distance. Beyond that, she had a plan. Her ticket home was from Hanoi, not from Ho Chi Minh City.

While the rest of us were packing our bikes and bags at the Metropole Hotel in HCMC, Nina was contemplating how she was going to bicycle back to Hanoi, alone. She was discussing final details, including matters of route and navigation, with Rick and others. She'd seen my two large maps from which I'd scanned and printed each day's travel and which are reproduced in this book.

Nina hesitatingly asked whether I'd consider selling them to her. No, I certainly would not! I gave them to her. I've only heard a little about her ride back to Hanoi. Her contemplated route through the central highlands and then down to the coast at Da Nang changed—she bicycled back via Laos and Thailand. Nina had bicycled in Vietnam before; she's an adventurous person upon whom youth had not been wasted. Jo, too, was adventurous. She'd cycled Rick's new Myanmar trip, which had ended just before our Cycle Vietnam trip began. Jo went from one to the other.

A floating restaurant-boat toured the harbor as we ate on board. What a variety of nationalities were displayed on the sterns of docked freighters! After our next and last dinner in HCMC, it turned out that our guide Hanh can sing!

School Days

Earlier in the trip, Nina and Dave had stopped about 10 km south of Thanh Hoa, still in northern Vietnam. Keith and Kevin, the documentary video makers who were with us partway in 1999, pulled up right then. They were joking about what they were going to film that day. As Dave told me later, he saw a long lane leading to a two-story school house.

"Hey," said Dave, "It'd be wild to go down and disrupt school! I bet all the kids would come pouring out!" That was a hot idea, so they walked their bikes down the lane to the school. They could hear the rising commotion inside. When they went through the arched gate into the courtyard, "the kids went nuts!" Laughing, joking kids whose English seemed limited to "hello" and "what's your name" quickly surrounded them.

Dave said they felt a little awkward because no one could communicate. But it "turned out we didn't really need to [talk] at all!" Keith had photos of his own kids and made friends by passing them around. Teachers came out and introduced themselves, and the visitors were soon "pulled into a classroom," as Dave put it. The teachers all came, shook hands, and sat around in a circle. Dave noticed a big drum there, apparently used to call the kids to school or perhaps to announce (as we'll see shortly) the beginnings or the ends of various assemblages.

The kids kept saying "headmaster," Dave told me. The headmaster was a shy man, but did come out to be photographed. He knew a little more English than the others. Then it was time to say good bye, but it had been good to see so many people smiling, grinning from ear to ear!

It is my impression that Vietnam in 1999 was at a stage where an educational disruption of this sort was fun! If a couple of foreign cyclists and a camera crew went unannounced to a school in England, Germany, Japan, or Kansas and caused a similar commotion, the headmaster's (or principal's) reaction would be very different. Perhaps (though their culture is very old) this was still a time of innocence and transition in Vietnam. If so, I hope it continues. But I know it might not.

Just south of Quang Tri is a school partly sponsored by Cycle the World. After experimenting elsewhere, Rick Bauman wanted to help a school near the route of his Vietnam trip so the participants could visit.

To the school we went, via a shortcut from the hotel along QL9 through Dong Ha, back to QL1, and south through Quang Tri. It was off the highway near Kilometer 774 where the V.Y.C bus was parked. We lifted our bikes over the train tracks beside QL1 and rode inland about a quarter mile on a dirt road through rice fields. We parked our bikes near where the kids park theirs, among trees outside the school.

Four or five young kids welcomed us at the gate by drumming. Here, I must reminisce for a moment: Years earlier in 1969, a U.S. Army band beside the airstrip at Camp Evans had seen us off one day to a place just inland from this school. Though that Army band was much better equipped than these kids were, their martial music had only filled me with suspicion. But on this day in 1999, I felt musically honored for the first time in Vietnam.

We crowded into what looked like a faculty meeting room. The assistant headmaster said a few words that were translated by Xuan Hung. Then a big drum sounded to end the meeting. We walked around the schoolyard and looked into classrooms.

Exercise time! All the students went into the central courtyard and lined up in rows and columns. Student-leaders captained them in a series of calisthenics that seemed aimed not at building great strength but at maintaining flexibility of the body.

Mathematical solutions to right triangles were written on a blackboard in one fifth grade classroom. I can solve right triangle problems, but I believe I learned that later than the fifth grade. In another classroom a few minutes later, the teacher had a group of kids recite that Ho Chi Minh quotation, declaring that Vietnam would last as long as the mountains stood and as long as the rivers flowed. When I was in the fifth grade, I remember learning Abraham Lincoln's Gettysburg Address for the purpose of recitation. But I didn't deliver it with nearly the leaning-forward, bright-eyed enthusiasm with which these kids quoted the modern father of their country. They spoke with extraordinary gusto, I suspect, because we were there. But still, these young students had joy and pride in their eyes.

Kids are kids, and the arrival of 20 foreigners in strange clothing did not make for a normal day at school. The teachers probably had a tough time of it, as did those other teachers north near Thanh Hoa earlier where Dave, Nina, and the film crew had visited. But in educational terms, I'm sure the disruptions were offset with learning for everyone. I doubt anyone thought otherwise; certainly not the kids.

I'm glad a little of my money went to help the Vietnamese. How much of our tax money had been used previously to destroy their country? Certainly, what Cycle the World is doing for the students at this school is better than what the U.S. military did to their parents and grandparents.

Down the road in the village of Phong Dien, I stopped to photograph where I'm sure I'd photographed 30 years earlier. Then, a crowd had gathered to await surplus food from the U.S. Army. Now, that same building is a school. Maybe it was then; I don't know. A wall has been built along QL1 where the railroad runs through the middle of the village. But right there, all that separated me from the school was a fence.

The school kids were just getting out for the day. They spotted me, and several of them made quick work of scaling that fence! I was soon surrounded, but I related to kids much better than I had a year earlier. These kids were friendly and curious as most kids in Vietnam had been. Having learned much about their country now, I felt completely comfortable with them and I made several photographs.

Communism and Capitalism

After 1975, as we have seen, hard-core communists dominated the government in Hanoi. Pure communism didn't work in Vietnam, just as it hasn't worked anywhere else. The Vietnamese were too independent for such a system of drab sameness and control. Due to economic nothingness, hungry people escaped to the sea in small boats.

Vietnam's present system mixes communism and capitalism. Can there really be such a mix? This is an on-going debate in Vietnam. Traditional communists think not and they contend with the "new thinkers," as we have seen. We must note that the purest form of capitalism doesn't work either, unless one approves of sweat shops, payment in script that's good only at the company store, trusts, price fixing, and similar injustices.

The government, Xuan Hung told us, had just debated whether there should be more than one political party in Vietnam. This had been an ongoing discussion for a while, according to Morley and Nishihara, editors and authors, in *Vietnam Joins the World,* 1997. The decision had been that only the Communist Party would be allowed. Hung told us that the manager of a private company may be a Party member, but the company owner may not be. Though communism certainly isn't a system I'd want in my own country, maybe the Vietnamese can modify it and make it work for them.

Getting It Done

It's a pragmatic thing. On the matter of trade and foreign investment, there seems to be indecision. Western businesses have established branches in Vietnam, but bureaucratic complications have forced many to withdraw. That discourages further investment. It seems the Vietnamese people will have to choose whether they want foreign business ties or not.

Several companies have manufacturing plants in Vietnam and some attract criticism. They pay wages that look low, but which would be astronomical in Vietnam.

Top, drummers
Bottom, the drummers go back
through the school's gate

There may be complaints about working conditions. A problem: The labor of Vietnamese employees can be resold elsewhere in the world for many times what it cost, with little of the difference returning to Vietnam.

Top right, a teacher at the school near Quang Tri

Top left, recitation: This was just an ordinary lesson, not the quotation from Ho Chi Minh. Some students were more interested in our presence than in their books. We did not make this an easy day for the teachers.

Vehicle restoration in Quang Tri

Exercise time at the school near Quang Tri

Below, the school in Phong Dien where I had photographed in 1970

Asian capital has been attracted to the country. Coke and Pepsi are both there and their products are widespread. All the computers I saw were running Microsoft Windows from the U.S. state of Washington. Vietnam's newest airliners (that I saw) were built in that same state by Boeing. Most capitalism in Vietnam looks small-time, like the roadside stands, and much is related to tourism in one form or another. Indeed, the government is making a big effort to attract more tourists, and Vietnam has much to offer. That new beachfront hotel in Nha Trang comes to mind, and the same company plans to open others. All over the country, the infrastructure (roads, bridges, pipes, wires, communication, etc.) is improving. I have heard stories about corruption in Vietnam and, since corruption hardly seems to be a rare thing in the world, there probably is corruption in Vietnam.

Reuters News Service in 1999 described barriers involving extra costs and much bureaucracy for foreign businesses. The English-language paper, Hanoi Viet Nam News (on the Internet at vietnamnews.vnagency.com.vn) reported very much the same thing,

Top, one of many such shops along QL1 throughout Vietnam

Houses south of Dalat are often surrounded by fields of commercially-grown flowers.

Bottom, a passenger alights from a cyclo in Ho Chi Minh City.

and suggested that the Vietnamese would fix the problem in a way beneficial to the Vietnamese and their culture. Hung Luong told me, "These people have been poor before and they'll be poor again before they lose their way of life." I certainly don't want to see an overly glitzy Vietnam. Life often moves more slowly there, and that can be good. Yet, change has been rapid.

Electronics

There was a real lack of e-mail in 1998, when I didn't see a single place from which to send messages. In 1999, e-mail and Internet access seemed to be everywhere! Many hotels had *business centers* (which they tended to misspell as "bussiness center"). From these, I could send several e-mails for a low price. On layover days in Hoi An and Nha Trang, I received replies from friends in the U.S. Two of our V.Y.C guides have personal e-mail addresses, so it's been possible to correspond with them.

A variety of conveyances on QL1 near Dong Hoi

I could readily send faxes from Vietnam on both trips, but in 1998 I didn't have anyone's fax number. In 1999, I discovered that just one fax cost about nine dollars, so I didn't do that very often. I received a fax from my sister at Bo Trach. Xuan Hung used his cell phone in many places throughout the country.

Michael Nörtemann, a visiting amateur radio licensee, took portable equipment to Laos and then to Vietnam in March 1999, according to his November article in *CQ*, a ham radio magazine. When he arrived, he was granted a temporary license to communicate from both Hanoi and Ho Chi Minh City.

A Cham tower in central Vietnam

Near Ho Chi Minh City, broken glass was cemented along the top of a wall around a house—only there were such things seen.

What If...

I asked Xuan Hung what his country might have been like if South Vietnam had prevailed against the north. He replied that most people believe they'd be more prosperous. I didn't get the impression, though, that anyone wished that had happened. I questioned further: Might this perception have come from all the money the United States pumped into South Vietnam while the latter existed, and from the years of economic failure after 1975? Hung thought this was very possible.

The Vietnamese brand of communism is simply not that drab picture we used to see in places like East Germany. It's not the picture we still see in North Korea. This is a communism without the horrible repression we've seen elsewhere, and Vietnam has no apparent interest in dominating other countries. Considerable individual initiative has been injected into the Vietnamese version.

Some would have us believe that the southern Vietnamese are now unfree because they live in a communist country. As though they were free under Diem and those subsequent dictators! I saw a goodly amount of personal, day-to-day freedom in evidence. Freedom of expression in particular may be revocable, but we in the U.S. have to watch out for that, too. The Vietnamese, we must remember, have never been used to freedom of a political nature. These things will continue to evolve. Vietnam has been doing that for a long time.

Jerry Brown ascends steps to a Cham tower near Phan Rang

The People Are Happy

The Vietnamese people I know are intensely proud of their nation. They are proud of being Vietnamese. Hanh told me she wants to learn more about her country and be "really Vietnamese." Xuan Hung, at the time of publication, is studying in the United States. After that, he'll return to Vietnam to serve his country. This is his "aim of life." Hung Luong told me the people of Vietnam are satisfied with their government. He added, simply, "The people are happy and they grow rice."

Drawing by My, Cham Museum, Da Nang

Rocks, Creatures, Cultures, and Wildness
Vietnam's Geologic Past

How did this part of the world come to exist? Why does it have its present form? These questions arose while bicycling among the varying rocks and landforms there. Here we must turn up the academic temperature a few degrees!

Vietnam, Laos, Cambodia, and much of Thailand all are parts of a well-defined tectonic unit—the Indochina Platform. Tectonics is the part of geology dealing with the *structure* of the crust and crustal movements, more than with its *composition*.

The Sunda Shelf is the largest undersea, continental shelf of its type in the world. Around Indochina and mostly south, the ocean is shallow enough for there to have been extensive land bridges when sea level was down. This happened about 18,000 years ago, according to Ekatarini Semendeferi who researched this region and, as a geologist, was part of an expedition there.

From Indochina and from the Malay Peninsula, the shelf extends under the sea all the way south down to the Indonesian Archipelago that includes Sumatra and Java. It surrounds Borneo and extends from there toward the Philippines. Straight to the east, the Sunda Shelf is bounded by oceanic floor of the South China Sea. Westward, the platform meets other oceanic floor and the terrain of Myanmar.

To the north, the Indochina Platform is bounded by the South China Platform, which extends into northeastern Vietnam. The geologic structure is similar there, but a geosynclinal zone (a broad downfolded area of the earth's crust) lies between the two landmasses.

Ciochon, Olson, and James carried out their paleoanthropological investigations in karst tower terrain southwest of Hanoi. Karst, as we shall see, derives from limestone—vast amounts of which exist in northern Vietnam. The name comes from the Karst region of the Adriatic coast in Europe; similar topography is widespread across southern China and northern Vietnam. It reaches one scenic climax east of Hanoi in Ha Long Bay, where over a thousand limestone towers rise out of the sea.

How does this topography form? Imagine a thick limestone elevated above sea level. Rainwater, made slightly acidic in the soil, will make its way down through cracks and fissures to the water table and then will move laterally through the fissures toward surface streams. The fissures slowly grow larger and become passages that interconnect. Karst is where groundwater has partially dissolved the rock (usually limestone, though that isn't absolute) into a whole system of caves, fissures, solution valleys, and sinkholes. During this process, the surface streams fed by the cave system are constantly eroding downward and lowering the water table, so there is a "downward trend" to the dissolution.

At the same time, erosion of higher areas proceeds as usual, particularly along weaknesses produced earlier by the honeycombing effect of the seeping water. Those areas tend to erode along the lines of the fissures into just the sort of karst towers we see today in Ha Long Bay and elsewhere. Karst is fruitful topography for paleoanthropologists because of all the cave openings where ancient people lived.

Sediments lie in many places across the Indochina Peninsula. In Vietnam, the entire Mekong Delta is of Quaternary sediments, as is most of the coastal plain up to and including the Red River Delta around Hanoi. There are massive, cross-bedded sandstones, conglomerates, shales, and lagoonal deposits. Some sediments rest *unconformably* upon other sediments, which means with a time-gap represented between them. Some rest upon igneous intrusions or upon blocks of older metamorphic rocks. *Synclines* (low places) were filled with sediment. Conditions of deposition may have changed laterally from continental redbeds (red sediments usually indicate deposition on land) to undersea shelf, and then to deeper water sediments—resulting in possible *facies changes* in a given layer of rock.

The Dalat series is the most extensive set of earlier Paleozoic Era sedimentary formations, dating from Cambrian through Silurian time (approximately 580 to 415 million years ago). Widespread submergence, according to Workman, occurred a little later in the Paleozoic during Devonian time (approximately 415 to 360 million years ago). Prolonged, extensive marine sedimentation ensued, interrupted in places by emergence of land, erosion, and folding. Earlier metamorphic massifs tended to remain elevated, defining sedimentation in the areas around them. Sedimentation continued as a regional process into the Mesozoic Era (approximately 255 to 63 million years ago at which time dinosaurs lived on the earth). Large blocks of limestone, which may contain cave systems, are found mainly in the northern part of the country.

The so-called "basement complex" of the region consists largely of high-grade metamorphic rocks—those subjected to sufficient heat and pressure so that most minerals were changed on the atomic level into new minerals that were more stable under such severe conditions. Though there are several exposures of this probably-Precambrian rock from north to south, the largest block is the Kontum massif (*massif* not capitalized by Workman or by others) in central Vietnam, which includes some younger granite, rhyolite, and other igneous material.

On a geologic map of Vietnam, the Kontum massif extends southward from the Da Nang area to a little north of Qui Nhon, and inland from there across Vietnam into Laos. This covers much of Quang Nam, Quang Ngai, Kon Tum, and Binh Dinh Provinces. It is a model for other, smaller exposures of its type. There are fingers of the metamorphic rock in several places. Many bodies of igneous rock lie south of the Kontum massif.

There are lobes of younger granite apparently associated with the massif. One such lobe extends toward Hoi An, which probably explains the granite building blocks I saw while bicycling back to QL1 from there. A larger lobe of granite (or perhaps part of the same one, separated on the surface by an area of sediment) is mapped as forming the headland north of Da Nang crossed by Hai Van Pass. I thought the rock looked igneous up there! That granite forms the high country of Bach Ma National Park, located inland along the same headland. Farther north, it forms the northeastern flank of the A Shau Valley.

I admit that I was still insensitive to rock types when I first visited the A Shau Valley three decades earlier. Besides, I recall mostly soil instead of bare rock. That warm, moist climate surely favors *chemical weathering* near the surface. That is, any fresh rock exposure will soon, in the geologic scheme of time, turn geochemically to dirt—oh, all right; clay and other minerals! I might have seen a sliver of basalt (a dark, eruptive, igneous rock) between the valley and Hue if I'd known to look while flying in that area.

The valley floor is mapped as Quaternary (quite recent) alluvium, as we would expect. Other rocks in the mountains between the A Shau and the coast are mapped mostly as various sediments of Devonian age, that time of widespread sedimentation.

Central and southern Vietnam looked rather igneous as we traveled south from Hai Van Pass. Igneous rock extends well south down the country's spine, about as far as the southern Truong Son Range goes. The headland crossed by Ca Pass south of Tuy Hoa is of granite, as is the big hill we climbed northwest of Phan Rang.

That second climb on our high route to Dalat consists of other types of igneous rock, though the high plateau itself along that route (where those vegetables grow) is mapped as various Paleozoic sediments. The steep hill down from Dalat traverses igneous rock, as does that final plunge on QL20 from Bao Loc down toward HCMC.

East of HCMC, near Bao Loc, across the Cambodian border, and northward in Vietnam along the border, are large areas of dark, igneous basalt. One such area is centered on Pleiku. From there, it extends north to the city of Kontum. Smaller areas of basalt are spread around Vietnam. From a bicycle, some rock in the south sure looked basaltic.

How did the northern and southern Truong Son Ranges get there? Apparently, five episodes of *orogeny* (mountain building) affected the Indochina Platform. Some rocks were affected by more than one of these. Other rocks were affected by just one orogeny, or by none at all.

A Precambrian or early Paleozoic orogeny may have occurred—along with emplacement of the Kontum massif. Then there were the Hercynian, the Orosinian I and II, and the Himalayan orogenies.

The Hercynian Orogeny occurred in the late Paleozoic (which ended about 255 million years ago). When Workman wrote, not much was known about it. It seems to have affected much of the area along the coast from just north of Nha Trang, south to Vung Tau near HCMC, and inland to include the region around Dalat. The largest movements happened in the northeast, with *thrust faulting* (movement with strongly horizontal as well as vertical components, where one block rides up and over another along a sharply tilted fault plane) against the land of the Kontum massif. A landmass called Annamia resulted from Hercynian folding. It included central and southern Vietnam, as well as much of the present-day adjoining countries.

The Orosinian Orogeny, parts I and II, had much to do with shaping the Indochina Platform. A major result was the landmass called Indosinia. This block, like Annamia, has remained fairly stable up through the present. Orosinian folding in Vietnam is found in a zone in northern Vietnam, and between Dalat and the Kontum massif.

Effects of the Himalayan Orogeny extended from the high mountains themselves through Myanmar, Indonesia, and as far as the Philippines and Japan. The effects included broad regional folding and faulting. India broke free to drift from the south about 100 million years ago, and regional effects began to be felt. India's collision with Asia began in the Cenozoic Era about 40 million years ago, and the orogeny that built Mt. Everest reached a peak only 10 million years ago, which is about when cutting of Arizona's Grand Canyon began.

The modern shape of the Indochina peninsula was determined during Cenzoic time by tilting and downfaulting that formed the South China Sea and the Gulf of Thailand. So, we then had the Indochina Peninsula, reasonably close to how it was when we bicycled it.

Flooding in the fall of 1999 near Hue, while very tragic in human terms, was part of the process by which the river deltas and the coastal plain are still being built. Indeed, the entire crust of our planet is changing. Because our time on earth is but a moment, we only get a brief look.

Sources included: David Workman, *Geology of Laos, Cambodia, South Vietnam and the Eastern Part of Thailand,* 1977; Nguyen Trong Dieu, *Geography of Vietnam,* 1995; Ciochon, Olson, and James, *Other Origins,* 1990; and the Master's thesis of Ekatarini Semendeferi, *Upper Paleolithic Cultures in Late Pleistocene Cave Sites in Tower Karst Formations in Southeast Asia,* University of Iowa, 1989. Also, I obtained a geologic map of Vietnam published by the National Geographic Directorate of Vietnam, 1971.

Creatures of Prehistory

About half a million years ago, the region became part of the habitat for *Homo erectus,* a direct evolutionary ancestor of modern humans. *Homo* lived throughout Southeast Asia, southern parts of present-day China, and many other places too.

In Vietnam, *Homo* lived in the Lang Trang Caves near the Ba (Horse) River in the western part of Thanh Hoa Province, not far from Laos. The city of Thanh Hoa is near the coast, a long day's bicycle journey south of Hanoi. The caves are inland, northwest of there, in karst tower topography formed in Devonian-age limestone, according to Semendeferi.

Homo was not alone. From about five million years earlier, and extending into the time of *Homo,* the region had been home to *Gigantopithecus.* This ape probably stood about 10 feet tall and ate mostly bamboo. In 1965, Vietnamese paleontologists had found the remains of *Homo* and *Gigantopithecus* together in the same cave, as had researchers in China. *Homo erectus* certainly encountered *Gigantopithecus* at some point. Their meeting was a large impetus for paleoarcheological and paleoanthropological investigations carried out in Vietnam by Russell Ciochon, John Olson, and writer Jamie James, and described in *Other Origins,* 1990.

What we know about *Gigantopithecus* is based not on complete skeletons, but on teeth and a few jawbones. Yet, by a process of extrapolation, we can know much about the ape. From the jaw, we know what kind of animal we're dealing with. We know about how large the head was. We know the usual head-to-body-size ratio in that type of animal, and we know similar ratios for the length of limbs. According to Ciochon, et al, these are conservative estimates. Still, the results are amazing.

How can we tell what the giant ape ate? That's a detective story in itself, told by Ciachon, et al. Growing plants take up many things from the soil, including silica. The silica, a very hard substance, ends up forming nearly indestructible *phytoliths* around the cells of the plant. Ever cut yourself on the edge of a blade of grass, ask the authors? Phytoliths were responsible for that. By examining a phytolith, it is often possible to tell what sort of plant it came from.

A student at the University of Iowa asked Professor Ciochon one day whether phytoliths might not be found embedded in *Gigantopithecus* teeth, and thus reveal what the creature ate? Hmmmm! There had been some related work earlier on this sort of thing.

Electron microscopy showed embedded phytoliths in *Gigantopithecus* teeth. It even revealed one embedded at the end of a gouge in the tooth enamel. The phytoliths found were consistent with a bamboo diet. A 1200-pound animal (perhaps half of that for females) must eat a great deal of something, and bamboo was the plant readily available to them. *Giganto* almost certainly ate large quantities of bamboo and probably not much else except a few fruits.

Other Origins includes a section about the role of bamboo in Asian culture. The authors begin, saying, "Nowhere else in the world has a single plant had as dominant an impact on the evolution of life and human development as bamboo has had in East Asia." The plant "seems almost to have entered into the Asian soul." "Bamboo" lumps together roughly

1200 related species, and makes Southeast Asia ecologically unique. Chopsticks, mats, baskets, watercraft, building materials, early paper, and much else: What part of life there does not somehow involve bamboo? Significantly, bamboo can be considered a key to the connection between *Homo erectus* and *Gigantopithecus,* according to Ciochon, et al.

When did these creatures live? Some of the teeth recovered from the Lang Trang Caves were subjected to electron spin resonance (ESR) dating by Henry Schwarcz of McMaster University in Hamilton, Ontario, Canada. This technique dates a fossil directly rather than determining a date from nearby volcanic rock, even where there is such. ESR works well on teeth, and that is what the team had brought from Vietnam. The numerical result from a pig tooth placed the fossils from the Lang Trang Caves at 440,000 to 520,000 years before the present.

The authors warn that such a range of dates can only be understood using statistical methods involving the standard deviation. In statistics, that number expresses how much the actual age of a fossil from a given site is likely to differ from its measured age. There is a 67% chance that the actual age is within one standard deviation of its measured age, and a 95% chance that it is within two standard deviations. Standard deviation generally decreases (the age-determination becomes more precise) as the number of samples from the site increases.

Fascinating speculation and myth accompany the science in *Other Origins*. Scientists can delve into this if they wish, as long as they're clear about it. The human imagination has long been full of myth about giant man-like creatures. There are stories about Yeti (the Abominable Snowman in Asia), Sasquatch (Bigfoot of the U.S. Pacific Northwest), and other such creatures. Is it possible these stories began because of contact between *Homo erectus* and *Gigantopithecus* in Vietnam or elsewhere? The authors consider it possible for such memories to persist long enough. Could *Giganto* have been the origin of Sasquatch legends?

Gigantopithecus preceded *Homo erectus* in Vietnam. *Homo,* after his arrival, may even have hunted *Giganto*. For several reasons, *Homo* could have been a final blow on *Giganto's* pathway to extinction. The authors discuss the meaning of extinction, which is a more sophisticated notion than merely noting that the last member of a species dropped dead. It has to do with continued viability of a species, and *Giganto* was no longer viable. But does he still survive somewhere? That is interesting speculation.

Other Origins draws a parallel between *Giganto* and the giant panda. Formerly widespread, the range of the giant panda has been drastically reduced to a small area in China. There, the small remaining population is highly valued, as was demonstrated by the capture and execution of two panda poachers.

The newly independent nation of Vietnam was struggling to create working relationships with visiting scientists: The scientific quest of Ciochon, Olson, and James was the first by Americans permitted after the Vietnam War.

The Cham People

Homo erectus gave way to *Homo sapiens* about 200,000 years ago. The Son Vi culture arose around 20,000 years ago and the Hoa Binh about 12,000 years ago. Other cultures followed through the final four millenniums BC, according to a timeline at www.viettouch.com, which is Chi D. Nguyen's informative website.

Bronze age cultures, the Dong Son in particular, made large bronze drums. The very elaborate, almost perfectly done, lost wax casting technique apparently began in Southeast Asia and later spread to China, which is the reverse of prior thinking. Just the sculpted pictures cast into the tympani provide a look at several parts of life (daily, spiritual, and ceremonial) in the Dong Son culture, according to Chi D. Nguyen.

The Sa Huynh culture preceded the Cham in central Vietnam. Many artifacts have been recovered from over 50 sites near that village. Evidence indicates that the Sa Huynh, another bronze-age culture, had a large influence on the culture of Champa.

Who were the Cham people, those builders of the several towers we saw throughout central Vietnam? The Kingdom of Champa once existed from Ngang Pass—that topographic and cultural divide north of Dong Hoi—all the way south to the end of the central mountains in Vietnam. Cham lived near Phan Thiet along the coast, and perhaps into the Mekong Delta, too. They lived in that part of Vietnam well before the Vietnamese (the Viet) did.

Our visit to the Cham Museum in Da Nang was enlightening. A year earlier, several of us decided our layover day had been full enough already; we'd climbed one of the Marble Mountains and had visited China Beach. We skipped the Museum then—but our tour went there first in 1999.

Much of what I'll relate here comes from Ho Xuan Tinh, *Cham Relics in Quang Nam* [Province], 1998. I purchased this book at the Cham museum. The two drawings I've used were purchased at the museum directly from My, the artist who created them.

The Cham were known for what they made. Their products, according to Chinese trade records, included sandalwood, cinnamon, pepper, ivory, rhinoceros horn, sea turtle, silk from silkworms, and cloth made from jute or cotton. Of metals, besides tools and weapons, the Cham made gold, silver, and bronze ornaments. Their products have turned up in Thailand, Taiwan, and the Philippines, so they must have traded over land and ocean routes. Their society was mostly agricultural, but some Cham were fishers and seafarers. Their soldiers were paid in rice.

First noted in Chinese historical writings in 192 AD, the Cham occupied the area near present-day Phan Thiet, a city along the southern coast but not quite to the Delta. In a temporary third-century military breakout,

Champa expanded far northward into Vietnamese territory then ruled by China, including Thang Long (present-day Hanoi) on the Red River Delta, and even into parts of southern China.

In the fourth and fifth centuries, the tide changed. The Chinese pushed the Cham southward and the kingdom of Champa grew smaller and smaller. By the eighth century, Champa only occupied present-day central and southern Vietnam. In the tenth century, Vietnam invaded Champa from the north, but the Cham held their territory. The Khmers from the west (present-day Cambodia) invaded during the twelfth century and occupied the Mekong Delta. That's eight centuries! Note the slower pace of such things then. An individual citizen of Champa might have lived an entire lifespan without seeing much change, yet change came.

A northern Cham civilization came to be centered in the present-day Da Nang–Quang Ngai region. A southern civilization centered around Phan Rang, including those who settled the Nha Trang area. These states united in the seventh century to become the Kingdom of Champa, with a capital geographically located between them. In the year 1,000, the capital was transferred to a town just north of present-day Qui Nhon. Whole groups of ruins (left by the northern Cham and described by Ho Xuan Tinh) are near My Son village, just south of Da Nang and inland from Hoi An. The U.S. Air Force bombed some of the best of these in 1969.

In the thirteenth century, the Khmers and the Cham united against the Vietnamese and defeated them. The Khmers then withdrew from the Delta. Still in the same century, the Mongols of Kublai Khan occupied Champa for five years until the Vietnamese came in 1287 and defeated them. By 1306, the Vietnamese would come to control all territory south to Hai Van Pass. This is an even more prominent topographic and cultural divider that's well south of Ngang Pass.

Cham history seems to have included an almost constant battle with the Vietnamese. Advantage shifted north and south. It involved foreign intervention at least twice (by the Khmers and the Mongols). In 1468-69, Cham armies attacked the Vietnamese whose civilization was by then spreading southward.

In 1471, the Vietnamese invaded Champa. This time, they captured the capital and the king, and massacred thousands. Champa was finished as a kingdom then, especially after the Vietnamese came back in the seventeenth century and captured the lands around present-day Tuy Hoa and Nha Trang. By 1832, the Vietnamese takeover was complete all the way to the southernmost tip of the Delta. The Cham people eventually became just another of the 54 minority groups in Vietnam.

We remember the Cham largely for the several towers that still stand. Similar to corresponding religious structures in India, Cambodia, and Indonesia, Cham towers aren't as large. But they were often placed on high ground where some still stand with distinction.

India influenced the Cham people greatly, including the organization of their state. The Cham worshipped Hindu gods. Writing came from Sanskrit. Place names were of Indian origin, as were the titles of Cham kings. Sculpture and architecture were influenced by Hindu art.

That decisive 1471 Vietnamese attack on Champa happened nearly 500 years before I'd see that same country as best I could through the small windows of Air Force C-130s. Three more decades would pass before I had even the slightest idea what had transpired down there. By the year of the attack, Christopher Columbus was 20 years old. Had he possibly done some thinking about crossing broad oceans?

The Cham survive in Vietnam. Some live in areas where a bit of their culture remains; others have been assimilated. On the way from the Cham Museum, which centers mostly on Cham art, Hung Luong commented that not much had been presented on the history of the Cham, or about the process by which they'd been displaced by the Vietnamese. "How did that happen?" I asked.

"We chopped them up!" replied Hung truthfully, with an appropriately severe expression.

Wild Vietnam

Beautiful, wild parts of Vietnam exist. Exotic wildlife abounds. The Vietnamese government, to its credit, is mindful of this and has set aside national parks and "protected areas." In 1969, President Ho Chi Minh, in one of his last official acts, established a research station, museum, and arboretum in what would become, in 1985, Cuc Phuong National Park.

As I learned about these areas, I received much help from people in Vietnam. Ms. Nguyen Diep Hoa, Communications Manager, WWF Indochina Programme, sent me about eight megabytes (a notebook-full) of information attached to e-mails. I'd ask questions late at night and would receive answers from her the next morning. Day and night are reversed, roughly, between the U.S. and Vietnam, so she must have answered during her working day, almost upon receipt. Gert Polet of WWF at Cat Tien National Park shared information and stories with me. I found other helpful documents, written by Ina Becker (wife of Gert) at Cat Tien, on that park's website at www.blakup.demon.nl/cat_tien.

WWF stands for World Wide Fund for Nature, which was previously known as World Wildlife Fund. In the United States it is still called the latter since the U.S. chapter chose not to follow the name change, Polet told me. The organization was founded in 1965; its first president was Prince Bernhard of The Netherlands.

Here, I share a WWF document sent me by Nguyen Diep Hoa. It states the objective of conservation in Vietnam and a few of the problems that exist for the nation. Words in brackets summarize a longer passage:

World Wide Fund for Nature in Vietnam

WWF was one of the first international nongovernment organizations to work in Vietnam. Representatives from WWF first came to Vietnam in the early 1980s and visits were made to what are now Cat Tien, Yok Don and Cuc Phuong national parks. In 1985, together with IUCN, WWF helped develop a national conservation strategy for Vietnam. A draft of this report was published in 1986, and a national biodiversity action plan was endorsed by the prime minister in 1995.

In 1991 WWF decided to expand its activities in Vietnam and an office was set up in Hanoi. Since then, the Indochina Programme office has coordinated the growing portfolio of projects in the country, established relations with the various government agencies, local research institutes, and NGOs involved in nature conservation in Vietnam, and facilitated the provision of funds and technical assistance for various field-level activities. It also helps to manage and expand on projects in Cambodia and Laos by working with WWF offices in Phnom Penh and Vientiane.

The presence of the WWF office in Hanoi has enabled the organization to respond more quickly and effectively to local conservation needs. Today, WWF's strategy involves helping to develop a functional network of well-managed protected areas, encouraging more sustainable resource-use patterns, minimizing the negative environmental impact of economic development, promoting conservation awareness, and building local expertise in nature conservation.

Biological Significance

Vietnam has been identified as one of Asia's most biologically important countries. Its wide range of habitats—from the myriad and varied coastal regions to the rugged central highlands, and from the flat swampy deltas of the Mekong and Red rivers to the temperate mountains of the northwest—are home to rich and diverse wildlife populations, many of which are endemic to the region.

Approximately 7,000 plant species have been identified out of an estimated 12,000. As many as 2,300 plant species are valuable as food, medicine, animal fodder, and timber. Much of Vietnam's flora takes on distinctive local forms, with many endemic species confined to small areas and occurring in small numbers, thus making them highly susceptible to extinction.

The wild fauna of Vietnam includes 275 species of mammal, 180 reptiles, and 80 amphibious species. (It is worth noting that these numbers, as well as those quoted above for flora, are largely scientific guesswork, but even as such they attest to the biological richness of the country.) Like the flora of Vietnam, these fauna show a high degree of local distinctiveness. Large and spectacular animals can be found throughout the country, including Asian Elephant (Elephas maximus), Tiger (Panthera tigris), Leopard (Panthera pardus), Kouprey (Bos sauveli), Gaur (Bos gaurus), and Banteng (Bos javanicus), all of which are endangered species.

Important endemic species include the Vietnamese Pheasant (Lophura hatinhensis), Edward's Pheasant (Lophura edwardsi), and the Tonkin Snub-nosed Monkey (Pygathrix avunculus). Near-endemic species (those found only in Vietnam and one or two adjacent countries) include the Douc Langur (Pygathrix nemaeus), Crested Gibbon (Hylobates concolor), Francois Leaf Monkey (Presbytis francoisi), Owston's Banded Civet (Chrotogale owstoni), Pygmy Loris (Nycitcebus pygmaeus), and Germain's Peacock Pheasant (Polyplectron germaini).

Most impressive, however, is doubtless the fact that four new large mammal species, previously unknown to science, have been described from observations made in Vietnam this decade. The Saola (Pseudoryx nghetinhensis), the Giant Muntjac (Megamuntiacus vuquangensis), the Khting Vor (Pseudonovibos spiralis), and the Truong Son Muntjac (Muntiacus truongsonensis) are four of only seven new large mammal species worldwide that have been described by scientists this century. Such developments indicate that the country's natural wealth and biological importance could be even greater that previously thought.

Conservation Threats

Overpopulation and the fallout from rapid economic growth are clearly the most serious threats to Vietnam's biodiversity. Currently, there are estimated to be about 78 million people in the country, with a population doubling time of only 31 years. This burgeoning population will put even greater pressure on the country's natural resources in the future.

Already, commercial logging, mass planned and spontaneous migration to rural areas, and the growing demand for agricultural land has led to the loss of all but a small percentage of Vietnam's forests—in 1943, 43% of the country was forested; today, forest cover is estimated to be approximately 19%. Remote-sensing data indicates that only two million hectares of primary forest remain, and that 100,000 to 200,000 ha [hectares, each 10,000 square meters or 2.471 acres] are lost annually. In addition, deforestation and habitat loss due to unsustainable resource-use patterns has precipitated the decline of many of Vietnam's rare and endemic species.

Moreover, as the doors to economic opportunity swing open in Vietnam, the ever-growing wildlife trade threatens the survival of many species, particularly because the trade targets rare and endangered species for their high market values. The wildlife trade continues to grow despite domestic and international legislation on International Trade in Endangered Species of Fauna and Flora (CITES). [There has been] difficulty enforcing the convention.

A Look Ahead

Sprawling construction sites, newly-outfitted industrial plants, Honda motorbikes, and a range of new consumer products are signs of the economic "tiger" Vietnam is looking to become. But the past decade has brought more than economic advances—the government of Vietnam has done much to advance the cause of nature conservation as well. Still, a substantial amount of work remains to be done if Vietnam is to conserve its wealth of biodiversity. Institutional support and capacity building are required if the country is to ensure the long-term viability of its forests, wetlands and marine areas. This will not be an easy endeavor, especially for a developing country in the throes of change. With this in mind, WWF offers continuing support to the people and the government of Vietnam in seeking to implement programs and launch initiatives aimed at realizing conservation goals.

Parks and Reserves

I've not been to any of the 11 parks or reserves in person, but I believe a series of photographic investigations on my part is called for. I've long been fascinated by the wild side of Vietnam.

The photographs here were taken by either Karen or Alan Robinson, who live only a few miles from me in Colorado. Alan travels to Vietnam to help set up national parks, since that is his area of expertise. Karen sometimes goes, too, and they pass the camera back and forth between them. Hence, I was asked to attribute the photographs to both.

Cat Ba is an island national park near Ha Long Bay. There's an archipelago of small islands near Haiphong, which is east of Hanoi on the coast. On the main island are areas of karst topography. As described earlier, that's where limestone is so full of caves and fissures that the rock resembles Swiss cheese with the holes connected, and can be eroded along those fissures into towers. There are 366 small islands and Ha Long Bay where—either because the sea has risen or the land has subsided—towers of limestone rise spectacularly from the sea.

On the islands, most rainwater flows into systems of caves. Most stream channels aren't perennial and flow only after tropical rainstorms. There is a diversity of landscape: beaches, mangrove forest, swamp forest, forested hills, and several lakes.

Con Dao National Park is far to the south on Con Son, the largest of the Con Dao Islands, nearly 100 km from the Mekong delta. If a line were drawn along the final course of that river and extended seaward, the islands would be just a little south of it.

Cuc Phuong was the first national park in Vietnam, designated in 1985. It had been made a forest preserve in 1960. It's in the foothills of the northern Truong Son Range, about 100 km south of Hanoi and west of Ninh Binh. That city was our first lunch stop on both bicycle trips; I had no idea then that a national park was fairly near. In a broad valley between two sets of limestone hills, the cliffs narrow eastward to form a canyon and build into larger mountains. Cave systems and underground rivers are present; little water flows on the surface. Hang Dang Cave can only be reached by climbing a 600-rung ladder. Luxurious flora there may be a relic of a time when the tropical forest of Indochina extended farther north than it does today, said a WWF document.

The park receives about 7,000 visitors each year, of which roughly a third are foreigners. Of those, most are scientists. A guest house there can accommodate about a dozen people. About 2,000 Muong hill people still live within the park. Accommodating their rural livelihoods and preserving their culture are the park's largest management problems.

Ba Be National Park is in the far north. It includes Vietnam's only mountain lake, which is surrounded by tropical rain forest. There is a channel between it and the Nang River such that when the river is high, water enters the lake and is stored. When the river is low, the opposite occurs, regulating the water supply used by the local people. The Dau Dang series of waterfalls, which extends for 10 km with some falls as high as 45 meters, is not far away. The park has numerous limestone caves, including Phuong Grotto. This area will be developed as a tour destination, which will provide an economic boost locally.

Limestone and Forests

When I saw the Perfume Pagoda near Hanoi, I suspected there must be other limestone caves in Vietnam. Are there ever! Park descriptions speak of karst topography, "limestone forests," caves, grottos, and streams that disappear into underground cavern systems.

Much of Vietnam's remaining forest is near its border with Laos and Cambodia. A program exists to link ecosystem protection between Vietnam and Laos in the Phong Nha-Ke Bang complex where certain species live only on certain hills or in certain caves. Some of them, particularly bats, are very beneficial as pollinators of crops or as insect predators.

In the limestone forests, growth of flora is very slow; 70% of those forests have been damaged without great hope of recovery. The government is attempting to protect what's left. When I walked in Vietnamese forests 30 years ago they seemed limitless; but that wasn't so even then and it's much less so now. It's not just because of defoliants the U.S. military, in one of its most evil acts, sprayed on southern Vietnam for several years, though that's part. It's also because of logging and land-clearing. Both are pressures from a rapidly increasing population.

Biodiversity in Lost Worlds

Described as a "lost world," Vu Quang Nature Reserve is an area along the Laotian border. It may be Indochina's most famous protected area where, in 1992, the saola was discovered. This bovid (sort of a goat/antelope) was previously unknown to science. While scientists were studying the saolo, the giant muntjac, which also had been unknown to science, was found. Hence, a mystique of wildlife and otherworldliness has sprung up around Vu Quang!

The best known, though seldom-seen, resident of Cat Tien National Park is the Javan rhinoceros. There are only two places in the world where this highly endangered large animal survives. About 10 rhinos live in Cat Tien; their other home is a national park in western Java (Indonesia).

Cat Tien is known as one of the world's biodiversity hotspots. Other large mammals live there, too, including the tiger, the elephant, and the gauer (a very impressive cattle/bison bovine, according to Gert Polet). In total, it has about 400 known plant species, 310 species of birds, 62 mammals, 22 reptiles, and 14 amphibians. Cat Tien has multi-canopy rain forest and one of the few remaining large areas of lowland tropical forest.

The same pressures exist in this area as elsewhere—commercial logging, clearing, poaching, and the aforementioned defoliants. In 1986, the Vietnamese government began designating protected areas in what is now Cat Tien National Park. There, population migration into the area had transformed vast forested areas into agricultural land. Protecting the land while preserving the livelihood of the local population is of huge importance, as elsewhere.

Bach Ma National Park

Of significance to me is Bach Ma National Park, on the same mountain spur that projects eastward to form Hai Van Pass between Hue and Da Nang. It isn't far from where the U.S. Army sent me walking. I thought then those forests and mountains had national park stature. I was right.

I know personally about monkeys and leeches, though we at least had insect repellent to use on the latter. Gert Polet assured me the descendants of the leeches are still there, though a grim story about a Vietnamese soldier being "sucked empty" is probably overstated! What other animals were there?

Conservation Efforts

In Vietnam, forest guards (rangers) from the Forest Protection Department have gone out to schools to talk with students about the importance of conservation. Illegal poaching has been a large problem. Tigers poached or captured, for example, can bring more money than a villager might otherwise earn in a year.

Some believe tigers and other animals have medicinal—including aphrodisiac—value. That is false. But large-animal poaching continues and must be reigned in through anti-poaching patrols and public awareness campaigns. The Thua Tien Hue (province) Forest Protection Department has undertaken public awareness activities, particularly on behalf of the tiger. Forest guards from the Chu Mom Ray Nature Reserve in Kontum Province—rugged country near the meeting of the borders of Vietnam, Cambodia, and Laos—have done similarly. Chu Mom Ray is part of a tri-national complex of protected areas designated as a high priority Tiger Conservation Unit.

National parks in Vietnam are operated by the national government. Nature reserves are operated by the provinces. Setting aside land hasn't been without problems in Vietnam, as elsewhere. But the governments involved do care; they are taking action to preserve what Vietnam has.

The Ho Chi Minh Highway

The government of Vietnam is building a new north-south highway to connect the northern part of the nation with the existing highway (QL14) that goes north from HCMC not far from the Cambodian border. The new road will go inland through the mountains, keeping the country from being divided in two each monsoon (flood) season. The new Ho Chi Minh Highway will link in places with the existing highway (QL1) along the coast. But most of it will follow the old wartime supply route known as the Ho Chi Minh Trail.

Environmental concerns are that the new highway will pass through some of the forested, wild areas that still remain in central Vietnam and even through a corner of Cuc Phuong National Park. I hope the Vietnamese government is mindful of this, as it is about other conservation concerns. I must add, the new route will make a fascinating bicycle trip.

The Truong Son Veterans

There is another concern, too. David Lamb of the *Los Angeles Times* wrote about veterans of the Truong Son Road, which is known to others as the Ho Chi Minh Trail. This writer and this newspaper are to be commended for adding so often and so well to our understanding of modern Vietnam. I have drawn upon Lamb's articles several times in this book; they have been highly informative and insightful. His story about the Truong Son veterans was all of that—and very moving, too.

The Truong Son veterans—those who traveled the route many times— endured long isolation, hunger, malaria, accidents, danger of snakebite, and bombing. We know about that. But theirs was also a struggle among beautiful forest and peaks; forest that seemed to share their emotions. It's about a lasting respect and love for one another that developed. The route is sacred to those who labored there, as the workers building the new road are very much aware. Some Truong Son veterans, whose memories of years there may now be all they have, would like this route to remain forever unchanged and untouched. I certainly understand that.

Tigers in Vietnam

I wrote earlier about an infantryman in Quang Tri Province who said he met a tiger at one of our night positions and climbed a tree because of it. I now stand convinced that he may indeed have met one! Clearly tigers live in Vietnam, though they are endangered. The following account is used with permission of the WWF Indochina Programme.

Lam Nhi—The Tiger Who Couldn't Go Home

Newspaper reports in the Vietnamese national press refer to the "Hue Tiger" as the wildlife story of the year. Her terrible plight and the coordinated efforts of the Hue Forest Protection Department, Hanoi Zoo and WWF to save her life have captured the imagination of people throughout the country.

While a tiger confiscation might not be the story of choice for a WWF Tiger awareness campaign, the fact that this female tiger cub has overcome the injuries and trauma inflicted upon her by hunters and wildlife traders underscores the continuing peril for tigers and other wildlife in Vietnam. That she is now the center of national attention and affection is a major success for Tiger conservation.

Emergency in Thua Thien-Hue

WWF's involvement with the plight of this young cub began in July 1998 when she was found in the trunk of a taxi, along with an Asian black bear. The two animals were found by forest guards from Phong Dien District, who were informed by local people alarmed by the fact that a taxi was driving through a remote forest some 50km from Hue, Vietnam's former imperial capital.

After questioning the nervous taxi driver and the wildlife traders cum passengers, the guards found the tiger and the bear in the trunk, stuffed into small wire cages normally used for transporting pigs to market, an indignity for such marvelous wild creatures. Unfortunately, due to severe mistreatment by the traders, the 70 kg bear died shortly after it was found.

But the young tiger survived. Indeed, she proved to be quite strong and resilient, considering the trauma she had experienced. She was kept for several weeks by the Hue Forest Protection Department (FPD) while local staff tended to the wounds on her front legs inflicted by the steel trap in which the hunters had caught her. Tips on diet and medicine were provided by staff from the Hanoi Zoo.

Mr. Hoang Ngoc Khanh, Director of the Hue FPD, contacted the WWF office in Hanoi soon after the tiger was found. Two representatives from WWF went immediately to Hue to begin the process of caring for the tiger. The WWF representatives invited a film crew and reporter from VTV-1 (the official national television station) to accompany them in order to start the public awareness campaign.

After consultation with Tiger experts, it became clear that to release the young female cub back into the forest could prove dangerous. This decision was not an easy one. But it was clear that she was probably too young to survive on her own, and even if she were to be reunited with her mother, she would probably be rejected due to her close contact with humans. Even if she were to survive on her own, she would most likely become a danger to humans, considering her experience with the wildlife traders. So, with some reluctance, WWF and the Hue FPD decided she must spend the rest of her life in captivity.

On Wednesday 26 August, a handing over ceremony took place in Hue. This ceremony was organized to draw attention to the tiger's plight and the cooperation between the Hue FPD and the Hanoi Zoo. Again, two representatives from the WWF Hanoi office made the trip down to the old capital to lend WWF's support and spearhead the public awareness activities. Auspiciously, news coverage of the event was given a prime spot, airing between the two opening football matches (and only a few minutes before the opening ceremonies) of the Tiger Cup, the first international football tournament to take place in Vietnam. Most of the country was tuned in. A few days later, the nation watched as the tiger's arrival at the Hanoi Zoo was broadcast on television. Many people cheered as the small cub ventured out into her new home – taking her first steps in nearly six weeks.

To make the best of a decidedly bad situation, WWF initiated a public awareness campaign dubbed "the tiger who couldn't go home" upon her arrival at the Hanoi Zoo. A press conference was held at the zoo on 5 September with the (national) Forest Protection Department, and WWF produced postcards

A "walking stick"
Photo by Alan and Karen Robinson

with a picture of the tiger and a short paragraph (in Vietnamese and English) detailing her experience and stating briefly the situation for tigers in Vietnam. In addition, WWF and a local student/youth magazine organized a contest encouraging children to write letters naming the tiger and explaining the reasons behind the name. The newspaper, *Hoa Hoc Tro* (*The Pupils' Flower*), received some 10,000 letters from all over the country in less than a month's time. Clearly, this tiger had struck a chord with people throughout Vietnam. The contest's winner, Miss Nguyen Thi Chinh from Vinh Phuc Province (located 50 km northwest of Hanoi), gave the cub the name "Lam Nhi", meaning child of the forest.

   Lam Nhi rapidly became a main attraction at the Hanoi zoo, with a sign telling her story: Her capture, taxi ride, why she's there, and the wildlife officers' investigation of the smuggling ring that would have shipped her to China. Tigers worldwide are threatened by human pressure. Public awareness is central, helping people understand what is needed for tigers to survive. Something positive may still come from this mostly-sad story.

Bach Ma National Park: Photo by Alan and Karen Robinson

Expectations and Discoveries

When I first went to Vietnam in 1969, I expected to find a land of dirt, mud, and slime. War stories in the media had been full of that. I expected a flat and dull topography. What I found was exotic and mysterious beauty: seacoast, forested mountain terrain, streams, and a hidden valley. Lam Nhi the tiger cub would live close to where I walked those mountains. I also found a remarkable people. May it ever be so.

Boat, Ha Long Bay
Photo by Alan and Karen Robinson

Further Information and Resources
Bicycle Trip Outfitters: Cycle the World

Voters in Portland, Oregon, decided Rick Bauman needed a rest. After about 15 years in politics, Rick heartily agreed! His rest would include some solo bicycling, and he went to Vietnam in April 1993 to do it. Why Vietnam? This was a "totally mysterious" place at that time, Rick told me. He had come of age during war years, during which Vietnam had defined America politically and in other ways.

Rick went south to north on that trip, from Ho Chi Minh City to Hanoi, in accordance with the prevailing winds that time of year. He found Vietnam beautiful, and the people were "overwhelmingly generous, though they didn't have much to be generous with." Bicycling turned out to be a remarkable way to explore Vietnam because he "had the option all day long" to relate to the people. "A bus window gets in the way," he added.

While cycling, Rick decided he'd provide this experience to others. Following his lead, 57 bicyclists departed Hanoi in January 1994 for HCMC. Cycle Vietnam has gone almost every winter since then. Significant events along the way included President Clinton's 1994 lifting of the U.S. economic embargo. "That's when Coke and Pepsi appeared all over the place," Rick noted. By 1995, full diplomatic relations had been restored with Vietnam.

That first year, bicycle trips in Vietnam represented an "exploration on both sides." The Vietnamese saw that police escorts and a medical team weren't necessary, though a woman suffered a broken leg once in HCMC. On that occasion, the Cycle Vietnam rider was stopped at a traffic light in HCMC just three blocks from the last hotel after a trip of 1200 miles. A motorbike got away from someone there and fell over on her. She was soon flown out to Singapore.

V.Y.C is the third Vietnamese travel company Rick has dealt with. His last job in HCMC each year has been to schedule V.Y.C guide Xuan Hung as a guide for next year's trip.

Rick's comments on changes in Vietnam over the last few years: "Cities are changing dramatically and quickly" though "Hanoi is just a little behind HCMC." In smaller cities and towns, there are more subtle changes. E-mail and Internet capability are everywhere now.

Cycle Vietnam ran a "Back Roads of Vietnam" trip one time. Xuan Hung had been enthusiastic about the route, which went inland from Da Nang and south through Pleiku. But roads were bad and support for a group was quite difficult. Besides, the trip attracted a different clientele that tended to be more into "conquering the mountain" than getting to know the culture, according to Rick.

Rick also tried a trip from Da Nang, Vietnam to Singapore. The route made its way over the mountains into Laos, across Thailand, and down that long peninsula through Malaysia. But after doing it twice, the trip had "too many problems" to continue.

Jerry Brown did that Da Nang to Singapore trip. There would appear to be a tire lying on the road up ahead, she commented. Riding nearer, it wouldn't be a tire at all, but a huge, coiled snake! With a most serious expression, Jerry held her hands just a little bit apart and emphasized that "you don't go even *that far* into the jungle" for fear of discovering what lives in there.

Rick emphasized that his trips have gone from one end of a country (or a region) to the other, so participants can learn about the culture and come to know the place. It's not just travel around a small area, but pointed toward a broader view. Rick has tended toward places that are politically "on the edge," where a bicycle trip may be a little unusual.

Cycle Vietnam expanded to become Cycle the World, driven in large part by Cycle Vietnam veterans who wanted more. Rick has offered trips in Laos, Myanmar (formerly Burma), Bhutan, and South Africa. A trip called Exodus followed the storied route of the Israelites out of Egypt, with religious conclusions of course optional.

And things do change… Lives refocus in other directions. As I edit these words, Rick has decided not to offer bicycle trips anymore. He'll do the two trips already booked and then "fold his tent."

But thank you, Rick! It was a life-changing experience.

Bicycle Trip Outfitters: Common Ground Journeys

In February of 2001, Hung Luong organized his first annual bicycle trip in Vietnam. His are four weeks long, from Hanoi to HCMC with a liberal offering of side trips. Three nights of camping, shorter bicycling days, and more time for the various side trips were featured. Half-trips that end or begin in Hue are available for those with limited time. The first-half trip includes a visit to Hoi An, and then back north to Hue for departure.

One excursion visits Ha Long Bay. Another investigates the Sapa area of northwestern Vietnam. There's a look into a cave near Dong Hoi, and a day trip into the Mekong Delta. There are fine campsites along the way, one of which is near the Vinh Moc tunnels close to the mouth of the Ben Hai River (former DMZ). Exploring Vietnam continues south from Phan Rang along the coast through Phan Thiet, instead of climbing the big hill up to Dalat. It ends at the beach city of Vung Tau, from where a hydrofoil ferries participants to Ho Chi Minh City.

Hung's goal is to break even on his trips. The still-reasonable price includes a $500 donation that goes directly to benefit the Vietnamese people. He believes very strongly in doing what he can for them, and I note here: If individuals like Hung don't do something, who will?

The money is donated to recipients along the route, during the trip. In 2001, money was provided to a school near the Ben Hai River in central Vietnam, as was money for a village water pump farther south. The whole journey is organized around meeting the people and the culture, while seeing a lot of Vietnam along the way.

Hung's website is www.commongroundjourneys.com where much can be learned and any changes tracked. Contact Hung at 503-307-7524, fax at 810-821-7089, vnrider@home.com, or by mail at Common Ground Journeys, Inc., P.O. Box 8992, Portland, Oregon 97207.

Photos and Layout

All my bicycle trip photographs in this book were made on Fuji color negative film using a Nikon N-70 camera and a Tamron 28-200 zoom lens. Most film was ISO 400, though some in 1998 was ISO 100.

The two images by Gail Lowenstine were made on negative film. Those made by Alan and Karen Robinson were transparencies (slides). Photographs from the Vietnam War were made on various transparency films— much of which was Kodak Ektachrome. In older incarnations, this film was said to be quite unstable. But these images, kept cool and mostly in a dry climate, lasted remarkably well for 30 years. Other images were on Kodachrome, which is quite stable.

All bicycle trip film was hand carried on airliners. Leaving Ho Chi Minh City, the X-ray machine was arranged in such a way that I could see the monitor. Though I used a bag lined with lead foil, individual rolls of film were visible! Oh oh! But I could discern no damage to the photographs. At other places, I was sometimes asked to open the bag because the contents didn't show on the X-ray machine.

All images to be used, except the maps, were scanned onto Kodak Photo CD and imported into Adobe Photoshop in the lab color space. They were converted to CMYK color for the printing press. Photos were cropped, small defects such as dust spots were removed, then Photoshop image functions were applied as needed for proper brightness and contrast. Color balance was adjusted if necessary. Considerable help came from Test Strip, a Photoshop plug-in from Vivid Details. The Photoshop unsharp mask filter was applied to all the images, including the maps, to sharpen them.

Integrity of the images was maintained. Elements of the photos were not moved around, grouped together, or placed in front of other backgrounds. Colors were maintained. The photographs (and the maps, which were scanned on a flatbed scanner) were saved as tiff files in their final sizes, at a resolution of 300 dpi.

Adobe InDesign was used for all page and cover layout. Body text is 9.5 point Stone Sans, though the several long quotations are in 9 point Stone Sans. Text files were written in Microsoft Word. All design and computer work was done in Microsoft Windows by the author.

Rick Bauman, owner of Cycle the World, disassembles his bike in Ho Chi Minh City.

Hung Luong near Nha Trang

Sunset, Ha Long Bay: Photo by Alan and Karen Robinson

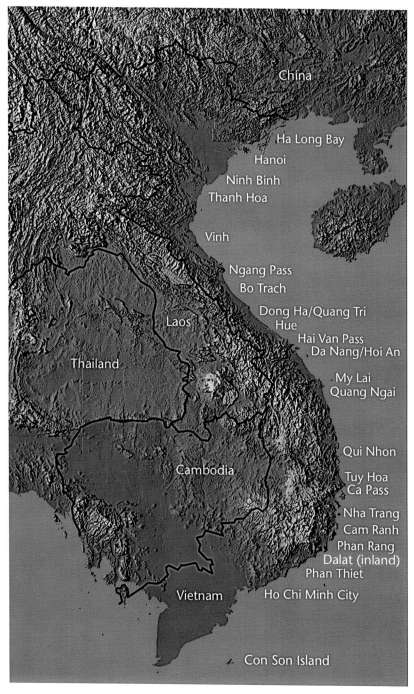

Regional map of Vietnam